"What if I told you th[...] packet of pumpkin s[...] cates that the original virus might have [been] made? A virus from another part of the world that was manipulated to act as an untraceable illness that killed quickly. A clever, malicious plot—"

"That's murder," Ben interrupted, then sat there and couldn't think of anything else to say. The word *murder* played over and over in his head. "Do you know for sure?"

"We're close enough. We'll know something for sure by next week."

"Who would want to kill pueblo people?"

"I don't know what we're looking for, but I have a feeling it's under our noses. We can't turn anything over to the feds until we get the official word from Atlanta."

Ben decided against telling Sandy he'd already been shot at. He'd be careful, but he wanted to know the killer—the person who had killed his grandmother and the others.

———————————— ★ ————————————

"This is a wonderful book with loveable heroes."
—*Library Journal*

"Slater's first novel holds the reader's interest with its brisk pace, well-rendered Arizona landscape, and challenging plot."

—*Booklist*

Forthcoming from Worldwide Mystery by
SUSAN SLATER

YELLOW LIES

THE PUMPKIN SEED MASSACRE

SUSAN SLATER

WORLDWIDE.

TORONTO • NEW YORK • LONDON
AMSTERDAM • PARIS • SYDNEY • HAMBURG
STOCKHOLM • ATHENS • TOKYO • MILAN
MADRID • WARSAW • BUDAPEST • AUCKLAND

THE PUMPKIN SEED MASSACRE

A Worldwide Mystery/February 2002

First published by Intrigue Press.

ISBN 0-373-26411-9

Printed in U.S.A.

To:
—Joan, for "seeing"
—Beth, Laura and Susan who supported the struggle
from the beginning

—Don, for his insight, ideas and laughing out loud
—All my friends in the Jemez Pueblo
who have enriched my life
and
—The countless students
who have made me a better writer

THANK YOU!

PROLOGUE

THE OWL WINGED noiselessly across the moon's path and settled on a pine bough above his head. He didn't look up. He knew the owl was there and knew its meaning. Death. His sweat evaporated in the dry, high-altitude crispness of the New Mexico night. Atop the mesa a fire kept him from chilling. He stared at the bright flames and didn't try to keep his mind from straying to what was wrong.

This wasn't the way it was supposed to be. He couldn't sleep and, like tonight, would take long walks calling upon the spirits to give him guidance. But they had deserted him. No longer did he feel their presence, their support. Yet, the answer was clear. He knew what he had to do. Much rested on his shoulders—responsibility, duty—but weren't they the same? Wasn't the future of the Tewa village in his hands? Someone who could assure all of a better life?

He put another cedar log on the fire; the orange warmth made his skin glow bronze. Then he untied the laces of his new Adidas, and pushed off first one shoe and then the other and rubbed his aching arches. Stripped to the waist, he wore designer jeans pleated below his black leather belt studded with buffalo nickels. But tonight he couldn't take pleasure in his clothes.

He sat back against a granite outcropping and let the fire warm the soles of his feet. He was beat. From his vantage point he looked out over the Indian Pueblo. Wisps of wood smoke stood straight up in barely waving columns above the roofs. On this windless night they acted as sentinels guarding each dwelling—the adobe houses huddled in an extended web of families and values dating back hundreds of years. He felt a surge of pride. These were his people. His to lead. His to protect. His to make rich.

He could make out the plaza ringed by houses flanked on the right by the Squash kiva and at the opposite end by the Turquoise kiva. The underground ceremonial chambers were privy to the secrets of centuries. Shadowy dancers floated over the hardpacked clay, putting one foot and then the other down in half steps to a drum beat. The long line of imaginary men and women shook pine boughs and turned in rhythm to the chanting of a circle of old men.

He would soon dance in celebration of summer. He couldn't remember ever missing a feast day. But he felt empty. He took little pleasure in performing the rituals of his ancestors.

Barking dogs brought his attention back to the houses below. Lights blinked on to his right. A group of young men had organized a hunt. A black bear had been seen in the foothills foraging for berries along the river, a male cub old enough to be abandoned by its mother. A black bear was powerful medicine. Would the taking of a yearling cub bring prosperity? Was this the sign he needed?

Someone hurried along the road leading to the Mission Church. As he watched, the door to the rectory was thrown open and he could just make out the long robes of Father Emerson before both figures were lost in the shadows of the path that led back to the center of the village. Attending those in need—a worthy profession—just not something he could do.

He couldn't check an involuntary shudder. He had to take action. Why hadn't he called? Told them for sure that he'd do it? He had been summoned to Santa Fe. Tomorrow he would meet with the investors. He had been dreading their accusations. They would think he was weak. But he wasn't.

A breeze suddenly tickled his nose. He sneezed. Startled, the owl rose mime-like and climbed high in the moon-bright sky. He watched death soar above him, blackly outlined, until the bird disappeared into the inky ceiling.

He felt a flutter of relief. It was the sign—death's visiting him this evening. He must act. He knew that now. No one could interfere with the way things were supposed to happen. Tomorrow, he would accept the packet of tainted seeds—lethal, untraceable, meant to kill the one man who stood in the way of progress. He pulled on the now-warm running shoes. Leaving the laces loose, he stood and jubilantly breathed in the cool night air.

He felt light-headed, calmed, but strangely excited. He would walk home along the river and take pleasure in how the giant cottonwoods shimmered silver above the water. The song of the rapids breaking gently over low rocks would keep him company. He bent down and scooped handfuls of dirt to smother the fire.

ONE

THE MORNING WAS HOT. Parched weeds grew on the roofs of the Pueblo houses. Lorenzo Loretto awakened at dawn to feel the stifling closeness of a day promising rain. He got up from his bed, a mattress on a sheet of plywood supported at the four corners by chunks of firewood. He would bathe in the river, but first, he had to pee.

He pulled the three pound coffee can from under the bed and watched as his stream of urine sometimes hit and sometimes missed the can. He would empty it in the alleyway behind the house and wait for his granddaughter to yell at him to rinse the can. She was up baking bread in the great horno in the courtyard to the side of the house. Already she was removing big crusty round loaves from the blackened opening of the adobe oven, each loaf secure in the center of a long wooden paddle squared at the end. From the covered basket beside her, she lifted a mound of dough. Patting it with her hands, she shaped it into a ball and placed it in the center of the paddle. Then, she thrust the paddle back into the oven gently sliding the dough off to rest on a shelf to bake. The aroma of fresh bread filled the air.

Behind the house, the clothesline sagged with flapping shirts, and jeans, and underwear. Wash day. If he didn't hurry, she'd come get the clothes he was wearing. Lorenzo put the coffee can down by the corner of the house. Luckily, he had his cane with him so he could continue down the narrow path between the houses and out of sight of his granddaughter.

Two thousand people lived in his village with one thousand trucks or cars. He waved his cane in the air as Marcus Toledo roared past in a new Jeep Cherokee. He hated automobiles. Always had. He never rode in one unless he needed to go a long distance. Lorenzo continued down the road by the Pueblo church shaking his cane at Sally Fragua's dogs who threatened to follow him.

He thought of himself as the eyes of his village. At ninety-six he kept watch over the births and deaths. At least, he thought he was ninety-six. He tried to verify his age for the clinic records last spring, but the mice ate the only paper that proved when he was born. Not that he could read English. He couldn't. But the paper had been issued by the tribe to his mother in 1952. When she died, he put the paper and the Bible from his first communion in a hole in the adobe wall behind his bed. Last winter had been cold and mice moved into the single adobe room attached to his granddaughter's house. They nested in the cardboard box of underwear under his bed and in the box of kindling, and in the hidey hole. His granddaughter hated mice. She chased them around the room when she came to clean, screaming that he'd die in such filth. He only sat in his rocker and looked straight ahead not hearing.

Tito Tsosie the rowdy rival from his youth and dead some fifty years, came up from the underworld slithering across the doorstep, his unmistakable beady eyes and wedge-shaped nose fastened to the body of a bull snake. Tito stayed with him until every mouse was gone. Eaten. At night he slept in the kindling box by the fire. Then, he left. Was Tito making amends? Lorenzo thought so. He liked Tito better in death than in life.

Lorenzo was less afraid of those from the dark side as he

got closer to leaving this earth. Many of his friends from the other world visited him daily now. They walked with him by the river or sat with him in the darkened sanctuary of the Mission Chapel. He talked with them, but speech was difficult. He heard little around him but his eyes were like the hawk's. He looked everywhere and saw everything.

The rectangular Pueblo church loomed in the distance. Its smooth tan adobe sides stretched upwards two stories with twin bell towers perched on the front corners above double hand-carved, fist-thick doors. The bells, now seldom used, were gifts from the Spaniards, cast bronze bigger than waste-baskets and securely tethered to a cross-bar embedded in the adobe bricks. The church had been restored twice, the first time over two hundred years ago. His mother had been married there; Lorenzo had been baptized there.

He stood for a moment at the churchyard cemetery. In the old days the dead were buried in the yard in front of the village church or for someone important—maybe a priest—under the wooden plank flooring of the sanctuary itself. This old cemetery was full; there were no spaces left. The elders had consecrated a new burial ground outside the village some years back.

But as Lorenzo watched, a man with a shovel and a man with a posthole digger leaned on their equipment while a third man unloaded the pointed slats of wood from his truck that would extend the picket boundary. They were enlarging the churchyard.

The tribe's fiscal officer, as the member of the Governor's Council in charge of village maintenance, ordered the quarter-acre enclosure around the graves to be expanded, the fence straightened, painted, made inviting to the hundreds of tourists who visited each summer. Teens policed the grounds for pop cans and candy wrappers and pulled upright the fallen grave markers. The sparse grass that sprouted hit and miss across the mounds was clipped close to the ground.

The new fence hugged the road and angled to the left. This created a dozen new burial spaces. Didn't the man know that he was begging death to visit the village by expanding the old cemetery, making room for more places of rest? Lorenzo watched as the men pounded the stakes in a straight line each leading farther to the north along the irrigation ditch. Lorenzo couldn't believe such foolishness. He knew that many didn't believe the way he did, but they would see. Death would come and he would fill his house before the dying stopped. It would be a time of anguish for his people. Lorenzo sighed. There was no way to undo what had been set in motion.

TWO

THE FIRST DEATH occurred on Monday, the second on Tuesday. Both would have gone unnoticed except for the fact that they kept Twila Runningfox, Physician's Assistant at the Tewa Pueblo, from attending an Indian Health Service meeting on Wednesday. As Twila reported, there was nothing out of the ordinary about the deaths of a sixty-three-year-old man and a seventy-one-year-old woman from flu symptoms—especially since both had a history of upper-respiratory problems and Dr. Sanford Black, Clinical Director of the Albuquerque Service unit, was the first to agree.

In fact, Sandy barely acknowledged Twila's excuse, thanked her for calling but dismissed her rather quickly. She was competent. There was no reason to dwell on routine deaths. He had a decision to make on adding a student intern and was already running behind schedule. He shuffled and reshuffled the applications and shifted his concentration from lower back pain to the stack of paperwork in front of him. Too much sitting in one position leaning over a desk—this was the part he least liked about his job—the bouts of forced inactivity.

He stared at the applications of five would-be interns. They were even beginning to sound alike—all well qualified, good undergraduate, strong masters studies in psychology, counseling, social work. So, what was he looking for? What did IHS need the most?

The counseling position in the Tewa Pueblo probably took priority. It might be wise to choose someone from that community. But Benson Pecos didn't exactly fit into that category. He hadn't spent much time there and he wasn't claiming Indian preference, either. He had a B.S. in Biology and an M.A. in psychology.

Sandy sighed and leaned back in his chair. Sunlight pushed through the tangle of grape ivy above his desk and zapped him in the right eye. He twisted his chair a half turn to the left. This wasn't getting him anywhere. He should ask his secretary. Gloria was from Tewa. He grabbed Ben's application and walked across the hall.

"Gloria, what do you know about a Ben Pecos?"

"He's really good looking."

"I was thinking of something a little more academic."

"Well, his mother was a famous Tewa artist and his father was Anglo, someone she met at school. When his mother died, a couple from Utah adopted him. He was five. He hasn't spent too much time in the Pueblo, mostly just summers with his grandmother."

"Is he well liked?"

"I like him."

"Gloria, if I consider him for the internship, I need a little broader application." He watched Gloria shrug. When she didn't seem to want to add anything else, he continued. "I like what I see on paper. If you can, check a couple of his references this afternoon. I think I'll invite him to the meeting in Tewa tomorrow morning. Maybe I'll give this kid a try."

"You won't be sorry." Gloria said.

"How do you know?"

"I know." Gloria turned back to the wordprocessor in front of her.

BEN'S GRANDMOTHER didn't have a phone, not many of the Tewa village elders did. One of the kids who hung out at the civic center down by the highway brought the message late in the afternoon—an invitation from Dr. Black to attend a meeting at the Tewa Pueblo clinic in the morning.

It must mean that they were interested in him—he just wished that he could return the enthusiasm. He'd applied, hadn't he? Then he'd had about a thousand second thoughts. But he called back and accepted, confirmed that he would be there and thanked Dr. Black for his consideration.

But now in the morning, Ben wasn't feeling any more certain. He wiped a spot of toothpaste off the mirror. He still had an hour before the meeting. He inspected his face. Ben Pecos, the anomaly. That wasn't original. Someone had called him that. His second year psychology professor at Stanford. A German woman who tried to make him fit some kind of mold for Native Americanism. She had a knack for making it sound like a national movement, something one aspired to, wasn't born into without a choice.

"No tepees? No feathers on the head?" She'd roll over in bed and propped on an elbow, run a finger over his prominent cheekbones.

"I'm a Pueblo Indian. Mud houses. Farming. The Spanish Conquistadors brought us the Catholic religion."

"Not even the horses to ride like the wind? Arrows? Spears to run through the enemy?" She'd tease but sound vaguely disappointed with his answer. Usually his hormones would end any further conversation.

Her curiosity was real; her understanding limited. He always thought he'd see her get off a tourist bus in the Pueblo someday 'ooing and ahhing' about primitivism—pointing to the adobe ovens beside the squat houses, watching a dance, buying some trinkets marked 'Handmade by Indians' and then go back to California thinking she'd had a real experience.

Cynicism. Could you become a cynic at twenty-six? Probably. And if he were lucky it would edge out any idealism he might have. While there was still a chance, he should chuck the idea of returning to his place of birth, of helping a people who only half-heartedly claimed him, still looked at him with suspicion because he didn't know their language or ceremonies...and, do what?

His grandmother wasn't surprised when he told her he might come back. She nodded and said that his mother followed the Navajo tradition and buried his umbilical cord between the river and the mesa. He would always call this place home. He couldn't help it.

He showered. The water was tepid and the white spots of alkaline on the shower curtain had fused to form a powdery hem. He wrapped a towel around his waist and walked to the kitchen. His grandmother had gone into Albuquerque with his aunt. The city was some hour's drive away but offered the closest decent shopping. He opened a window and felt a breeze skip across his face. Already hot and dry. He closed the window.

He unwrapped the plate of fry bread beside the plastic bear of honey, then wrapped it again. It was one less thing to feel guilty about. He wasn't used to a lot of starch and fat calories and the grease-soaked pastries would sit like a lump in his stomach. He walked back to his bedroom to dress. He was doing everything but let himself think. If he was offered an internship, would he accept? His counselor called it "the perfect opportunity, a chance to make up your mind about working with your people." He'd see. He hadn't received the offer yet.

THE ROOM WAS CROWDED with twenty-odd health care workers. Some he knew; others were probably from surrounding Pueblos or Albuquerque. Dr. Black motioned for him to join them and pointed at a table holding three open boxes of doughnuts. Ben declined and took a chair by the window.

"I think we're all here. Twila won't be with us this morning." Dr. Black was looking at his notes.

"Could we discuss the lunch program for Headstart?" A plump woman in the front row asked.

A man two rows back stood and turned towards the group then waited until he had everyone's attention before he spoke. "Doc, I shouldn't need to remind you how important it is to discuss the allocation of Federal monies for a new alcohol program. The Governor of the Pueblo has personally asked me to report to him what is being planned."

Johnson Yepa, the Lieutenant Governor of the Pueblo—Ben remembered the short, stocky man from his youth. What a blow-hard. There's one in every group, he thought, and sat back to see how Dr. Black would handle the situation.

"Johnson, I want to hear the reports of my clinic personnel, first. We'll tackle how we want to spend the grant in small group discussions later."

Great. Johnson wasn't going to get away with anything. Dr. Black was staying in control. A good leader. Ben watched Johnson, who seemed to be studying something on the floor.

"I don't want to tell you your business, Doc, but something as big as alcohol, as meaningful to this Pueblo, should be getting your full attention." Johnson's voice rose to a sonorous pitch. He paused for emphasis, then with a sweeping gesture included the group. "There isn't a family in this room who shouldn't be concerned about this killer. Some of our leading citizens and artists have died because of the bottle."

Johnson looked around. Ben suddenly had the sinking feeling that he was going to be singled out.

"Some in this group have suffered grave personal loss." Johnson meaningfully dropped his voice and almost indiscernibly pointed his chin towards Ben. There was shuffling of feet and some in the group uncomfortably shifted in their chairs and looked at the floor. Everyone knew that Ben's mother had died of alcoholism.

This was a surprise. Ben hadn't expected his interpersonal communication skills to be tested so quickly, but he had to do something, defuse the situation.

"Dr. Black, I'd like to volunteer to lead a small group. I've just finished doing work with teens who drink and have some ideas to share. Mr. Yepa, I'd welcome your input. It's good to see our community leaders supporting alcohol programs." Ben thought Johnson looked surprised, maybe deflated, but he nodded his acceptance.

"Great. We can benefit from a new perspective." Dr. Black beamed his approval. "Let's move on to training for the paramedics. Earnest? Do you have an update?"

Ben listened to the reports. These were dedicated people who enjoyed what they were doing, who felt what they did was making a difference. Somewhere between the discussion to add more vegetables and decrease the pasta in the pre-school lunch menu and the vote to expand the capacity of the on-site computer; Ben made a decision.

"I appreciated the way you derailed Johnson but kept the focus on the topic." Dr. Black stood beside him as the others left the room after the meeting. "How 'bout joining us? I'd like you to take the internship."

"Thanks," Ben said, "I'd like to give it a try."

"Meet me at my office—nine tomorrow. And, one other thing, call me Sandy."

IT HAD STARTED OUT to be a bad day and had the feel of a bad rest of the week. Sandy walked into his office at six thirty a.m.—extra time to tackle the ever-present paper-work when he got a call from Twila. It was the end of her shift at the clinic; she should have been on her way home. He felt that little twinge of sixth sense; something wasn't right.

"Two more elderly people died last night. The fourth death since Monday."

Sandy sat forward. Four deaths in four days—that was a flag for an infectious disease specialist.

"Give me the symptoms again."

"Simple flu—dry coughs, aching joints, low grade fever, fatigue. One had pink eye. Then it progresses to a kind of pneumonia."

"Ages?"

"Sixty-three to seventy-four."

"Incubation time?" Sandy heard Twila take a deep breath.

"It's got to be less than twenty-four hours. But, that seems impossible."

"Send me their medical records—at least, your notes from when you examined them."

Sandy waited by the fax sipping his second cup of machine-coffee, white. He placed the papers in four neat stacks across the conference table in the nurses' lounge and sat down to consider the variables. A summer virus outside the spectrum of flu shots? Maybe. Could all four have had a history of upper respiratory? A quick check ruled that out, only the first two.

Plague was always a worry but there hadn't been any cases reported so far this year. Then he separated the last sheet from each pile, the certificate of death, and stared at the four identical causes—fluid on the lungs—suffocation.

Finding answers wouldn't be easy. The Pueblo people probably attributed these deaths to witch-craft. He needed to sit down with the Governor, apply pressure if necessary, to be able to do whatever was needed, including autopsy if there was another death. Maybe it would be a good idea to get Ben Pecos involved. He could help interview the families. Yes. He'd get Ben started right away.

THE ALBUQUERQUE Indian Hospital looked out of place, an afterthought set back as it was off of Lomas Blvd. just east of University Avenue. But it had been there first, built in the thirties, a lone tuberculosis sanitarium nestled among seedling pines that then marked the outskirts of town. Any crowding now was the fault of something else—the University of New Mexico Medical Center—the health care conglomerate next door continued to spread upward and outward and finally dwarfed the four story building. People even forgot that IHS was still there. "On Lomas? An Indian hospital? I don't remember one." Ben had stopped twice for directions.

He parked his uncle's blue Dakota under a towering evergreen and hoped that any dots of pitch would come off in the carwash. He was humming as he took the hospital steps two at a time. Once the decision had been made, it felt right, this internship; he even admitted that he was looking forward to it. His grandmother was pleased. He wasn't sure that she didn't take responsibility for it—probably paid a medicine man to cast a spell.

He got directions from the receptionist and stopped at Gloria's office.

"I'm glad you're with us. Dr. Black will see you now."

Ben thanked her and walked across the hall. Sandy was glued to a computer monitor. Ben cleared his throat.

"Ben. Come in." Sandy shot up to remove an open book from the chair beside him. "How about a change of assignment? It'll put that alcohol counseling job on the back burner for awhile, but I'd like your help on this." Sandy filled him in on Twila's news. It crossed Ben's mind to mention the cemetery and the newly provided burial spaces. Half the village, mostly the old people including his grandmother, blamed the fiscal officer. He didn't, but at least his grandmother would be pleased that he was aware of Indian thinking.

"Interview each of the families. Note anything unusual but also get the mundane stuff, what they did prior to death, what they ate. As you know, we're always concerned about plague in those areas. Make sure you don't get in the way of any customs, but I guess I don't have to tell you that."

"My grandmother keeps me straight." Ben smiled ruefully not wanting to admit how little he did know. The meeting was short. He felt Sandy was preoccupied with the illness thing. So he did a few errands in town and headed back to the reservation.

He parked the truck by the side of the house and watched a dust devil skip along the side of the irrigation ditch. It started slowly, gathered speed, sucked up bits of sand into its cone, then circled once or twice more, before it flattened and "died" silently in the weeds.

Within the fourth day of a death, wind was suspect. His grandmother believed that the wind was the soul of the departed trying to regain entry into this world. Sal Toledo had died Monday night. Had he just seen some part of Sal whirling drunkenly only to commit hari-kari in an outcropping of buffalo grass? He didn't think so.

He got out of the truck. Was there any hope for him? His lack of training in Indian ways was a source of anguish for his grandmother. She fretted that he wouldn't be careful.

"If the soul becomes lonely, it will return to take someone with it."

Four of her friends had died. He knew his grandmother believed that Sal had returned for company—taking his three friends to the other side with him. She warned his daughters and nieces to watch their children. Children could not be left in a room by themselves during this time and the houses of the dead had to be occupied by at least two people so that the souls did not reclaim their old homes. So much to remember.

His grandmother sat at the kitchen table snapping the ends off of plump green beans. Ben pulled up a chair and offered to help.

"Sal visited me last night."

Ben didn't say anything. Sometimes she saw her dead friends in her dreams.

"He said nothing but I know what he wants. He beckoned me to follow."

Ben shivered. Was this because she was old? Seventy-eight her last birthday. Did she see her own death? He didn't want to think that his time with her might be running out. He pulled a handful of beans out of the colander and waited, but she didn't say anymore.

Sal Toledo's "releasing" ritual would be performed this evening, the fourth night after his death. Sal was the husband of his grandmother's younger sister, and Ben had promised to take his grandmother to the ceremony. The house was filled with smells of his grandmother's cooking. The ritual involved all the relatives of the person, and for someone like Sal, there were generations to be fed.

THE EVENING turned cool once the sun slipped behind the mesas. Ben helped his grandmother open the windows of her house so that the adobe would gather the coolness and store it within the two foot thick walls well into the next day. When they were ready to go, she walked in front letting him carry the basket of food and bring up the rear with his uncles, aunts, and nieces. It would be easy to lose patience with his grandmother. She refused to use even a cane to help her navigate the washboard surface of the Pueblo roads.

Sal's house, a flat-roofed, boxy adobe connected on the north to his daughter's house and on the west to his brother's house was filled with people. All of the furniture had been removed from the front room, a combination living room/dining room, and food was placed in a row down the center of the floor. Paste wax and elbow grease made the linoleum shine but didn't cover up the tiny bumps in the surface. Originally, the dirt floor had been prepared with a mixture of goat's blood and ashes spread evenly into all corners, but eventually the small rocks had worked their way through the dried paste. Three pieces of linoleum covered the two rooms, their mismatched geometric patterns faded and cracked at the edges.

Ben watched as Sal's brother sat on the floor at one end of the food. A new cooking pot was placed in front of him.

Carefully, with his left hand, he scooped small portions of each kind of food that had been brought and put it into the pot then lit a cigarette made of native tobacco. He inhaled and exhaled directly over the pot and when he was finished, dropped the glowing butt into the food.

Pushing himself to his feet, he took a short-handled broom and made sweeping motions over the heads of each person in the room, standing tip toe to clear Ben's hair. Walking to the fireplace, he pulled out a cold lump of charcoal and placed it under his tongue.

After wrapping himself in a blanket, he stooped and picked up the cooking pot, put it under his left arm and walked to the door. Sal's wife and older relatives began to wrap themselves in blankets. They would follow the offering to a shrine outside the village. His grandmother tugged on his arm. She expected Ben to accompany her.

The night was still and moonless. Ben could hear frogs gallantly attracting mates along the river. The shrouded row of mourners walked single-file past the church and on toward the fields. He and his grandmother brought up the rear. Just before they reached the shrine, Sal's brother purposely dropped the pot. It exploded scattering food in a large circle. Sal's brother next drew four lines in the earth and spit out a bit of charcoal. Each follower also drew four lines. After a sharp look from his grandmother, Ben squatted and did the same the hard sandy soil resisting his efforts.

The procession turned to go back to the house and stopped a third of the way and repeated the drawing of four lines. Sal's brother again spat out a bit of charcoal. This was done two more times before the procedure was repeated in front of the door and under each window of Sal's house. At this point the brother turned to the group and offered the following prayer:

We have separated ourselves by smoke
We have painted the world between us gray
We face each other from the sides of steep arroyos
Do not, we beseech you, look upon us with longing,
but release us
let us go so that we may prosper
and you, likewise, may be free
And this, our life, will be contented.

After this final release of the soul, the members of the procession washed their hands in a bowl of water set out for them by the door. The wish of "May you have life" was met with "Let it be so" as each person reentered the house. Sal's brother picked up the handbroom, poked it into the fireplace and dusted each person with ashes and then blew ashes into the four corners of the room. With a "Now, you can eat," everyone filled his plate.

On the way home his grandmother quizzed him about what he knew of the ceremony they had just celebrated correcting him, which seemed often, when he got something wrong. Instead of going directly home, she asked him to walk with her by an abandoned house at the edge of the village. He remembered the house and a little of its story, enough to recall that as a child he knew better than to play near it.

She told him again how that family hadn't had a releasing rite after the death of their daughter. How at night they began to hear whispering and felt someone walk through the house. At last, at wit's end, they fled, abandoning their home. No one had been able to live in it since—not even today, some twenty years later.

They stood quietly, then his grandmother reached out and took his hand. "I worry that your time on this earth has been troubled. I worry that you have lost the way of your people. Your mother would be proud of you, but she would not want you to put aside your heritage. If I had been strong, they would not have taken you from me."

Ben didn't know what words would comfort his grandmother so he simply said, "I'm home now." He thought she nodded. The chirp of crickets and the distant yip of coyotes filled in the silence. At last his grandmother turned to go. She allowed him to hold her elbow when it became difficult to walk over the ruts. A minor victory. Tomorrow he would interview Sal's family and start a data bank of information hoping to find something that the four flu victims had in common.

JULIE MIGHT BE fresh out of school with a Masters in Journalism from the University of New Mexico, but she was good, the best investigative reporter in her class. Granted, her time in the field was limited but she trusted her instincts, and they were seldom wrong. So when all her feelers screamed that something was up, it was.

The Albuquerque TV station newsroom buzzed with activity, faxes, phone calls—Santa Fe had called twice that morning. First, the Tourist Bureau, then the Office of Economic Affairs, both with veiled warnings about not broadcasting something inflammatory—adopting a wait and see approach. They didn't have to worry. Her boss wanted to do just that—keep this one out of the news until they were certain. He was not a reactionary. That might explain why his station had the top ratings—consistently the top for almost ten years. That was an honor you earned, Julie knew.

"There's a meeting in my office in five minutes." It was the boss himself who walked down the narrow aisle between the twenty-odd cubicles summoning his crew.

"You think this has something to do with the mystery flu?" Julie fell into step behind a fellow reporter.

"What's your best guess?"

They both found seats in the back of Bob Crenshaw's spacious office and watched as the room filled.

"Do you ever wonder about the dress code around here? What's good for the gander isn't acceptable for the geese."

The reporter beside her had been hired on when she had and both of them were in tailored suits and heels—while the boss wore a Harley-Davidson tee shirt and Levi's.

"He's making a statement," Julie offered.

"Honey, at his age that statement should have been made long before this."

The woman seemed truly irked. Eccentricity never bothered Julie, and Bob was probably somewhere in his fifties. Couldn't he be an old Hippie? Some leftover from Woodstock? It was a little before her time. She might feel old but twenty-four years was awfully young sometimes. Besides, Bob liked to get his hands dirty, work the technical side, move a camera around once in a while. Everyone respected him for that and he wasn't going to dress in a suit to do it.

As she watched he slipped a jacket on over the black short-sleeved tee-shirt and covered the motor-cycle company's emblem. Grapevine had it that Hogs were his passion. There was no wife, no family, just inherited family money—lots of it and a really awesome road bike. Julie guessed he could do what he wanted.

Julie looked around as Bob called roll—two program directors, three editors, a couple technical folks, reporters, including herself—a well represented meeting.

"Okay. Let's get started. I don't know where to begin, but here's what I know so far. Public Health officials in Santa Fe have been notified of the fourth death in five days in the Tewa Pueblo." He paused and watched the reaction of his audience. "No one wants to call it an epidemic, not in a state that depends upon tourism for its livelihood. It seems localized and already under control, but I want to get a reporter on it right away. Julie Conlin?" He paused, looked her way and made eye contact. "I want you to take this one. After the meeting let's talk for a few minutes, I have a suggestion as to where to start."

Julie was elated and shocked. Why her? This smacked of senior level stuff. What a coup. She certainly wasn't going to turn it down. Two of the editors gave her a thumbs up sign and the reporter next to her squeezed her arm.

Bob finished up with information on the upcoming Rocky Mountain Broadcasting awards. Channel Nine had been nominated in eight categories. There was a lot of cheering and hugging and jumping up and down. After some questions about the competition, the room cleared quickly.

"Let's sit over here." Bob motioned to the conference table in the corner as he punched the intercom. "Hold my calls." He picked up a couple phone slips and then joined Julie.

"It's probably time we had a little heart to heart. How long have you been here? Three, four months?"

"Two and a half," Julie said.

"I really don't think this Tewa death thing is something to worry about. All the deaths have been people over sixty. But I'd like you to do a little snooping. If there is a problem— some outbreak of plague—I want us to be on top of it." He stared at her and lightly drummed his fingers on the table. She sat forward.

"Start with the Indian Hospital. Find out what they know and how they're going to proceed on this. Just a minute, I have the name of the contact over there." Bob looked at the phone slips on the table. "Here it is. Dr. Sanford Black. He's the honcho. Don't be afraid of a little aggressive journalism." He paused while she copied the number. "The State Tourism department is interested. They'd like to put a lid on it, of course. There's no use upsetting the public. In fact, they're hoping to delay letting the papers get it—not a cover-up, just a delay." Bob hastened to add.

"I understand. No problem," she said.

"And, kiddo, run whatever you get by me. Don't want the boys in Santa Fe upset any more than they are, and maybe I can grease some wheels if we need it." He leaned over and gave her a fatherly pat on the arm.

"This could be your chance to carve out a niche for yourself. Anchor spots are never cast in iron."

She was surprised, but she didn't let on. Anchor spot? It was every junior reporter's dream. But this was so sudden. She didn't kid herself. She'd been here two months and had completed a half dozen nondescript stories—not bad ones, just good everyday news—but not the kind that got you noticed. He let his hand linger a minute before removing it, and Julie willed herself not to squirm away. So this was the reason. She hated this barely veiled sexual approach. Was an anchor spot just the dangling of bait? I'll do something for you, sweetheart, and you do something for me.

She smiled sweetly—not a come-on—she'd treat his interest as some paternal blessing then knock his socks off with her talent. And that might not be too far from the truth. She knew she could do this story. It was a dream come true. So she got a chance at it because of her looks. So what? A pair of legs and half-way decent boobs should be worth something.

"Doings," Gloria said. She stood in the doorway to Sandy's office.

"Doings? Today?"

Sandy groaned inwardly about lost time and having to retrieve his own files. Indian ceremonies demanded attendance and were unpredictable. They happened with some regularity but little warning.

"I'll be leaving at noon."

"Anything I should know about?"

"Some woman from *Channel Nine News* called. She wants information about the deaths in the Pueblo."

"What did you tell her?" Sandy could never be certain how Gloria would handle something. Her idea of taking charge could be different than his.

"I told her to stop by this morning. You had that cancellation with the UNM people. She'll be here at ten."

Damn. He'd be rich if he had a nickel for every time he'd asked her to check with him first before making appointments.

"Did you get a name?"

"Julie Conlin. She sounded pretty."

"Sounded pretty?"

"You know, sort of young and bouncy."

"Are you trying to tempt a married man?"

"No."

Sandy wondered at the literal level of Gloria's functioning. He took off his reading glasses and pinched the bridge of his nose.

"Did she say anything else?"

"She wanted to know how she could interview people in the Pueblo. Maybe someone at the clinic."

"What did you tell her?"

"I said you could help her."

"Thanks."

"That's Okay. You'll like her."

Sandy choked back "How do you know?" because, of course, Gloria would have an answer.

JULIE CONLIN AWOKE before dawn. She could not believe her good fortune. Two months in the field—more correctly, two months out of school—and she had landed a plum. She had a feeling this story would be a headliner. She'd get air time, the kind of exposure most rookies didn't get without two years experience, and what had Bob said? "Anchor spots aren't cast in iron." Next year at this time, she'd be doing those goofy local celebrity things—ribbon cuttings, dedications, maybe a product sponsorship.

She took a step towards the bathroom, and put her weight down hard on something buried in the shag carpeting. She switched on the table lamp. Oh God, Wayne's keys—the extra set to her town house. She sat back down to rub out the sharp indentations left in the bottom of her foot. The fight had been a good one. Somewhere imbedded in the shag carpeting should be the half carat diamond engagement ring that she'd thrown at him. No, Wayne would have taken that. He would have combed the carpet on hands and knees for anything of value that might remotely be his.

She didn't care. She didn't want any reminders. She had slammed out of the house and told him to be gone by ten. She'd even given him an extra hour—stayed in the Library until closing, then got a cup of coffee. They'd been together three years and had set a wedding date twice. Then both let it drag on knowing it was never going to work, hoping it would die in some unattended way releasing them without bitterness.

But it was the bitterness and envy, yes, envy that had put a cork in it last night. Instead of congratulating her on her good fortune, Wayne had peevishly suggested that maybe it had taken something besides talent to land the assignment. Maybe, a little leg, a crotch shot ala Sharon Stone, some promise of better things to come. And she'd lost it. Somewhere between the kitchen and the dining room was a set of fake Fiesta ware in six jillion pieces.

She switched on the bathroom light, drank three glasses of water and rinsed her mouth. Her teeth seemed coated with Espresso. Would she miss the relationship? Was she in for some delayed reaction that would leave her bereft and grieving in a week? Probably not. The feeling of relief was too strong. And in all honesty, the sex hadn't been that great. Comfortable, a couple good moves, but not great. So, would she know great? Or had she read too many romance novels? Or, as her mother would say, "Honey, your expectations are just too high"

Wayne would be her cure. No more Prince Charmings, just hard work. This assignment was perfect, right time, right topic. She could really do a lot with background on Indians. Play up other epidemics. Rattle some cages with the old smallpox massacres. It would be easy to swear off men. She'd be too busy to notice.

JULIE WALKED THROUGH the sliding glass doors of the Indian Hospital at exactly five minutes to ten. The Navajo man behind the receptionist's desk looked up.

"Is Dr. Black in? I'm Julie Conlin with *Channel Nine News.*"

"Do you have an appointment?" The question was perfunctory, not hostile.

"At ten." Julie smiled and took off her sunglasses. In a comb-like sweep, she placed them on her head and left them to act as a headband in a vain attempt to tame the tumble of red-gold curls. The young man behind the desk paused to watch her, then adjusted his headset, and pushed an extension on the board in front of him.

"Doc? I got a woman down here from Channel Nine. You want to see her? What was your name again?"

"Julie Conlin."

"Okay. Go up these stairs and turn right. First door."

She could feel the young man's eyes on the back of her legs as she climbed the stairs. Fleetingly, she wished that she had worn a suit with a little longer skirt and not the above-the-knee navy. Too late now. The door to Dr. Black's office was open. She tugged her skirt down as far as it would go and walked in.

There were books everywhere. What wasn't covered by a book held a stack of papers.

Sandy turned from the computer and said. "Let me clear a space. You're here about the deaths in Tewa, right?"

"Yes." She watched the fortyish man in Dockers and madras plaid shirt clear a chair next to his desk.

"Research is my passion." He shrugged his shoulders and grinned. "I hope a little clutter doesn't bother you."

"Actually, I've never trusted anyone with a clean desk— sterile desk, sterile mind."

"Great answer." He looked at her appreciatively and leaned back in his chair. "Now, how can I help?"

"The Department of Tourism has been alerted that there may be a major medical problem in the Pueblo. Our information says four deaths in four days. Is this correct?"

"Yes. I'm reluctant to give it any inflammatory names like epidemic or plague, but we are looking at the possibility of plague." Sandy referred to a computer print-out. "All the deaths have been people over sixty. All were related. All deaths seem to follow the same pattern. Acute upper respiratory infection, lungs fill with fluid and the victim suffocates."

"What makes you suspect plague?"

"I'm not sure that I do. It's just one consideration. The illness so far doesn't present itself as anything we know. For one thing, it works quickly. Unbelievably quickly. All of its victims have died within 24 hours of showing symptoms."

The phone interrupted Julie's next question.

"Yes, Twila. When? The same age group as the others?" Sandy had tucked the receiver under his chin and was entering information on his computer. "Spell Persingula for me. Persingula Pecos, age seventy-eight. Symptoms? Fatigue, shortness of breath, aching joints—" Sandy paused. "His grandmother? I'm sorry. This is going to be rough for him but we need permission to run some tests. I'm not saying autopsy. Our chances of getting that—" Sandy turned to look at Julie.

He wishes I weren't here, she thought. But wasn't this what good journalism was all about? The luck to be in the right place at the right time?

"Ask him to meet us at his grandmother's house in an hour. I'll alert the Office of Medical Investigation." Sandy hung up.

"Number five?"

Sandy nodded. "I'd like you to be sensitive to Indian customs. The thing about the autopsies—I don't want to watch the news tonight and hear how we're shirking our duty, how we should have brought pressure."

Julie smiled. "I understand. Is there someone at the clinic in Tewa who could help me? Make sure I'm not treading on toes?"

"Yeah. Maybe there is. Here's the clinic number; ask for Ben Pecos."

Julie thanked him and put the slip of paper in her purse. She'd call the clinic when she got back to the office.

BEN MET SANDY in front of his grandmother's house. Relatives had gathered to prepare the body. His uncles had gone to the *fiscal* to request "a corner for their elder," a request that could not be turned down. The uncles would then continue to the rectory and ask Father Emerson for a requiem mass.

"I'm sorry," Sandy said.

"I still can't believe it. She woke up feeling ill this morning. I guess more tired and achy, than sick. We had gone to a ceremony last night and I thought she had overdone things, stayed out too late. I insisted that she go to the clinic." Ben paused to take a deep breath. "Twila also thought she might be reacting to a change in her schedule. There were no other symptoms to make us even suspect this mystery flu. When we got home, I insisted that she lie down. And that's how I found her. She died in her sleep.'' Ben's voice cracked. ''Twila came right away.''

''We need to take your grandmother into Albuquerque for tests. I won't use a word like autopsy. We simply need to run some tests. Something that will give us answers. Can you make the decision?''

''Not by myself. My uncles and great aunts would also need to say 'yes.' I know it should be done, but it won't be easy to get permission.''

Ben asked the senior family members to join them in the kitchen. He cleared the formica-topped table and brought in two chairs from the dining room to add to the four assorted chrome and plastic upholstered ones. Twila Runningfox motioned to him that she'd lean against the sink.

''First, let me offer my condolences. And say that my request comes from the need to put an end to the dying, the mystery killer.'' Sandy paused to look at the solemn group in front of him. ''I would like to take Ben's grandmother to Albuquerque for tests.''

''What will they do?'' an aunt asked.

''Take samples of blood, tissue, and fluids,'' Sandy said.

''This is the fifth death this week. We've got to know what we're up against to save the lives of others,'' Ben added.

''No.'' His uncle's fist hit the table.

''Won't you help us stop the dying?'' Twila stepped away from the sink. ''Dr. Black could take the body into the lab this afternoon and bring it back before sundown.'' She looked questioningly at Sandy.

''I drove the hospital van and called the Office of Medical Investigation before I left. They just need two hours. They're set up to start as soon as we get there.''

''I'll go with the body. I could bring my grandmother back this afternoon.'' Ben looked at his uncle. There was a long pause. Everyone waited. A muscle twitched in the uncle's jaw.

''I don't care. Do what you have to do.'' The uncle pushed

back from the table and slammed from the house, knocking the fragile screen door from its mountings.

Sandy and Ben unloaded the aluminum box with the plastic liner and carried it into the house. Sandy went back to the clinic to fill out papers and call the OMI to give them a time of arrival. Ben's aunts dressed his grandmother in her best skirt and blouse but not in traditional Tewa clothing, that would come later. Ben told himself not to forget to remove the turquoise nugget necklace and earrings before they reached the hospital. He decided it wouldn't be a good idea to tell his aunts that the jewelry might disappear. Ben helped his uncles carry the box from the house and balance it on the four Samsonite folding chairs he borrowed from the community center. He stood beside his grandmother and waited for Sandy. A breeze made the afternoon bearable but lifted a cloud of powdery dust from the unpaved road and coated the box. Ben traced his finger around the rim and left a shiny grit-free line. It was like writing in sand on a beach. Before he had finished, the line had faded. He wrote "I miss you" and watched the words disappear.

He had come home. Was that enough for his grandmother? To know that he called this place home and would try to discover his roots? Try to put it all in perspective? He didn't know. The hot breeze dried the tears that escaped and ran down his cheeks. Once again, he had run out of time. Someone he loved had left him behind to sort out the pieces.

JULIE HATED HOSPITALS. And the Office of Medical Investigation was worse than a hospital. Housed in the basement of the Dental Clinic behind the University of New Mexico Medical center, this was the first stop for someone who died of unknown causes. The sophisticated lab would begin a series of tests that might mean sending body parts on to pathology. Not the kind of place she enjoyed spending an afternoon. But if it meant getting a story, she'd go anywhere. Well, almost. She wasn't about to disappoint Bob Crenshaw. The thought of junior anchor hovered like a subliminal carrot.

The clinic in Tewa had said that Ben Pecos would be at the

OMI lab at four-thirty. It was four forty-five. She hoped she hadn't missed him.

She took a deep breath, pushed the double doors open and walked as quickly as heels would permit on the thick rubber mat that covered the tile floor. The place smelled too clean. The curving corridor reeked of sterilization processes. And everything was spotless—floors, walls, doors—even the elevator was scrubbed to a shine. You could eat off the floor.

Yuk. Not a good idea. But she had always heard lab technicians were so insensitive to their surroundings that they could have a jelly doughnut in one hand and cut with the other. Disgusting, but probably true.

The corridor angled to the right and ended at a set of double doors. There was a makeshift waiting room outside with two chrome and black leather chairs, an ashtray that looked like a miniature space needle and a smoke-gray plastic magazine rack fastened to the wall. Someone's attempt to be homey, Julie thought, but it didn't quite make it.

There was a man standing beside a silver colored box, some kind of lab casket, she supposed, strapped to a gurney. There were two more lined up behind that one. The man was young, tall, and even from the side strikingly handsome with high cheekbones. A shock of unruly brown straight thick hair fell over his right eye. He absently pushed it away. His 501's and tee shirt hugged a muscular physique. "Oh God," Julie prayed, "let me be clever." She stepped forward.

"I'm sure if that one's taken, they could find you an empty before sunrise." She let a teasing smile linger a moment.

The man turned to look at her. His eyes moved slowly over her face. In anger? Disgust? Dismissal? She couldn't read his expression. Finally, he turned back towards the box and said, "This is my grandmother."

Julie hoped if she just waited the sky might fall, in this case, rows and rows of florescent lights in the ceiling would explode all around her and bury her in rubble. How could she have been so stupid, so callous? What was worse, now she couldn't seem to find anything to say.

She was saved by an older man in a white lab coat who

pushed through the double doors. He noticed Julie and glanced from one to the other before he decided that they were not together.

"Can I help you?" he said to Julie.

"I'm here to meet Ben Pecos. The clinic in Tewa said that I could find him at the OMI."

"I think you already have. Ben, when you're finished, I need to see you inside."

Julie watched the doors swing shut; the rubber molding held them perfectly aligned. Julie wished the man had stayed, wished she didn't have to turn around. Ben Pecos. She needed a really big favor from someone she had just insulted. She took a deep breath and turned to face him.

"I'm sorry. My remark earlier was thoughtless. I was expecting someone who looked more...."

"Indian?"

Julie nodded and wished she could take the remark back. Why was she making such a mess of things?

"Could we start over? I really feel awful." She thought she detected the hint of a smile. "I'm Julie Conlin, *Channel Nine News*." She held out her card. "Dr. Black thought you could help me in reporting on the mystery illness—keep me from putting my foot in my mouth. Which can be a full time job if you hadn't noticed."

This time a laugh. Yes. He was smiling. She met his gaze and found herself hoping he liked her, had forgiven her at least, because the queasy feeling in the pit of her stomach never lied. She was attracted to this man.

"What do you need?"

"An interview with clinic personnel, maybe someone on the tribal counsel."

"When?"

"As soon as possible. I'm doing a brief spot tonight at ten, background mostly, but need to follow it up with something in depth tomorrow."

"Meet me at the clinic in the afternoon. Two o'clock. Do you know how to get there? I-25 to Bernalillo, through town on highway 44 then take highway 4 out of San Isidro. Second turn to the left after you see the Tewa village sign.''

"I'll find it." Julie smiled and held out her hand. She knew he was watching her navigate the rubber mat as she walked back up the corridor. She willed herself to exit professionally and not get a heel caught. For the first time that day, she was glad she had on the shorter skirt.

"YOU GET RID of the girl already? Nothing personal, but I'd rather look at her than you." The man laughed showing an upper row of uneven, stained teeth. A smoker, Ben thought, probably explains the ashtray in the hall.

"I need your John Henry here," the man pointed to the top page of a stack of papers then flipped to a sheet near the back, "and here. Date both entries, and you're on your way."

"How soon will you have the results?" Ben asked.

"Hard to say. I know this is priority, but don't expect much before the first of next week. C'mon. I'll give you a hand getting the box in your van."

This wasn't the way he should be taking his grandmother back to the Pueblo. Her frailness under the sheet on the table inside had made him feel sick. He hadn't been able to help her. Had he, in some way, let this happen? He slammed the back doors of the van shut and climbed behind the wheel. He looked down the driveway at the sun still well above the tops of the trees. There would be time to prepare his grandmother for burial before it set.

Ben usually didn't mind the drive from Albuquerque to the Pueblo. New Mexico 44 was a long stretch of highway without the usual visual distractions of signs, or gas stations, or even residences. Winding through the flat land before gently rising to meet the mesas, the asphalt was flanked by blue-green clumps of chamisa and sage. In the distance the mesas rose like leavened cakes high above the desert floor, their flattened tops dotted with pinon. The sprinkling of green stood out in sharp contrast to the reds of their steep rock sides.

This was his heritage; this country that Coronado discovered four hundred years ago. He had come in search of the seven cities of Cibola, golden cities of great wealth. What he found were several sun-baked adobe farming villages with the names of Halona, Hawikuh, Matsake, Kiakima, Kawkina, and Kianawa. What he left was religion, oppression, illness...death.

Maybe he should make a commitment to help his people. Accept an IHS grant and return to school in January to continue in psychology. Didn't he owe his grandmother that? Even if it meant a payback after he graduated—working in some god-forsaken place. A place he might not want to live? Like Pawnee, Oklahoma or Rosebud, South Dakota? He sighed. The internship would help him make up his mind.

In the meantime, he wondered what he would tell the reporter, Julie. He found himself looking forward to seeing her again. Would she be upset if she knew that a medicine man had already planned a communal cleansing rite? A rite that required that the man enter a clairvoyant trance to seek out the witches who had done this evil? Ben smiled. He'd stick to the conventional stuff.

His aunts met him at the house. Already people were bringing food. His two uncles carried the coffin into the bedroom and his aunts shooed everyone out in order to prepare the body. If they were surprised to find the body sealed in a plastic ziplock freezer bag, no one said. Ben had remembered to put the jewelry in the box beside his grandmother.

The grave had been dug and three of the four *fiscales* came to the house to take the body to the church. The fourth *fiscal* remained in the grave to insure that witches would not jump in and claim it as their own or plant evil objects. Ben joined the procession and walked numbly to the cemetery. The Catholic rites were short. The priest sprinkled holy water, offered a prayer, and threw a handful of dirt into the grave with his left hand. A bundle of his grandmother's prized possessions were placed under her head including the pot used in her naming ceremony.

The *fiscal* stood at the head of the grave and told the mourners that Ben's grandmother had gone to the place of "endless cicada singing." He told them not to be sad or let the death divide their home. Ben forced himself back from the pain and concentrated on the late summer afternoon. He watched the flame-red sun sink behind the trees along the river. A breeze teased the leaves of the cottonwoods twisting each individually, their green-gold heart shapes fluttering, then falling still. Away, beyond the river the mesas formed a stairway—a now purple-black silhouette of giant stepping stones.

Ben stepped to the back of the group of mourners. He felt suffocated. He would say his good-byes later. He closed his eyes and breathed three long abdominal intakes of air. He stood a moment in the shade of a cluster of Russian Olive before walking back to the house.

He set aside the screen door that was propped in the doorway. Ben smelled the house's mustiness that even the platters of fried chicken and casseroles of enchiladas couldn't mask. His aunt had left a shoebox of belongings his grandmother had wanted him to have on the table. His name was scrawled across the lid. He toyed with opening it, then pushed the box to one side and got a glass of water. The water looked faintly yellow with a hint of sediment swirling in it. He put the glass down without taking a drink. Not unusual. The water purification system often had problems. He was certain that the team of health specialists had already taken samples.

What a relief if the cause of the illnesses turned out to be something like the water. Something that could be changed, controlled. Something the tribal lawyers could have a field day with—as if they needed an excuse for litigation.

He walked back to his bedroom. The room seemed crowded, cramped with only a dresser and single bed. The chenille bedspread, its fuzzy lines and dots worn smooth along the top, looked dinghy. Ben walked to the window and opened the curtains. It didn't seem to help. The room needed paint and bright colors and a child's happiness. And that was something it had never had. At least not for a long time. His earliest memories were of hiding behind the door and crying when his mother would come home drunk. His grandmother had been the one to comfort him and shield him from the scenes—the screaming, the anger, the sickness.

His mother had started college but was pregnant before

Christmas. The father could have been anyone. A classmate. A professor. She gave birth to Ben in this house and made pottery bowls intricately designed with black and white patterns on smooth clay to support the two of them. But after awhile the selling trips to Santa Fe and Albuquerque stretched into weeks of partying. When the money ran out, she came home and made more pots. Later she made storytellers, small clay women with babies sitting on laps, hanging from necks, clinging, adoring, loving.

Ben hated the storytellers. In their cloying stillness they mocked the essence of a mother that he had never had. On his senior trip in high school he visited the Smithsonian and stood and stared at his mother's work. Fourteen years later and two thousand miles from home, he stood and studied the perfectly crafted figure of the storyteller and could not hold back the sobs of anguish—for the mother he had never known and the artist who had died so young.

No one knew the father of the baby his mother lost that spring when he was four. Maybe the Mescalero Apache bull rider who hung around during the summer with a mending clavicle. The pregnancy sobered his mother, and she did her best work that winter. She was ill much of the time. The alcohol weakened her body. She stayed at home and played with her son and created. It was the happiest winter of Ben's life only to be shattered in late April when his mother was taken to the hospital and didn't return.

Ben walked back to the kitchen and opened the fridge. A six-pack of Dr. Pepper sat on the second shelf. Not his favorite, but better than tap water. He sat at the kitchen table. Had his grandmother been right to let him be adopted? What would he have done had he stayed?

Idly, he flipped the top of the shoebox to one side and pulled away the layers of tissue paper, and caught his breath. The storyteller was on its side but he could tell it was one of his mother's best. He gingerly placed it on the table and moved it so that the figure sat squarely in the middle of a shaft of light. He turned it to the right and back to the left. A mother and child—the child standing on the woman's lap, arms around her neck—a baby boy close to his mother's heart with brown hair and Anglo features.

JULIE TURNED AT the second left after the sign that welcomed visitors to the Pueblo. The short incline of dirt road leveled immediately and continued until it widened to form a parking lot in front of the community center, public health clinic, and tribal offices. All the buildings looked new and affected in their pretend-adobe styling. Only the fire station at the rear looked functional and unpretentious. A new red truck outfitted with flattened hoses that snaked around pegs on its side was being polished by two men in tribal-tan uniforms.

Ben was waiting for her and waved her to a spot in front of the Governor's office. Friendly, Julie thought. That's promising.

"Can I help with anything?" Ben leaned in the driverside window.

"No thanks." Julie turned to pull the laptop from under the front seat and then froze.

"Ben. Over there." Julie pointed through the windshield to the right of the car.

"Nothing to worry about. That's Lorenzo Loretto. Don't ask me how old he is, he's been around forever." They both watched as the bent figure passed in front of the car. Lorenzo waved his cane in the air and worked his puckered lips that were pulled back into the dark cavern of his mouth. Only nonsensible sounds came out.

"Ya-tee. Na, na, na. Hey-toe, na. Yaha nee."

"He'd look better with teeth," Ben said. "The clinic had a set made for him, but he lost them, or traded them for something he wanted."

"Is he all right?" Julie was pointing to Lorenzo's ragged blanket and soiled shirt. His deeply lined weathered skin hung from prominent cheekbones and left hollows where flesh should have been. Wispy, matted white hair stuck to his forehead held there by a rolled red bandanna that had slipped rakishly over one eyebrow. Droplets of drool left the corners of his mouth and followed the deep creases in his chin before sliding down his neck.

"There's probably no better place for him to be. Better here outside in the fresh air than locked up in a hospital or home. Everyone keeps an eye on him," he said.

"He seems a little eerie."

"I still say it's the teeth. A set of choppers and you've got Cary Grant."

"But is he harmless?" Julie watched as Lorenzo continued to wave his cane slicing the air in front of him.

"Only one blemish on his record—a breast-slapping incident involving a nun."

"What?" Ben had her full attention now.

"Two summers ago, coming out of church, one of the more well-endowed nuns had a June bug land on her chest. Lorenzo squashed it flat. He had witnesses. He was only trying to be helpful. Everyone thought it was funny, but the nun was pretty flustered."

"Are you pulling my leg?" Julie waited for him to laugh but his face was deadpan.

Suddenly, a short, plump Pueblo woman ran out of the tribal offices looking distraught.

"Help. Someone. Come quick. It's the Governor. He's collapsed."

Julie and Ben left the equipment and ran after her. The office was dark and it took Julie a moment to adjust to the dim light. An oversized walnut desk and two glass-fronted bookcases filled the back wall. On a Two Gray Hills Navajo rug in front of the desk lay the crumpled body of an elderly man. His bronze skin looked sallow and drawn. His eyes stared unseeing at the ceiling and his breath escaped through his mouth in raspy whispers.

Ben dropped to his side and loosened the constricting bolo tie and unbuttoned his shirt. He yelled at the Pueblo woman to get the paramedics.

"How's your CPR?" Ben asked, his fingers pressed against the carotid artery.

"Up to date, but I've never used it."

"Like it or not, I think you're going to get your chance. I'm not getting a pulse. Let's do this together; you take the chest." He reached up to grab a handful of Kleenex from the desk and swabbed the inside of the man's mouth to check for obstructions. "All Clear. Okay. Here we go, on a four count. Me first." Ben bent forward over the man's mouth, pinched his nostrils shut and inflated his lungs with air.

Julie placed the heel of her right hand on the back of her left hand and rested both lightly on the Governor's chest. She leaned over the body with her elbows bent poised above the sternum. On cue and counting under her breath, she let her body's weight fall forward and down in quick thrusts. A brittle rib gave way with a snap. The rubber dummies never did that, she thought. Noticing her grimace, Ben said reassuringly, "Ignore. Bones heal, but you have to be alive first." She watched as he again filled the man's lungs with air and she waited to repeat her routine. Pausing, Ben checked for vitals.

"Okay. Let's go again."

"He wasn't even sick." The Pueblo woman had reappeared in the door. "He started coughing yesterday." She twisted a Kleenex and shifted her weight from one foot to the other. "He said that he hadn't slept last night, the coughing kept him up. And then he started to walk around his desk and fell to the floor." Her voice ended in sobs.

Julie's turn to rest. Rocking back on her ankles, she shook her forearms and hands and bent forward on cue pushing with her weight. She didn't see the paramedics rush into the room but scrambled out of the way as two uniformed men dropped to the rug beside her. She suddenly didn't have the strength to stand, so she leaned against a wall away from the frenzied activity in front of her. The wall felt cool against the sweaty dampness of her blouse. She pulled her knees up and rested her chin on crossed forearms. She felt drained and helpless.

Ben leaned against the opposite wall. A lock of damp hair stuck to his forehead. The scene between them was barely controlled bedlam. The two paramedics and the Governor were part of a jumble of wires and paddles and metal cases of dials and electronic graphs all beeping out information in a code foreign to her. With a press of a button, the old man flew into the air and flopped back grotesquely. Again, the electric zapping charged through his body. And, a third time. Suddenly, the room was quiet. Julie, Ben and the two paramedics formed a tableau. Each unbclieving, each reliving the scene before him, each questioning his part in its outcome.

"We've lost him," said one of the paramedics. His voice sounded hollow.

Julie stood and moved with Ben towards the door. The Indian woman cried softly at her desk.

"Is there anything we can help with, Mary?" Ben asked as the woman looked up.

"No. I can take care of things." She blew her nose. "Ben, thank you for trying to keep him with us."

As Julie stepped outside, she was blinded by the sunlight. The day was glorious. A slight breeze played with the hem of her skirt and tugged at her hair. She waited and hoped the numbness would pass. It didn't.

"I need to call the station." Julie said. "Bob will want to do something for the evening news. Is there a phone someplace out of the way?"

"The community center." Ben said.

Mary stood by her desk as the two Indian paramedics strapped the Governor's body to a gurney. She sent a young man from the community center to notify the man's family. His brothers needed to know so that they could meet at the house to dress the corpse in traditional Tewa ritual clothing. His moccasins would be reversed, and a bit of his favorite food, something that he enjoyed most in life, would be wrapped in cotton and placed in his left armpit.

Mary walked to his desk and gathered a few pumpkin seeds from the basket he always kept there and carefully folded them into a Kleenex. She would take them to the house and see that they made the journey to the next world with him. Everything in the after world or the world beneath this one was reversed. So, the amount of food sent with the man was in direct proportion to his station in this life. If an individual was not so highly regarded, or worse yet had not led a virtuous life, more food and even an extra pair of moccasins would be added because the road would have many turns and be rocky.

The governor would need very little of his favorite food for his journey because the road would be straight. A few pumpkin seeds would be perfect. This man was a good man much loved by his people. Mary stopped to find another Kleenex and dabbed at her eyes. She couldn't believe that she'd never see him alive again.

But, she needed to hurry. Tonight there would be a *velorio* and all the members of the village would come for a few minutes to pay their respects. Some relatives and close friends would stay the night. Meals would be served at all hours. Sometimes the family would sing Spanish funeral dirges and offer Spanish prayers.

Mary locked the office door and walked up the dirt path that led to the village. What did it mean that their Governor would take a space in the cemetery in front of the Church? One of the new spaces created by the expansion of the grounds. Would there be more deaths? Until the spaces were filled?

Mary paused before turning down the road that led to the Governor's house. The next four days were critical to the Governor's passing safely into the next world. She thought she had seen his soul leave his body. It had to leave through the mouth and Ben and his pretty lady friend were trying to bring him back. Mary sighed. She hoped they had not interfered.

The soul needed to move on to the next world. Nothing in this world should impede it. If the soul felt it had unfinished business on earth it would go around to all the people it owed something to and ask forgiveness. Mary suddenly thought of the five dollars she had loaned the Governor on Monday.

"I don't need the money. It was a gift." She shouted to an empty sky and turned down the road already lined with cars bringing mourners.

THE PAY PHONE was under the bleachers. Julie deposited a quarter then a dime and slumped against the wall. She was still shocked to see someone die. The assignment had suddenly lost its allure. When Bob answered, she outlined her ideas for a spot and got the go-ahead. She joined Ben on the bleachers and for a long time they sat side by side. Ben took her hand but didn't break the silence.

"Thanks for helping," he said finally.

"The outcome should have been different. I can't believe we lost him." Julie turned to face Ben. "I feel strongly about getting this information to the public. This was the sixth death. I've talked the station into sending a crew out. Is there somewhere we could film a spot for the six o'clock news?"

"Anywhere outside the village." Ben said.

"Will you let me interview you on camera?"

"I guess so if you think I can help."

THE SIX O'CLOCK NEWS opened with the electronic logo bursting onto the screen and the tag line, "Governor of Tewa Pueblo dies of unexplained illness, flood waters recede in the Midwest...all this and more, stay tuned for *Channel Nine News* with..." a cut to a commercial and then the two evening anchors began. "Channel Nine is on the scene this evening in the Tewa Pueblo where yet another unexplained death has occurred. We take you now live to Julie Conlin, our reporter in the field."

Julie stood beside the road that curved in back of her through the red rocks canyon. The long rays of the afternoon sun spread a rufus tint across the ground while above her high white cumulus clouds had exploded over the mesa's top, their billowy edges defined by the azure sky. She moved towards the camera.

"Dan, Margo," she began, "At 2:20 this afternoon, the Governor of the Tewa Pueblo died of an unexplained illness—the sixth person to die of the same symptoms. I've asked Ben Pecos to share with our viewing audience what this means..."

The camera zoomed in for a close-up of the man beside her and seemed to continue to glide into his large dark eyes. It sought his core and transmitted the raw pain to those watching. He was open and vulnerable and powerful and believable. He talked of Indian epidemics, curses of the past, and eulogized the elderly who had died that week taking with them the rich history of his people.

Julie knew the piece had been good, exactly right for the severity of the problem. People all over New Mexico—the United States, for that matter—were beginning to count the deaths on their fingers and put any plans to visit the area on hold.

THREE

HE WAS GOVERNOR. Johnson Yepa was Governor of the Tewa Pueblo. He repeated the title out loud… "Governor of the Tewa Pueblo." He would lead his people in this time of need. He would champion the rights of the abused, make opportunities available that had never been possible before. He would be written about, remembered as a modern savior. The village of his ancestors, of his peers, of his family would never be the same again.

There would be money for whatever his people wanted. Even new homes. No more fighting over HUD handouts, like that row of pitched-roof houses that flanked the village, the first thing that outsiders saw as they approached the Pueblo from the main highway—pointy-roofed houses that lined a paved road one quarter of a mile long aimed towards the mountains but going nowhere. It looked for all the world like a strip of suburbia had dropped from the sky—seventeen houses with slanted roofs, one block before the Tewa Industrial park (a corrugated steel sided building that housed a machine shop), the fire station, public health clinic, tribal offices, and two blocks before visitors saw four-hundred-year-old homes clustered around bare dirt arteries that wound in and out lacing the community together.

Johnson remembered all too well that the houses were a gift, although questionable, of the Department of Housing and Urban Development in the late 1970's. The Washington bureaucrats had promised to build a number of frame and stucco three-bedroom houses and gave the Indians a choice of flat or pitched roofs. All but one of the eighteen homes had a pitched roof. His people had become dependent upon handouts. The houses were just one example. But even the handouts had strings....

Besides the bickering about how the new houses would be allotted, the red-tape of just getting them done rivaled working with the Bureau of Indian Affairs. Many people from Tewa and the outside were genuinely incensed that the village allowed pitched roofs and ruined the esthetics of the centuries-old adobe structures in the village. Johnson and others simply pointed to the shoddy workmanship and stated that the HUD houses would fall down in twenty years anyway.

The anger and gossip seemed to dissipate as the first house was erected on its own slab a discreet distance from where its neighbor would be. Then envy set in. There was a waiting list and an elaborate scheme for choosing the owners. Those getting a new home stood in line to pick from the stacks of carpet swatches or decide the fate of their kitchens and bathrooms by peering at two inch squares of linoleum that fanned out from a key ring.

Johnson Yepa's mother had been eligible for one of the pitched-roof houses. When she died, he inherited it. It was his mother who put in the rose pink toilet, matching sink and bath-tub. He put in the split-rail fence and lawn, the only lawn on the street, the only lawn in the Pueblo—the strip of rough bermuda grass now sprinkled with dinnerplate-sized brown spots caused by the pee of the neighbor's dog.

Johnson squatted, then got down on all fours. Enough of this daydreaming, he needed to finish the job he'd started. Dragging the last of the forty-odd plastic milk bottles filled with water, he crawled to the edge of the lawn. Smoothing a circular resting place, he seated the gallon of water upright, and sat back to survey his handiwork. On hands and knees, he had spent most of the morning planting these guaranteed dog deterrents. The lawn now looked like it had sprouted small opaque statues each sporting a jaunty red or blue cap. Not bad. This should do it. His wife read in a magazine that this would work.

He stood and brushed loose bits of lawn clippings from his slacks and then retired to the porch. He was admiring the display when he saw the dog. It started toward the yard, stopped, loped to the corner where Johnson's property met the asphalt, trotted along the front of the split rail fence, dropped to its stomach and squirmed forward, under the bottom rail and onto the lawn. Johnson thought it tried to make eye contact before it picked out a perfectly green patch of grass and squatted, right in front of him, ignoring his shouting.

Johnson took one last look at the lawn. The hot desert sun, now overhead, made it uncomfortable to stay out much longer. He watched as the dog sniffed at half a dozen of the jugs before going home. The dog was probably too dumb to understand a warning. But maybe the bottles would work for smart dogs. He'd leave them.

Today the brown grass wasn't his only problem. He needed to plan. With the Governor dead, the honorable Johnson Yepa would sign the papers to put a casino on Indian land. His land. A real casino, no bingo palace with fake Vegas dancers in sequins and feathers. No grandmas who played twenty cards at a time and lost their welfare checks. No. This would be high class. Men in suits driving fancy cars. Men who would bet a hundred dollars at a time. And come back for more. He pulled open the screen door but turned back and decided to do what he did almost every day—walk to the site that he'd chosen for the casino, give life to his dream. The dream that would save his people from poverty.

Johnson would walk to the two acres down by the river, about a mile from where he was standing. His plan was to extend the street in front of his house. Make it go somewhere and keep the traffic from disturbing the old portion of Tewa. People wouldn't even realize they were in an Indian village. He had learned early on that living in HUD housing negated his heritage. Somehow you couldn't be the real thing if the roof of your house wasn't flat and the walls weren't made of earth. His wife sold frybread in front of their house every summer on weekends but never did as well as her sister who lived in an old adobe three blocks away. Anglos, who could figure them?

Sweat dotted his hairline as Johnson struck out behind his house cutting through a gully that connected with a hard packed dirt road leading to the river. Tumbleweeds, green and pliable, grew waist high in early August. Struggling up the rocky incline, Johnson waited at the top to catch his breath. His new oxblood brown Ropers were covered with red dust, but he hardly noticed. When he started out again, Johnson kicked a flattened Pepsi can, kept it going in a straight line down the middle of the road until he tired of the game and scooped it up to put in his pocket. He hated litter. He hated poverty. As Governor he would lead his people to jobs, status, the money to have a good education and health care.

As a little personal reward, he'd buy himself a powerboat and maybe that new Cadillac. A red convertible Cadillac. A little "up-front" money had been mentioned by the investors to the tune of two hundred thousand. Johnson could hardly contain his glee; he would be rich. A shadow flitted across the sun—a hawk—maybe something larger. Johnson paused but kept the thoughts of what he had done in order to become rich from pushing into his consciousness. It was best not to dwell on it.

"Almost there." Johnson said out loud and felt the excitement bubble up like it always did. A walk in 97 degree heat was no picnic. But any discomfort was always forgotten when he gazed upon the two acres that were soon to be transformed, made glorious by his careful planning. Johnson's hair, heavy with pomade, hugged his scalp and trapped droplets of sweat, but he couldn't scratch and disturb the high wave that circled up from his forehead. He pulled his brown polyester shirt out away from his skin and felt refreshed as a breeze skipped in to tickle his chest and dry the perspiration under his arms. He felt wilted. So, why did he come here every day? Suffer the heat and discomfort over and over—but he knew why. It was his dream, his life. He couldn't stay away.

The words of the investors echoed in his ears. "This is a good choice. Perfect for our plan." He remembered the first time the three of them had stood silently looking at the barren field. Johnson couldn't say what the others saw, but he was looking at his casino. Its parking lot alone would be an acre of asphalt. Johnson could see the towering lights that in pairs would spring up out of tiny islands of greenery. At midnight, it would be as bright as day. Millions of pieces of crushed mirrors would be imbedded in the facade of the building itself, each sliver reflecting a palette of primary colors as spotlights turned and scattered light through the cascading water of the twenty foot fountain. He would be able to drive a semi through the gilt edged, double-door entry.

The carpet inside would be thick and one inch deep. Purple, yes, he liked purple. Johnson hadn't decided whether he would wear a tuxedo in the evenings. He might wear a silk shirt with ballooning sleeves. What had the saleslady called it? A poet's shirt? He knew he would wear black patent leather loafers with a bar of gold trim across the instep and one and one half inch block heels. The shoes were in a box behind the seat of the Bronco. Sometimes his wife ridiculed his clothes and laughed with his sisters behind his back. So, she didn't need to know about the shoes. But who would have the last laugh when they saw him with movie stars and toasting his success among politicians?

"This could be another Inn of the Mountain Gods." Johnson recalled the remark that had made his heart beat wildly. There was nothing wrong in thinking big. The investors could see the possibilities. And Johnson liked the idea of duplicating the success of the Mescalero Apaches south of Ruidoso. Why not have a Pueblo get in on the tourist action? Attract a few rich Texans. The Pueblos didn't have timber or fishing rights to sell. No one would ever discover oil on their land. One pueblo grew blue corn for a line of London based body shop products, another opened a native-plants nursery, two operated sand and gravel pits; but not one really made money, not even the ones that had bingo—not big money, like a casino.

Johnson nervously picked at the cuticle on his thumb. There would be some who would say that the price of all this was too great, that he shouldn't have…shouldn't have done what was necessary. But what had he really done anyway? He'd just taken advantage of an opportunity. Isn't that the way the investors had phrased it? An opportunity—one that wouldn't come again.

He turned back and saw the white walls of the casino waver mirage-like in the distance and felt relief like a gentle wind carry away his concerns. He felt up-lifted. He believed that he had been called upon to make this possible. Yes. He would lead his people forward.

"SOMEONE'S HOLDING on one," Gloria said.

"I'll take it in my office."

Sandy walked past the four women at the switchboard. Sunday, and IHS had to staff the phones. The calls had started after the broadcast on Thursday. "Will I be exposed to the mystery illness if I visit New Mexico?" That wasn't so bad, but then some of the questions got ridiculous. "I was in Hobbs last week, should I get tested?" Tested. The illness didn't even have a name, let alone some way to predict it. The public expected medicine to have an answer to everything. How soon they forgot Legionnaires Disease or Toxic Shock Syndrome.

Sandy picked up his phone braced for the worst.

"Hey, pal, you're up to your eyeballs with this one." The voice was familiar.

"Pres!" Preston Samuels, Director of the Center for Disease Control in Atlanta, had been a mentor and supervisor.

"Tell me about this news conference tomorrow. I'm being encouraged to attend."

"Only if you have some news about the tissue and blood samples we sent."

"I don't want to sound crass, but I'm not sure you had our full attention until the last two deaths. It's not like we're sitting on our hands waiting for a new challenge."

"So, the answer's no?"

"Incomplete. We're still working, but don't get your hopes up. Looks like a pneumonia but difficult to classify."

"If we're lucky, we may already be out of the woods. We haven't had a death in four and a half days."

"Let's hope. But you know what they say about luck—it only applies to horseshoes."

THREE EPIDEMIOLOGISTS, including Preston Samuels from the CDC, an official from the State Health agency, a representative from the Bureau of Indian Affairs and Dr. Sanford Black, infectious disease specialist, sat on the dais in Woodard Hall at the University of New Mexico. All the big guns, Julie thought as she adjusted her recorder. The state was getting its ducks in a row pretty quickly on this one. But didn't it have to? The summer's tourism was probably already down the toilet.

She tested her equipment. She'd broadcast live from the auditorium for the noon news update. She had become an on-the-air regular, giving briefings daily, answering call-in questions. She hadn't been wrong about this story—it was making her career. Everyone was interested and judging from the packed auditorium in front of her, interest wouldn't diminish any time soon. But how could you expect interest to just disappear when lives appeared to be threatened. And nobody had any concrete answers. It was easy to panic over the unknown. She took a seat to the right of the podium when the moderator motioned that they were ready to begin.

Dr. Black gave an overview of the victims' symptoms and stressed that the illness seemed contained but that prompt medical treatment was essential—within the first six hours—if the mystery flu was suspected. Preston Samuels went next and gave a brief history of the CDC, how it's a maximum security prison for microorganisms and could assign over one hundred scientists in a round-the-clock research effort if the deaths continued.

Then one of the epidemiologists gave the illness a name: Unexplained Adult Respiratory Distress Syndrome or UARDS—pointing out that there were about three thousand cases of UARDS in the United States last year. Was he suggesting that they might not ever know what was causing the mystery flu? Not very comforting, Julie thought.

Another epidemiologist took the mike to explain that they were working to find out what it wasn't and reminded the audience that most discoveries were made by ruling things out. He went on to discuss how they were considering everything from plague to paraquat, an herbicide often used on marijuana plants. And he likened the "not knowing" to how it must have been before weather tracking when a tornado or hurricane could strike without warning. There were affirmative murmurs from the audience.

Finally, someone asked about autopsies. Dr. Black took the microphone. "We're working with the Pueblo and will honor their customs whenever we can. We've been able to run a fairly sophisticated set of tests on one of the victims and the results have been inconclusive. Let me ask the BIA representative to present the Native American viewpoint. Ed?"

A tall Indian man in red vest and blue jeans stood to address the audience. A Santo Domingo man, he was wearing the traditional chongo, a braiding process that left a vertical knot of ribbons intertwined with black hair at the nape of his neck. Three strands of pin shell and turquoise heishi gleamed under the harsh light bar set up for filming. He spoke clearly, but haltingly, and chose his English words carefully.

There was no doubt that Indian customs were complicating the search for answers, mused Julie. She listened as he described how some elders were blaming MTV, video games, and even fast food. Tewa medicine men were performing purification rites, but the BIA representative pledged Pueblo support of Western medicine in the future. There was polite applause when he sat down.

"Not a lot of answers." She hadn't seen Ben in the audience until he slipped into a seat beside her at the end.

"How are the family interviews going?" she asked.

"They haven't been productive yet. About the only thing that the victims shared recently was a Seniors' meeting at the community center. And four of them were in church on the Sunday before they died, including my grandmother."

"It sounds like it's going to take the CDC a while to come up with answers, too."

"Have time for coffee?"

"We're taping the spot for the noon news, and I've lined up one of the epidemiologists for an interview. Can I have a rain check?" Julie hoped she had flashed her most dazzling smile.

JOHNSON HAD MET the Hispanic foreman at the edge of the village Monday morning and directed the crew of five men to the parcel that needed clearing. Every day since then, he had stood at the edge of the field and watched their progress. He couldn't call it a ground breaking—not yet. It was just some preliminary road and site preparation. But he'd be signing the final papers soon. In a month the foundation would be laid for the casino.

He stepped aside as the tree movers pulled up. He had designated fifteen trees to be moved and saved. He would make sure the journalist who did the write up knew he was a conservationist. Anglos liked to think that Indians were close to the earth.

"Hey. You there." Johnson waved at the backhoe operator. "Don't leave all this dirt here in one pile. I want this spread evenly—" A cloud of exhaust fumes choked off the rest of his directions as the machine jolted dangerously close and then pulled away. Pig. Johnson swore softly under his breath.

The first young cottonwood found a new home. Johnson had hired a crew from the Pueblo to divert the irrigation ditch to run along side the building site. Two pinons and a mountain juniper followed. He had the crew plant them in a cluster to the right of the entrance where the long curve of asphalt would take cars back to the valet station. His nephew would be in charge of the valets. Every kid in the village with a driver's license would be wanting a job. Johnson would have killed as a teenager to drive BMW's, Mercedes and Lincolns—even if it had been just in and out of a parking space.

His dining room would attract only the discriminating. He would steal Mollie away from the Andersons. What did they call her? A domestic? Domestic or not, she was the best cook in New Mexico. He grinned. She was pretty good at a couple other things, too. Mollie's soft breasts swam before his eyes.

"Hey. Watch out. You wanna get killed?" The driver of the backhoe yelled down at him. The backhoe had come within six inches of hitting him. Johnson thought of flipping him off. He needed to show the prick who was in charge. Instead, he dusted off his slacks and walked back up the road towards his office.

Ben Pecos was interviewing Mary this morning about the death of the Governor. He'd better be there.

BEN WATCHED Johnson Yepa walk towards him. He really found it impossible to like the man. He was just a general pain in the ass with a knack for knowing how to irritate.

"Ben, how you doing?" Johnson held out his hand and looked up at him. "Ever get that alcohol program going? You know that's just the kind of thing we expect from IHS. A little preventive medicine."

Ben almost didn't extend his hand. He hated the moist grasping that Johnson called a handshake.

"Start up should be in October. But let's talk about today. I'll meet with Mary and then I'd like to ask you some questions. Will you be free in an hour?"

"Don't know. Hard to say. I don't think I can help." Johnson looked away, and Ben thought he feigned interest in something over by the highway.

"You don't think you can help because of time or you feel you might not know anything that might be helpful?"

God, the man could fidget; he had the attention span of a sparrow. And Ben knew that whatever came out of his mouth next would be a lie. He'd probably forgotten about being interviewed this morning. Mary had rolled her eyes when Ben had asked about the schedule.

"Both of you were with the Governor in the days before he died. I can start with you and then talk with Mary or the other way around."

"Uh, I just remembered I've got an important meeting in Albuquerque at ten." Well, there was the lie.

"Will you be sitting in on the interview with Mary?"

Ben waited at the door for Johnson to follow him inside.

"No. You go ahead."

Mary transferred her phone and motioned for him to follow her down the hall.

"We can meet in the lounge. Most of the staff have taken leave to prepare for the feast day on Monday. You won't be dancing?" she asked.

Ben tried to read the question. Chiding? Facetious?

"Not this time."

"Come to our house to eat. Bring your girlfriend."

Girlfriend? Julie. He'd forgotten that Mary had met her.

"Maybe I will." Actually that wasn't such a bad idea, Ben thought. He planned on seeing more of Julie but this mystery flu thing was taking up a lot of time—for both of them.

"Do you mind if I record our conversation? I'm not very good at taking notes." Mary nodded and he placed the compact recorder between them.

"I want to reconstruct the days preceding the Governor's death. I want to know things like his habits—did they change, did he complain of anything? I'm not just interested in aches and pains, I'd like to know about anything that seemed to upset him. Was he spending longer or shorter hours in the office? I want you to add anything that you think might be important or just something you think I might be interested in. I'll ask you about his diet—whether he ate at his desk, or went home for lunch. Do you have any questions before we start?"

Mary shook her head.

"Then, let's start with how long you knew the governor."

"All my life. He was the father of my best friend in school."

"Think about the week that he died. Was it a more stressful week than usual?"

Mary paused. "No. He was upset by the deaths of the old people. They were friends. He talked about…" Mary looked at Ben, then glanced away. "He talked about their spirits. There had been a warning."

"How was that?" Ben turned up the audio button. They still considered him an outsider. She was reluctant to talk about beliefs with him.

She looked up accusingly. "The cemetery. It has several new spaces, surely you know that they will be filled."

He'd flunked again. He wasn't thinking of that. Ben waited, but Mary didn't continue. He decided to change the subject.

"Tell me about his eating habits. Did he eat the same things everyday? Did he eat here at the office?"

Mary chuckled. "Everyday he ate frybread with beans. His

niece would pack his lunch and I would microwave it. It took him a long time to trust the microwave. One time he put some aluminum foil in, and it scared him.''

''What did he drink?''

''Always a Coke. He drank three, maybe four Cokes a day.''

''Junk food?''

''No. Not too much. He ate lots of seeds and nuts. He always kept a basket on his desk full of seeds, pumpkin or sunflower. Sometimes, he had pinon nuts.''

He spent an hour with Mary before walking home. The irrigation ditch was full. Three foot wide canals dispersed the water from the main artery and wound in and out of dirt-packed back yards under clotheslines and beside the Mission School playground. The water formed a cheerful little stream that gurgled and hurried along the edge of the village to reach the fields of corn. He paused by the cemetery and looked at the fresh mounds of earth. Three of the graves had new crosses. Doors and more than one chicken coop had given up planks for the carved wooden markers that dotted the quarter acre in front of the church. He had purchased the bronze plaque and marble headstone for his grandmother in Albuquerque. It looked out of place.

The older markers were bleached a slate blue from exposure. The plastic flowers tied to their bases gave a surreal touch that defied change. Their eternal reds and yellows were muted by a coating of dust. A row of fuchsia and white Cosmos leaned against the barbed wire boundary on his left. He'd plant flowers on his grandmother's grave next spring.

The hum of machinery about a half mile to the south caught Ben's attention. Through the dust he could just make out a Euclid and several backhoes. They were on Indian land. He followed the road that took him away from the village and towards the river and mountains and noises of civilization.

Large orange earthmovers lurched forward and turned, bounced backward and turned all the while churning up dust and sending bits of rock and hard clay sailing through the air. The machines whined and belched fumes that rippled around them in the still air. One of the drivers motioned him back and pointed to his head. Probably wants me to wear a hardhat, Ben surmised. He moved closer to the road and thought he'd watch a minute from a safe distance. Whatever was going on, it was a massive undertaking. This was an impressive collection of machines.

A man operating a roller stood in the cab and leaned out over his piece of equipment to check its progress before turning and flattening the strip of land to his right. He had taken his shirt off and his muscular back was streaked with sweat in half-dried yellow-orange clay stripes. The man had tied a bandanna around his mouth and nose. He leaned out once more to inspect the earth in front of his slow moving giant and then, as Ben watched, he toppled forward, over the machine and spilled spread-eagle onto the roller and under it. The roller barely paused as it ground his body into its freshly smoothed path. Continuing in a straight line, the machine lazily inched forward.

Ben screamed at the driver nearest him and bounded over the piled dirt. A burly older hispanic man had already reached the maverick roller and turned it off but not before its back wheels had also bounced over the body. Ben knew before he knelt beside the man that there was nothing he could do. Death had been instantaneous.

The body had been badly crushed but Ben checked for a pulse and noticed an elevated temperature. The man was burning up, and it wasn't from the sun. Then he noticed the bright pink cast to the man's left eye. Could death have occurred before the fall?

When the ambulance arrived, the men helped load the body. "Take him to the University Medical Center, the OMI. I'll call ahead; someone from the Indian Hospital, probably a Dr. Sanford Black, will meet you there." Ben watched the ambulance spin out of the soft dirt and tear off up the road with flashing lights and siren. That seemed anticlimactic. He turned back to the group of subdued men. "Anyone hear this man complain of feeling ill?"

"Yeah. He was sick yesterday but he needed the money bad so he came back today."

"What were his complaints?" Ben thought he knew before the man answered.

"He had the flu."

"Is he from around here?"

"Pena Blanca."

"How long have you been on this job?"

"'bout three, I guess, four days."

"Who's in charge?"

"I am." The older Hispanic man stepped forward.

"I'd like the address of the man's family."

"Sure. I can get it for you. Over here."

Ben followed the man to a pickup parked beside the road. The truck's side panel read Romero Construction. He jotted down the telephone number.

"You don't think we got a problem, do you? I mean, some people died here a couple weeks ago. Could we catch this sickness?"

"I don't know, but you might want to knock off for today anyway." Ben glanced at the group of men gathered a short distance behind them. In shock, all of them.

"Yeah. I'll do that." The foreman handed him a slip of paper with the man's name and address.

Ben needed to call Sandy, have him meet the ambulance at the OMI. So much for being lulled into thinking that this thing was over. Just a few deaths of old people and then nothing. Maybe they were looking for a virus, a killer that didn't discriminate among age groups after all, and if they were...Ben didn't want to think of the consequences.

FOUR

LORENZO HAD TWO favorite summer nap spots. One was under the four-hundred-year-old cottonwood beside the river and the

other was in the balcony of the Mission Church. He had wanted
to watch the big machines dig up the earth on his way to the
river, but the flashing lights had warned him away. He had
stood at the edge of the field and waited for them to leave. The
lights went around and around in jerky half circle splashes of
red and then rushed up the road to the highway. They went so
fast, Lorenzo could see a man's spirit had been left behind. Or
maybe the spirit was mad and was cursing that spot and those
machines. Lorenzo turned and hobbled back to the Mission
Church.

The cool darkness surrounded him as he climbed the curved
stairs to the balcony. The rough board benches were lined up
six deep with an aisle between. Lorenzo lowered himself to the
floor where he could look through the banister at the altar. A
four-foot-tall Virgin mother held out her arms in welcome. Her
blue plaster of Paris robes fell away from her body and formed
a base for the statue. Her hair was blonde, her hands pale cream
with pink nails. Someone had draped a rosary around one wrist
and there was a necklace made of corn kernels around her neck.

Lorenzo knew the Summer Mother and the Winter Mother
of his people. When they had lived beneath the lake in Sipo-
fene, supernaturals, men, women, and animals all lived together. There was no death. Now the blackness stalked his people. The medicine men would call upon their powers to chase
it from the village. But the blackness was strong.

Lorenzo thought of the beginning of a Tewa prayer; Within
and around the earth, within and around the hills, within and
around the mountains, your authority returns to you…. The
spirits were listening. When he was younger, he visited the
earth navels on the four sacred mountains, lakes or *nan sipu*
where the spirits lived. He would go to the spirits and ask for
their help. He must plan a trip to the mountains.

THE CONSTRUCTION WORKER had been rolled onto a table with
a drain in one end by the time Sandy got there.

"I'm waiting to get the go-ahead for an autopsy. There
shouldn't be a problem. Anything we should know about so

far?'' Sandy questioned the technician who was absently wiping his hands on the front of his lab coat.

"It was just like you thought. His lungs are filled with fluid."

"Want to venture a guess as to whether he had stopped breathing before or after the accident?" Sandy asked.

"I won't know for sure for awhile, but I think he was technically dead before he hit the ground. He must have stood up to get more air in his lungs and blacked out. I don't think he was breathing from that moment on."

"Can I use your office?" Sandy had already moved towards an open door to his right.

"Sure. I'm going to finish up a couple things. Let me know when I need to go to work on your guy here."

Sandy closed the door and dialed the number in Atlanta.

"Pres, glad I caught you. We've had our first death in the under sixty category, a construction worker."

"Indian man?"

"No, an Hispanic working a crew in the Pueblo."

"Same symptoms?"

"Exactly. Pres, if this is something new—a totally new virus—not on the books anywhere, what kind of time frame are we looking at from isolation to eradication?"

"Between you and me, months. Four to six maybe. It took five to track down Legionnaires. Things haven't changed that much when we're working from scratch."

"Damn. I just remembered; the feast day is Monday."

"A feast day?"

"Yeah. About five hundred or so tourists and the curious will be swarming all over Tewa to watch the dances and eat."

"Bad timing." Pres gave a low whistle. "I think based on the autopsy of the construction worker, you should talk the media into getting the word out. Do you have a contact? Someone you can trust to report accurately and not exploit the situation? It's pretty sensational stuff."

"There is someone. A young woman from one of the TV stations. Her reporting so far has been sympathetic. She's working with my intern in Tewa…she's been careful not to step on toes so far."

"She sounds perfect. Keep me updated. I'll assign whatever you send me top priority."

Sandy continued to hold the phone after Pres had hung up. What should he do? His intuition said an all-out warning, a media blitz. But was that wise? The state would lose. The Pueblo would lose. But the deaths couldn't be ignored. He dialed the TV station and asked for Julie Conlin.

JULIE SET UP a live interview with Dr. Black for that evening on the 10 o'clock news. Bob Crenshaw had been reluctant at first but after reading the *Tribune's* latest headline: "Are We Safe Here? Strange deaths leave Pueblo's residents bewildered," he sanctioned the plan and only asked that she run the script by him before air-time.

Julie worked on a set of questions before meeting with Dr. Black at eight-thirty. The station was at its usual frenzied best when he arrived so they met in Bob's office where they wouldn't be disturbed. Dr. Black seemed ill at ease in all the hustle but Bob's welcome had been effusive and almost genuine. Within two minutes formalities were dropped and everyone was on a first name basis. Bob asked to sit in on their discussion, which rankled, but was probably due to her inexperience, she concluded.

"So, what's the tactic? How are you going to inform the audience without needlessly scaring them?" Bob leaned back in his desk chair arms behind his head.

Julie ignored the "needlessly." There was every possibility that a good scare might be in order.

"I want Sandy to remind people of recent cases of unknown infectious killers. The examples need to be fairly current, nothing too much over ten years old. Let's start with the 'strep' bacteria that killed Jim Hensen in 1990." Julie stopped to make a note on her legal pad before resuming her pacing back and forth in front of his desk. "And then move to the E. coli that killed those kids in the Pacific Northwest—tainted hamburgers from Jack-in-the Box."

"I like that idea," Sandy said.

"Do you think we should do something stronger, maybe suggest that people stay away from this particular feast day?'' Julie paused in front of Bob but looked at Sandy.

"No. I'm adamant on that one. The evidence is still inconclusive and I don't want to go out on a limb with the station taking some inflammatory position," Bob interjected.

"For what it's worth, my gut level feeling is that we're just nosing around the tip of the proverbial iceberg." Sandy said.

"Listen, all due respect, Doc, but I think you're way off base. All you research types would like to see your specialty get some press. Means more money, doesn't it? Maybe time off for research?'' Julie thought of interrupting to say that a clinical director was in a little different position, but didn't. She couldn't be adversarial. Maybe if she joined forces.

"I agree with Sandy." Julie pulled up a chair and sat across from Sandy at the conference table. "I don't think we can rely on viewers reaching the conclusion we want them to. Good journalism doesn't just lead them by the hand, it gives them some conclusions, too.''

"Hey, kiddo, read my lips, I don't want to jeopardize the station's credibility.''

"Okay." Chalk up a loss, Julie thought. "I just don't want a rehashing of Legionnaires, or Toxic Shock or AIDS. What we tell them has to be current and has to be thought-provoking." Something they'll perceive as a warning, she thought.

"I agree," Sandy said. "I think that I should warn people not to be complacent. We thought we had won the war against infectious diseases in the 1950's but twenty years later, all hell broke loose. There's even been a resurgence of tuberculosis.''

"What does the latest research indicate?" Julie asked.

"The National Academy of Sciences has identified over fifty emerging infectious agents. It seems that disease begins to spread when man intrudes into nature.''

"What do you think?" Julie turned to Bob. "Is this more like what you had in mind?''

"I want you to stress that the disease doesn't appear to be highly contagious. Six old people and this construction worker; yet, no members of their families or any of the health workers have gotten sick. Wouldn't you say it's safe to conclude that the public isn't in danger?"

"So far that would seem true. I would probably have to admit that I have no evidence that anyone attending a dance in the Pueblo would truly be at risk," Sandy said.

"See? If we can't trust the good doctor, who can we trust?" Bob looked at Julie like he expected her to protest.

"But it doesn't mean there couldn't be a problem. All of the victims had the Pueblo in common. It's not an excuse for not being careful," Sandy said. "The CDC is taking this seriously."

"What are they doing?" Bob asked.

"We sent a number of samples of blood and tissue off this afternoon. They'll dedicate a team of twenty to sixty technicians to solving this mystery. That's not to say we won't get bumped by something bigger. But we have their attention on this one so far."

"When will you hear something?" Bob asked.

"Difficult to say, but maybe by mid-week."

"Can you think of anything else?" Julie asked Bob and hoped there was no trace of sarcasm.

"No. That should do it."

After a quick stop at makeup, Julie took Sandy to one of the sound technicians to be wired with a portable mike.

"Nervous?" she asked.

"A little." He grinned. "This is outside my job description."

"You'll be fine."

A man in the control booth motioned for them to stand by. Julie checked Sandy's mike and pointed out where they would be sitting. They would go on after the weather about twenty minutes into the broadcast. Julie hoped their viewers got the message to be careful.

The pudgy weatherman fumbled with his mike. What an idiot. Thought he was funny, too, Julie mused. Finally, he unsnapped the lapel mike and twirled it around by the cord a couple times faking a can-can dance. Then pushed his glasses in place with his middle finger. Hadn't someone talked to him about that? How it looked like he was giving the bird to a couple hundred thousand viewers? Once a nerd, always a nerd.

She nudged Sandy and mouthed, "We're next." His smile was confident. He would do well. The viewing audience would be able to make an intelligent decision about attending the feast day.

THERE HAD BEEN A BREAK in the dancing before lunchtime and Johnson had gone back to his house to rest. The mid-August sun sapped his strength and dancing used muscles he didn't know he had. He stretched out on the spare bed in his wife's sewing room after he spread a towel to keep the ceremonial paint on his body from staining the quilt. He opened the window and remembered the screen was off as three bright green bottle flies buzzed past him.

He dozed, awoke once to check the time, saw that he had another hour and settled down to sleep away his tired leg muscles. Johnson slept fitfully. First, he dreamed that the old Governor was performing in a carnival, pulling coins from behind the ears of delighted children who squealed for more. The Governor would grin, then hand a piece of gum, lollipop, or jawbreaker to each small member of his audience. The sun-baked skin around his eyes crinkled into deeply etched lines. He laughed often but then suddenly stopped and shook his finger at Johnson. And then Johnson saw himself—he was one of the children clamoring for candy, begging the Governor to make more money appear from their ears, or nose, or the corners of their eyes.

Johnson sat up and swallowed hard, then blinked to make the image of the old man go away. It had been so life-like. How many times had he watched the Governor entertain small guests. He'd always had time for youngsters.

The curtains had been sucked out the window with the breeze but that wasn't the sound that had roused him. No, it had been something else. He lay perfectly still and listened. He strained to hear the sound again and hoped it was his imagination. All was quiet in the house. In the distance the drums could be heard and the shouts of children playing along the irrigation ditch.

He heard cars turn down his street, then back up when they couldn't find a parking spot. He didn't move a muscle but continued to separate and categorize the sounds around him.

Then, it was there again. The tiny pings of pebbles as they danced across his roof. The staccato taps of someone wanting to do him harm. The work of a witch. Johnson broke out in a sweat. This wasn't the first time he had been under a spell. Two years ago it had cost him five hundred dollars to get rid of a recurring cold sore on his upper lip. It was best to act quickly when someone wished you evil.

The taps had stopped for a minute before starting somewhere by the front porch and continuing back towards the sewing room. His heart beat faster, and he found it difficult to breathe evenly. Then, just as suddenly as they had started, they stopped. He waited a long time before getting up.

He looked out the windows of the sewing room, the bathroom and kitchen and living room. No one was in sight. Then he opened the front door, caught his breath and fell backwards against the doorjamb. There in front of the door in a neat row, evenly spaced, were five round glistening balls of obsidian. The witches tools. He shut the door. He had to get out of his house.

He and his wife seldom used the back door. He backed the power mower into the wooden steps that leaned precariously against the house and for three years had somehow forgotten to fix them. Today he wouldn't mind the two foot jump. He tucked the two boughs of ceremonial evergreen into his armband and threw open the back door.

He saw them as he prepared to leap, leg in the air. Five shiny black pebbles that matched the ones on his front porch—or were they the same ones? He panicked. He had to get out. He could feel the spell surrounding him, making his breath come in short gasps. He had a weight on his head that pulled at the circle of feathers attached at the crown and made his ears tingle and go numb.

He rushed to the sewing room knocking over an end table full of magazines. He pushed a trunk under the window and clamoring up, threw a leg over the window sill and looked at the ground below. Nothing. Sand and dirt, and that was it.

The white buckskin skirt of his costume caught on the casing and held him until he pulled it free. Then he tumbled forward and hit the ground with a thud.

Something hurt, he ignored it and struggled to his feet. He brushed the dirt from his costume and his arms and legs and then inspected the leather kilt-like skirt. Not too much damage done. But the red ocher paint on his chest and back had run down to stain the top of the white buckskin around his waist. His wife knew how to get the stains out. It would be all right. He was breathing easier now.

Someone was parallel parking a car between two others in front of his house—all had their wheels on Johnson's lawn. Maybe if he put in curbing the cars would stay in the street. Johnson would have to think about that. But, for now, he had to get back to the dances.

THE SMELLS ASSAULTED Ben's senses: corndogs, tamales, tortillas, frybread, dust, and car exhaust mixed with the heat and drifted over the crowd. As usual, about a thousand visitors lined the plaza; the summer feasts or corn dances were always popular. It was a common sight to him, but Julie couldn't get enough of the carnival atmosphere. It had been a good idea to ask her to come. He'd forgotten what fun it was to share the dances with someone who had never seen them before.

Vendors were everywhere. Trays of silver and turquoise jewelry covered tables, shaded by bright umbrellas filling the already crowded streets. Julie paused to hold up a pair of stamped sterling conchos to her ears and squinted into a mirror tacked to the pole that held the sunshade.

As they made their way to the plaza, they skirted a merry-go-round of molded plastic rabbits, turtles, skunks and squealing preschoolers. Souvenir tee shirts fluttered in the breeze. Trash barrels overflowed with melon rind, corn cobs and the usual assortment of paper plates and cups. They slipped into the crowd at the west end of the plaza and worked their way forward for a better view. Julie stood on tiptoe to see over the rows of people in front of her.

The dancers seemed oblivious—to the crowd, the heat, the

noise; they turned and swayed, placing moccasined feet in precision steps to the beat of the drums. Only the streaks of sweat across chests and running down arms belied their susceptibility to the heat of the breeze-less day. Some women were barefoot with nothing to cushion the jolt of hitting the hard hot clay of the plaza's flooring.

"Look. Something happened to one of the dancers." Julie was pointing to a group of men almost in front of them. Ben pushed through the crowd and saw Twila Runningfox kneeling beside a fallen dancer.

"Heat exhaustion, I think." Twila said. "We need to get him inside."

Ben helped the man struggle to his feet.

"His aunt lives two streets over," she said.

The man leaned heavily against Ben and seemed dazed as they walked slowly away from the plaza. Julie fell in behind and walked with Twila. Parked cars and vendors' booths slowed their progress. Pueblos might have to close their dances to the public eventually, Ben thought. No one could have anticipated their popularity or the Anglo's insatiable curiosity. A group of tourists pushed past them, then stopped to peer into the windows of a house.

"We're here." Twila opened the back door and Ben half carried the man through the kitchen where two Indian women were arranging thick slices of ham on a Melmac platter. They dried their hands quickly on paper towels and talked excitedly in Tewa while directing the group through the arched doorway and into the living room.

The man slumped onto a sagging sofa and sat with his head in his hands. One women brought him a glass of water while another threw a light shawl around his shoulders. Twila sat beside him, first checking his pulse and then feeling his forehead. She was asking one of the woman some questions and writing down her answers in a pocket-sized notebook.

"Chills." Twila was standing now and the word with its dreaded implications seemed to hang in the air. "I'd like to get him into Albuquerque. I don't think we should take any chances."

"I'll get the paramedics and the clinic van and call IHS. Can you follow us?" Ben asked Julie.

IT WAS LATE in the afternoon by the time Ben reached the hospital in Albuquerque. Julie waited for him in the reception area as he briefed Sandy. Peter Tenorio was a long-distance runner famous in New Mexico for conquering La Luz Trail in the Sandias—running the trail up and back in the fastest time ever recorded. And now he was fighting for his life. A twenty-eight-year-old man fit and in his prime—it didn't make sense.

"Do you need to get back right away?" Julie asked.

"I probably should. I need to meet with the family. I can catch a ride with the paramedics."

"I don't mind driving back." Julie smiled and took his hand and they walked back out to the parking lot.

He was a little cramped in Julie's Miata but didn't notice the discomfort as she drew him out, encouraged him to talk about his family and his future. And it was a friend he was sharing things with, not a reporter. He learned about Wayne, and the promise made by her boss that dangled the prize of becoming an anchor-woman under her nose, and the Mom and Dad in Phoenix who liked to get involved every once in awhile— whether they were invited or not.

He watched the way the setting sun turned her hair to copper-gold and warmed her hazel eyes. He stretched and left an arm along the back of the bucket seat and felt her hair brush against his skin. She smelled fresh, a breeze carrying rain. For all the heat of the day, she looked crisp—not that that was really the way he'd describe her, but crisp wasn't wrong.

He talked about his mother and the story-teller and promised to show her the piece of pottery. And Julie was interested in his heritage—in him. Ever so slightly, she squared her shoulders so that bare skin touched his arm. He fought back thoughts of the two of them naked, standing pressed together before he explored her body with fingers, tongue...

"Is this it?" Julie had turned down a dirt road lined with adobe houses. A little help with directions and she pulled up in front of his grandmother's house. There were fewer cars than earlier but the road was still clogged in places. A Feast was a long full-day event.

"Do you want to come in?" Ben didn't move to get out of the car.

"Probably shouldn't." Julie paused, then quickly added, "I have an early day tomorrow." But he didn't think that was the real reason that she turned him down. He leaned towards her and hands cupping her face, drew her to him. Her lips parted and her arms went around his neck. The kiss was long and he could feel her breath quicken keeping up with his own excitement. She pulled away.

"I'm going to be a real prude and say that I really need to be going." She sounded a little breathless. "And maybe some little voice is telling me to keep our relationship on more of a business level."

"Is that what you want?" Ben asked.

"Doesn't have anything to do with wanting. I just think it's best," she finished ruefully.

"There's always a chance that things might change." Ben smiled, then opened the car door. "I'm not going any place."

"I guess I'm not either."

This time the kiss was chaste—almost, anyway—and then he got out of the car and started across the sandy dirt along the front of his grandmother's house before he turned to wave.

THE SHRILLNESS poked at Sandy's consciousness. Sprawled on his stomach, he waved it off and scrunched the pillow against his ear. His wife stirred, then turned to face the wall. Tuesday morning. Why was the alarm going off while it was still dark? He made a swipe at the clock's glow-in-the-dark face and smirked when it clattered to the floor. He turned on his back as the ringing started again. The phone. He sat up, awake, and looked at the floor. The clock had stopped at four a.m.

"Yes?"

"Dr. Black, that young man they brought in this afternoon has gotten worse. The doctor would like you to be here." The night nurse sounded harried.

"Who's on call?"

"Dr. Burns."

An older physician, not an alarmist. It must be serious. He was in the car before he remembered his beeper. A nagging reminder of reality, but he was the one who insisted all the docs wear one. He found it on the kitchen table, snapped it to his belt and checked the batteries.

A young man near death. They had struggled to save him. Could they have done more? Flying blind and nailing a target with a broad spectrum drug was like flinging a handful of sand at a wall hoping to hit a pin-sized villain. The chances were almost too minuscule to hope for success. So far, the CDC was still reporting that their tests were inconclusive. Inconclusive. If a word could make him crazy, that was it.

The predawn light robbed the Indian hospital of color and it stood pale and somber. Sandy parked in the far corner and jogged across the empty lot. Six cars lined the semi-circle emergency drive. Must be relatives.

He was at the top of the stairs when he saw members of the young man's family waiting in the hall. He stopped and put a hand on a man's shoulder and offered a few encouraging words to a young woman leaning against the wall. He could only hope that he wasn't lying.

He pushed open the door to the examining room and nodded to Dr. Burns. The man on the table was on a respirator and hooked to IV's. Dr. Burns said something to one of the nurses and followed Sandy back out the door into the hall.

"Can we talk in your office?"

Sandy could tell by his expression that things weren't going well. Stepping into his office, he pulled the door closed behind them.

"It doesn't look good. Can you believe that a long distance runner, in top condition, could be fighting for his life?"

"Was there any warning?" Sandy asked.

"None, really. The family just thought he was tired from dancing. He had been fasting the week before the ceremony. So, it didn't seem unusual that he would be fatigued. And it was hot out there yesterday." Dr. Burns refused the chair that

Sandy had cleared. "I need to speak with the family. Prepare them."

"Let me know if there's any change." Sandy said.

He watched Dr. Burns leave, then turned in his chair to face the computer. First, the mystery disease needed to be called an epidemic. Not a word that he'd get past the State Health Agencies easily, but it was time. Next, he'd have to meet with maintenance to seal off a ward at the back of the Fourth floor. He thought they could manage a ten bed area. Sandy only hoped that it would be enough. Maintenance would also have to vent that area. New duct-work, new compressors. The air in the ward could not be recirculated. All air from that area would have to be released to the outside. That was pretty much standard procedure for isolation wards. He hoped that the remodeling done a few years back had not complicated rerouting some of the ductwork.

He checked his watch. Four thirty-five. A tap on the door, Sandy looked around as it swung open. Dr. Burns stood in the doorway and catching Sandy's eye, shook his head before turning back into the hallway.

Gone. A young man in his twenties. Sandy reached for the phone. Pres usually got to the lab early. They needed to mobilize. Set up a lab in New Mexico. Probably at IHS on hospital grounds. The cement block maintenance building would be the easiest to remodel.

"I agree with having a base there. I can reassign lab techs and have you staffed by Friday. The same with equipment; we'll have everything you'll need in place by the weekend."

Pres assured him he would get back to Sandy with details. But Sandy needed to get his crew started on the remodeling. Thank God, he had everyone on beepers. He dialed the chief of maintenance. Sandy needed to get the ward set up by noon. He wrote himself a note. He'd have the nurse on duty check the supply of disposable masks, gloves and gowns and hold a seven-thirty staff meeting.

The chief of maintenance called back immediately. Yes, the remodeling had made allowance for redirecting air flow from certain areas of the hospital. He thought the fourth floor ward would be no problem. The chief was reading from a set of plans that he had at home but would confirm once he got to the hospital. The maintenance building would need the same venting, reinforced doors, possibly its two windows blocked. He hadn't sounded happy about the deadline, seventy-two hours, but Sandy knew he'd try to make it. He'd have a report before noon.

There could be no visitors allowed in the ward. Sandy would have warnings posted at the reception desk. He'd have to increase staff at the Tewa clinic. Maybe another ambulance. He'd check with Twila. The Docs at IHS in Albuquerque needed to be briefed and schedules changed to allow two doctors on duty at night. He hoped they wouldn't need more.

They had blood and tissue samples from Ben's grandmother, the Hispanic construction worker, and now Peter Tenorio. And, there had been the five previous deaths including the Governor. There was no reason to think they were not related. The symptoms were the same, only the age group was now different. The death toll was at eight.

He'd put a rush on equipment. He knew the hospital needed a minimum of two new ventilators. He'd make certain that the clinic in Tewa had one. The mechanical device that forced air into the lungs while it forced fluid out would probably save lives if used in time. Time. It was the one thing they didn't seem to have.

"SANTA FE IS ON line one." Gloria said from the doorway.

"Who in Santa Fe?" Sandy was still in the dockers and sweatshirt he'd put on at 4 a.m. He checked his watch, eleven-thirty.

"Someone important."

"Did you get a name?" Sandy tried to keep his exasperation from showing.

"No names but I got a title."

"And?"

"She's a director."

"Thanks." Sandy pressed the blinking button.

"Dr. Black, here."

"Sharon Walters, New Mexico Department of Tourism. If I can believe the papers, we've had another death?" She didn't wait for his answer. "And, if I can believe the papers, you have no idea what is killing people. Just what are you people doing besides scaring everyone half to death?" Her voice rose and wobbled slightly, but it was apparent that she would continue. "I've gotten calls from all over the United States. Four of the major hotels in Albuquerque are reporting a forty per cent drop in reservations compared to last year at this time."

She stopped to take a breath. "We have the Fair coming up, the Balloon Fiesta; this is the busiest time of the year for New Mexico. Some merchants make enough during the balloon fiesta to live on the rest of the year. This is the height of summer visitors to our national parks and monuments before kids have to start school. The next thirty to sixty days will make or break this state's economy. Do you understand that?" Sandy listened to the frenzied tone of her voice and wished he wasn't so tired himself. In a state where fifty thousand people got paychecks generated by the 2.8 billion dollar tourist industry, he could empathize.

"I don't think it's a matter of understanding the hardship of the situation. An epidemic always..."

"Epidemic? You're using words like epidemic?" Sandy held the receiver an inch from his ear. Better. "*ABC World News Tonight* aired a special that quoted some half-assed medical professional who warned would-be tourists away from New Mexico. And now you're using the word 'epidemic'? Just join forces and let outsiders shut this state down? Do you have any idea how long it will take New Mexico to bounce back from this type of adverse publicity?"

"Has anyone contacted *ABC World News* about a retraction?"

"Peter Jennings has promised to 'rephrase' what the consultant said, but the damage has been done." Sandy thought her voice sounded deflated. The hurricane had run its course.

"How can I assure you that we're acting as quickly as we can and as responsibly? Forty government physicians and public health officials will be meeting at the New Mexico State

Laboratory this weekend to plan a strategy for investigation and control. I will personally let you know our decisions.'' Sandy braced for another harangue and wasn't prepared to hear a click on the other end of the line. Hung up. She actually hung up. He didn't like the feeling of hysteria.

"Dr. Black? They want you upstairs right away." Gloria said. Her short roundness filled the doorway.

"What's wrong?"

"Another person with the mystery flu. Peter Tenorio's fiancée. They just brought her in."

"I'm on my way."

The second floor looked the same as it had at four a.m., only the faces of the relatives huddled in the hall had changed. Sandy nodded in greeting and pushed through the doors to the examining room. The young woman was still in street clothes, but he recognized her as the one standing in the hall last night. She had not been unstrapped from the gurney.

"Too late." One of the new doctors pulled his mask down and walked toward Sandy.

"Symptoms?" Sandy asked.

"The same. She collapsed at the funeral for her fiancé."

"Makes you suspect exposure to a common carrier," Sandy said.

THE SQUAT block building, once gray and unobtrusive, hidden behind the hospital, now sparkled with shiny ductwork on its flat roof and a fresh coat of white paint. Twelve specialists took turns around the clock entering data—test results, Ben's interviews, case histories of UARDS victims from across the United States—anything that might prove helpful in narrowing the search. Disease transmission and risk factors were pressing issues.

Another half dozen specialists ran tests, blood, tissue, secretions from noses and throats. Both groups looked for common links. Sandy balanced managing the clinic with as much time behind a microscope as he could spare.

"Hey everybody, I'm still short two dollars; the pizza guy's waiting."

A young lab tech had been in charge of dinner. Sandy grimaced. Wasn't this the third evening in a row they'd had pizza? Judging by the age of the group around him, he might be the only one watching his cholesterol. But he wasn't pointing a finger. He might differ with them over food choice, but he couldn't fault their tenacity and brilliance when it came to research.

In the week since the lab had been set up, a normal repertoire of respiratory viruses had been examined and eliminated. First, influenza, then adenoviruses, cytomegaloviruses and so on. Next, they investigated toxins— herbicides, heavy metals, poisonous gases—and came up with nothing; then, plague, Brucellosis and Q fever; and again, the same dead end. No one wanted to say that it might be something "new" until every other possibility was exhausted.

As they started the second week, Sandy thought the group was edgy; frustration was high, joking minimal. Between the lab in Albuquerque and the CDC in Atlanta, a total of 25 diseases had been tested for and eliminated. The sudden flooding of the patient's lungs was the symptom linking the victims, but it was also the major stumbling block. No hemorrhagic fevers were known to be native to North America. And not one of the victims had traveled overseas or entertained foreigners.

FIVE

JOHNSON WAS CLEAR-HEADED that morning. He'd slept like a baby for the first time in days. This was the moment. The day he'd been waiting for—no, had worked for. Even his wife seemed relieved that he hadn't awakened in the middle of the night and wandered about the house. She didn't even comment when he whistled off-key in the shower. He ate a big breakfast of ham and eggs and tortillas and beans, then took an extra fifteen minutes to fix his hair. Suddenly the world was a beautiful place.

The white Chevy Suburban handled like a tank. He'd rather drive his Ford Bronco any day, but this was official tribal business. He needed to drive the official car with the tribal seal on the sides. He was going to meet with the Andersons in Santa Fe. By the end of the day he'd be a rich man. A very rich man. This was the day. He could hardly contain himself. As the honorable Johnson Yepa, new Governor of the Tewa Pueblo, he would sign the papers that would bring gambling to Indian land. The first casino gambling for a Pueblo.

Johnson maneuvered the 4-wheel Drive vehicle through traffic on Interstate 25. He was going to be late. But then he was on Indian time. Everyone knew Indians never watched the clock. Being ''on time'' had no meaning. Besides, what were they going to do? They needed him as much as he needed them. He'd made all this possible, hadn't he? They knew they needed to be nice to him. They knew they needed to pay him.

Johnson's thoughts lingered a moment on his wish-list. The powerboat was still number one. He had almost made his decision. One of those thirty foot jobs with lots of horsepower. Something he could pull over to Arizona, maybe take a couple friends along, or just park at Elephant Butte and enjoy whenever he wanted. But then a car was tempting, a red convertible. He'd definitely decided on that new Caddy.

The turnoffs to Santo Domingo and San Felipe Pueblo flashed by. He laughed. He really had his foot in the ol' Chevy's gas tank today. Maybe he'd make the Pueblo buy him a Caddy and put the official seals on its doors. They ought to. He was going to bring in seventy-five to a hundred new jobs, maybe more. The old Governor had thought gambling would ruin the village. How many times had Johnson seen neighboring Pueblos turn down offers to get out of poverty. He'd show them. Six months from now, his people would be thanking him. Praising him.

The siren caught him off guard. He pulled to the side of the highway and got all of his papers together. The cop who approached was young. Johnson didn't know him. Too bad. He usually didn't get tickets when he was on business.

"Sir, your driver's license."

"Something wrong, son?" Johnson used his best "I couldn't possibly have been doing something wrong" voice, but he had a hunch it wouldn't work with this kid.

"Well, I clocked you doing 89 miles per hour. This stretch of I-25 is posted 75 miles per hour. You seem in a big hurry to get somewhere, sir." Johnson handed him his license and vehicle registration. "Let me check these and I'll be right back." The young officer walked back to his patrol car. Johnson waited. He didn't want to think about the Andersons. Father and son were both clock watchers and it seemed like the cop was taking a long time. Johnson watched a jackrabbit hop from one thicket of chamisa to another.

It did give him time to gather his thoughts, decide what he was going to say about what had happened. How could he explain nine deaths when only the Governor was supposed to die? That afternoon was so clear in his mind. The Governor stood by the door waiting to talk with Johnson before he walked across the parking lot to attend the senior's meeting at the community center. Johnson stepped into his office with the packet of seeds in his hand. The seeds that had come from the investment group—pumpkin seeds, a favorite of the old man, only these were special, treated in a lab to cause illness and death.

Johnson shivered. He could hear the Governor asking if he wanted to go to the meeting. Johnson promised to stop by later and he could still remember the prickle of sweat that had popped out on his upper lip when he'd opened the foil pouch and offered the Governor the seeds. "Very plump," the Governor had said.

Then, in a scenario that Johnson relived over and over, the Governor took the bag—the whole packet—and deftly dumped its contents into a basket on his desk already filled with cream-beige flat seeds and mixed the contents by shaking the basket up and down a couple times. With that he spun on his heel and walked out the door, the basket under his arm.

Johnson had been shocked into inactivity. What should he have done? Before he could make a decision, Mary, the secretary, stuck her head in the door and said she needed Johnson's signature on some travel vouchers—right then—before he went to the meeting. He followed her back into the reception area.

He hadn't had time to think. He couldn't arouse suspicion by grabbing the basket away from the Governor—not after he'd made a gift of the seeds. And how would he have been able to tell the difference between tainted and fresh? His hands were sweaty now thinking about it; he was leaving damp smudges on the steering wheel.

When the tourists walked in looking for the Indian arts and crafts center, he jumped at a chance to get out of the building. He walked out into the sunshine with them and stood in the parking lot and chatted about what they might want to look for—what was a good value, what they should have to pay for some items. They thanked him profusely and drove away; the two children leaned out the side window and waved.

And that's when he remembered the packet. He, at least, had been thinking clearly by then—enough to know that he needed to get the packet and destroy it. The Governor had put it down on the corner of his desk. The packet was the only thing that could get anyone in trouble. The only thing that could be traced to a lab. The Governor had the seeds. That part of the plan had been completed. He burst into the Governor's office and strode to the desk.

But it wasn't there. He sucked in his breath, closed his eyes, counted to ten and opened them. It simply wasn't there. The shiny foil packet wasn't anywhere. He dropped to the floor to run a hand under the edge of the heavy mahogany desk. He'd crawled around to the back snagging his slacks on the plastic carpet protector under the chair. The beating of his heart rose to make his ears throb, and he hadn't heard Mary walk in until she'd asked him if he'd lost something.

He picked up a business envelope from the desk and told her he was looking for an aluminum pouch about that size. But she'd been down the hall and hadn't seen anything. Any further questions were stalled by the Governor walking in. There hadn't been a quorum and the meeting had been postponed. Johnson remembered how elated he was to see the basket of seeds in his hand.

Johnson's legs had almost failed him, but he'd managed to leave the room and walk back to his office. He'd sat and swiveled in his chair, the motion soothed his jangled nerves. And then the cleaning lady interrupted his reverie by asking to empty his trash. And he knew at that moment, beyond any doubt that she had taken the original packet—it had been empty, hadn't it? It looked like trash. He'd fought an urge to embrace the dumpy woman who stood in front of him, apron askew.

But that didn't explain the deaths of Peter Tenorio and his fiancée or the Hispanic construction worker. The five old people had probably been at the seniors meeting with the Governor. He must have shared the basket of seeds. So what about the others? How could this mystery flu have become contagious? But wasn't it all due to the expansion of the cemetery anyway? Something beyond Johnson's understanding and certainly beyond his control—and there would be only three more deaths. There were only three more spaces to be filled. He needed to remind himself of that.

"Everything seems in order. Sir? Sir?" The young cop shook his shoulder. "I need your signature here." The patrolman leaned into the car and pointed to a dotted line on the side of the ticket pad.

Johnson wiped his perspiring hands on a paper towel that was stuck in the cup caddy on the dash. "I have a very important meeting with Anderson and Anderson Investors in Santa Fe." His voice sounded a little weak, Johnson thought, but gained strength when he said, "I am the Governor of the Tewa Pueblo." He then pulled himself up to sit tall behind the steering wheel and added, "I'm on official tribal business." He emphasized the "tribal" and waited. The cop stood there. "I'd think that this ticket could just be forgotten." This time Johnson smiled but not wide enough to show the missing first molar.

"Well, sir, I appreciate your thinking that. I understand your predicament. But, I'm not allowed to alter a ticket. I will make a note of the fact that you're on official business." The patrolman balanced the ticket pad on the door and made a notation. "Now, sir, if I could just have your signature right here." Again, he pointed to the dotted line. Johnson signed, put his driver's license back in his billfold, and tossed the registration in the glove compartment along with the ticket. He let the cop pull out first.

JOHNSON WAS forty-five minutes late when he pulled up in front of the sprawling adobe office complex of Anderson and Anderson on Cerillos Road. He admired himself in the bronzed glass as he walked toward the handcarved mahogany doors. He liked the way the band on his chocolate-brown polyester Farah slacks hugged his waist. The matching cocoa silk shirt gaped open and showed the heavy gold chain with gold nugget and turquoise pendant. He was glad that he had put half inch lifts in his Ropers. The extra height was noticeable. He felt like a man about to become rich.

The Anderson's secretary, a thin elegant woman in her late forties, was saying something into her headset and motioned him toward the walnut door to her right. Johnson smiled and nodded and knew he would be ignored. There was no love lost between them. He had asked her out to lunch once and she had barely contained her disgust. Johnson still wondered why he had asked her out. The challenge, he guessed. Everything about her was severe, hair pulled back in a bun, collars always buttoned to the neck, absolutely no breasts. There's a woman who hasn't spread her legs in awhile, he thought. He pushed open the door.

The Andersons, Douglas and Junior, were standing by the window, both dressed alike and both glaring at him. Johnson opened his mouth to speak and then thought better of it, and closed his mouth.

"Don't even think of giving me that Indian time crap. You're fucking forty-five minutes late." The old man's face was flushed but his eyes were a clear, cold blue. Like the eyes in that Australian shepherd puppy that his daughter dragged home. The one that got hit by the car.

"The governor's dead." Johnson finally found his voice.

"And how many other fucking people?" The veins stood out above the elder Anderson's eyes and Johnson struggled not to stare. Out of respect, he looked at the carpet.

"Are you listening to me?"

Johnson glanced up. Anglos always wanted eye contact. His ears and eyes could work separately; staring at someone didn't make him hear better.

"You tell me…" The old man was sputtering now. "You tell me how this could happen."

Johnson shrugged. "They were mostly old people. No one knows exactly what happened. The tests run on—"

"That's another thing. You lied. You said there wouldn't be any fucking tests." The words were almost a shriek now. "You told us it was against your Indian religion to defile the dead. Said your people had to have the bodies in the ground by sundown."

"Yeah." Johnson traced a flower in the carpet with the toe of a Roper. The much dreamed about power boat was fast becoming a canoe without paddles. "We sort of got cornered on that one. Some infectious disease hotshot at IHS wanted to make sure."

"Make sure? Make sure of what?" Johnson noticed the elder Anderson's clenched fists. His knuckles were white.

"Dad, calm down. This may not be as bad as you think. Six of the people were elderly. There is such a thing as coincidence."

"Nine fucking coincidences? Is that what you think, Junior?" Douglas, Sr. swung to face his son. Johnson eyed the door and expected "no-boobs" to burst in any moment. He hoped she couldn't hear them.

"Was there any guarantee from your lab guy that the illness couldn't be spread?" Johnson asked.

The senior Anderson swung back to eye Johnson but didn't answer. Johnson knew he had him on this one. Who was to say it had to be Johnson's fault—all his fault? In one split second Johnson knew that the elder Anderson didn't trust his source one hundred percent.

"Dad, let's sit down. We need to hear what Johnson has to say." Finally, the elder Anderson glanced away and followed his son to the couch. The Andersons sat at opposite ends of a burnt orange leather monstrosity and faced the chair that they expected him to take. Johnson sat down. This was better. He swallowed.

"One of the tests just confirmed that an old woman died. She was seventy-eight and had a history of weak lungs. There's no way she could have gotten the…the sickness," he finished lamely. Johnson realized that no one wanted to talk about the hermetically sealed packet of pumpkin seeds—not by contents anyway.

"Do you have the packet with you?" This from the younger Anderson.

"Threw it away."

"Are you telling us the truth?" The elder Anderson peered closely at him. Johnson wished he wouldn't stare like that. He always felt funny after these meetings. With those eyes the man was probably a witch.

"Shouldn't we sign the papers?" Johnson took a chance and tried to change the subject. He crossed his fingers that it would work.

"We'll finalize the papers today, your agreement to have the casino on Tewa land; but Dad and I would rather wait until this thing, these deaths, blow over to have any hoop-la. I know there hasn't been any sickness for the last ten days, but a press conference might not look right. Do you agree with me, Dad?"

"Yes. The important thing is not to call too much attention to ourselves."

"We're completing negotiations with the State for a Class III permit. We don't anticipate any problems. We have the support of several other Pueblo Governors and Dad's in tight with state legislators. If all goes as we anticipate, we'll bring the earth movers back in Monday, start slow, get some of the preliminary work done before we announce it. How about it? Does that sound okay, Johnson?"

Johnson nodded. He didn't know whether he'd buy the boat or the Caddy first. No, he'd stick with the boat.

"We're prepared to make a down payment on the sum we agreed upon, say, one hundred thousand today and the rest the day the casino opens." Junior said. The elder Anderson cut in, "We're in up to our eyeballs. Do you understand that?" He watched Johnson. His eyes seemed to burn into Johnson's forehead. "Tell me again that we have nothing to worry about. Tell me you took every precaution."

"Sure. Everything's fine." Johnson almost looked him in the eye but didn't, and he almost told him that the cemetery was close to full now; that the deaths were under control now. But, he didn't. He just thought about what he'd buy with the one hundred thousand. It was better than nothing. And in a few months he would get the rest. He could wait. The old man walked to his desk and returned with a bulging manila envelope.

"Here. A first installment." He sounded gruff, but almost civil. Johnson took the envelope and left.

PART TWO

SIX

THE SANTA FE MORNING was bright and hot. Larry Bernowich stepped back into the shade of the portal and wiped his forehead. Who said that dry heat would be better than the humidity in Peoria? Hot was hot with or without humidity. There wasn't even a breeze. He looked at the flags in front of The Palace of the Governors. Limp. Not unlike a certain part of his anatomy, he noted. Vacations and hanky-panky might go together. Vacations, sex and two children did not. He looked appreciatively at the backside of his wife as she squatted in front of an Indian vendor. A little broad in the beam but still a good looking woman.

He checked his watch. Oops. That wasn't allowed on this vacation. Marilyn's orders. Checking just one more time, he popped the clasp and stuffed the watch in his pocket. It was eleven o'clock. They were stopping in Albuquerque so that Marilyn could call her aunt; that meant that they wouldn't get to Carlsbad before evening.

The driving trip to New Mexico had been Marilyn's idea. She wanted the trip to be leisurely. Stop and go whenever they wanted. She had insisted on renting a large van so that everyone had plenty of room. Larry thought her idea was all right in theory, but the last five days had driven him nuts.

He looked at his wrist and wondered how long it would take him to remember his watch was in his pocket. He wished Marilyn and the kids would hurry. Back home right now, Frank would be calling in that big parts order. Larry hoped he wouldn't have any problems with the supplier. He knew Marilyn wanted him to forget work; he had said he would try. He had promised to stand in the shade and keep an eye out for movie stars. He didn't go to enough movies to know who was who. He absently worked over the cuticle on his index finger with his teeth.

"Dad. Dad. Look what I got." Seven-year-old Ryan ran towards him holding what looked to be a spear with feathers and leather lacings twisted up the sides. Larry breathed a sigh of relief; the point was rubber.

"That's great, son."

"Me, too. Me, too." Amy had been close behind her brother. Now her short legs were propelling her upward in bouncing hops landing each time on top of his Nikes.

"I got sum pin." She opened her sweaty fist and showed her father the dozen or so cream-colored pumpkin seeds stuck to her palm.

"Pun tin sees."

"Pumpkin seeds. Pump-kin-seeds." Her brother enunciated carefully.

"Pun-tin-sees." Amy defiantly repeated also drawing out the syllables, her voice rising at the end.

"Okay, okay, Sweetheart. Let's see what you have." Larry scooped the child up in his arms. "Where did she get these?" he asked Marilyn who had just walked up.

"The Indian lady where I bought this bracelet." Marilyn admired a silver band with insets of large blue stones. "She had a basket full of them."

"Are they edible?" Larry asked.

"Of course, they're like sunflower seeds. But, I think we need to save our appetites for lunch. Amy, let's put your seeds in a plastic bag and save them for later." Marilyn took a bag from her purse and helped Amy scrape the seeds into it. "Now, put this in your pocket."

Larry had expected a wail of protest. At three, Amy seldom wanted to do anything anyone wanted her to do. Surprisingly, this time she followed her mother's instructions.

Marilyn checked her watch. "It's eleven twenty. It will take us over an hour to get to Albuquerque. I think we should eat here. What do you think, hon?"

Larry sighed, but nodded.

LARRY AWOKE AT five a.m. He could tell it was going to be a terrible-Amy day. She had awakened twice in the night. The first time she wanted a drink of water; the second, she complained about being hot. He volunteered to get up with her. The air-conditioner in the window of their motel room in Carlsbad put out more noise than cool air. So, he told Amy that he would make it rain on her bed and she would be cool. He got a glass of water and lightly sprinkled the sheets on her side of the queen-sized bed. It had been a game and Amy helped by generously dousing her pillow. Five minutes after Larry turned out the lights, Amy sat up and screamed that her bed was "icky." This time Marilyn got up and declared that if watering the sheets was so wonderful, he could sleep on them. Amy was placed on his side of the other queen-sized bed beside Marilyn and he crawled in beside Ryan. Amy had been absolutely correct; the sheets were icky. Larry gathered a light blanket around him and pushed two arm chairs together with a coffee table in between. It wasn't much of a bed, but it was dry.

Larry leaned against the bathroom sink and stared in the mirror. He was amazed that he couldn't see the cobwebs. He decided that an early morning walk would get rid of his throbbing headache. This feeling might be tolerable if he'd had a few beers last night. Maybe he'd think of an excuse to get out of going underground to look at stalagmites and just crash for a few hours. Maybe he could catch a Cub's game on TV.

He glanced at the bed and saw that Marilyn's nightgown had worked its way up to her waist. One plump leg dangled seductively over the side of the bed. Damn. Any other time and that would be an open invitation. Better to not even think about it. Larry opened the motel room door and locked it behind him.

He was gone less than an hour. As he turned onto the long strip of asphalt that would take him back to Room 122, he saw the ambulance. He began to run and reached the door just as the paramedics pulled a gurney over the sill and turned to load it into the ambulance. The small form was wrapped in a blanket and strapped to the bed. Amy. An oxygen mask hid her face. Marilyn thrust Amy's teddy bear into his arms and grabbed Ryan's hand.

"We'll follow in the van," she said.

Larry was too stunned to ask questions. He unlocked the van; Ryan rode beside him in the front; Marilyn behind him. He could see her eyes in the rear view mirror. They were wide with the terror of not knowing.

"What…." Larry had started to ask her what had happened, but she quickly shook her head and pointed at Ryan. Probably best not to upset him more than he was. Larry concentrated on keeping the van reasonably close to the ambulance and ran two stop lights to do so.

"Wow, Dad. That was really neat."

"Ryan, put your seat belt on." Marilyn's voice was shrill and uneven. When they pulled into the emergency entrance, she was out of the van before Larry could say anything. He watched her run towards the ambulance. The paramedics worked in one fluid motion. They pulled the gurney out, balanced it between them and snapped the legs in place; then ran, pushing it ahead of them through the sliding glass doors. Then they were gone, swallowed up by the four story white building. Larry hurriedly parked the van and met Marilyn in the corridor outside an examining room.

"They asked me to wait here. Larry, I couldn't get her to wake up this morning. Her breathing was so ragged."

He put his arms around her. He pulled her into his chest as her body convulsed in sobs. He had never felt so helpless. He tried to give Ryan a "buck-up" kind of smile, but he felt it fail.

A white-masked man emerged from the room and noticing them pulled his mask down and offered Larry his hand.

"I'm Dr. Randolph. I don't have any news just yet, but she's holding her own. She's a plucky little fighter. Why don't I have one of the nurses show you to the waiting room and get you some coffee if you'd like. I'll join you as soon as I know something."

Two hours later, the doctor was pulling up a chair beside them. "Frankly, I'm baffled by this one. My suspicion is that she contracted a pretty virulent upper respiratory infection that moved quickly to her lungs. Size and age are big factors here. At the moment she's stable. I'd like to airlift her to Albuquerque for tests. They have the equipment to monitor her and, hopefully, find the culprit.''

"Will she be all right?" Larry and Marilyn held hands and searched the doctor's face for the truth.

"There are a couple things on her side. Age is a plus, and I think we've caught whatever it is in the early stages. I've called ahead to the University Medical Center; they're expecting her. We'll know more tonight.''

Guarded, Larry thought. They never want to go out on a limb. "Could her mother go with her?" Marilyn jumped up at the doctor's nod. This wasn't exactly the vacation they had anticipated, but anything that would bring back their little girl had to be done.

Six a.m. Sandy circled the parking lot at the hospital three times. There were no parking spaces, not even any reserved for hospital personnel. Finally, the chief of security opened the gates that kept the maintenance area, including the lab in back of the hospital, off limits. Good idea. Sandy would put a guard there and let hospital personnel park by the back door.

Sandy watched a man in the yard doing something to the end of a sheet metal tunnel. Additional duct work. Just a precaution. The man had snapped on a visor and was welding two long pieces together. The blue flame of the torch wavered over the seam.

Sandy pulled open the heavy basement door. All the trapped smells that meant hospital pushed past him, antiseptic, Lysol, the cafeteria's Thursday special, liver and onions. He walked down the ramp to the elevator and noticed that it was stopped on the second floor. The thing was unpredictable. Out-of-order half the time. He'd take the stairs. He wondered why he didn't think of taking the stairs first? Great role model for those he counseled to lose weight by increasing exercise.

The reception and waiting area was already full. There had to be thirty people seated against the wall and another half dozen waiting to sign in. The receptionist waved at him with a handful of pink phone slips.

"The one on top. A Dr. Randolph from Carlsbad has called three times."

"Randolph? Doesn't ring a bell. I'll get back to him."

Sandy looked down at the reception area as he climbed the stairs to the second floor. He had never seen a crisis like this one. Not in his twelve years with Public Health Service. He scanned the phone messages. Mostly from outlying IHS facilities, Gallup, Crownpoint, Santa Fe. It was conceivable that he'd have to use other hospitals in the system if this thing got bigger. From a lifetime of habit, he opened the blinds on his office's east window and stood a moment enjoying the reddish pink tint to the morning sky. He had probably enjoyed more sunrises in his life than sunsets. This might be the only quiet moment he'd have all day. There was a phone slip scotch-taped to his computer screen, this Dr. Randolph, again. Sandy reached for the phone. Ted Randolph answered on the third ring.

"Dr. Randolph? Sandy Black, here. I was expecting to get voice mail at this hour. I have a message to give you a call?"

"Thanks for getting back. This may be nothing, or it may be helpful. I'm sure you're following every lead to the cause of the UARDS outbreak."

"Have there been cases in Carlsbad?"

"Maybe. I didn't think there was a connection at the time but in hindsight, I may have treated the second non-Indian case." Sandy could hear the shuffle of papers. "A three-year-old girl was brought to emergency at 5:30 a.m. Sunday morning, comatose and suffering from inflammation of the lungs. Her lungs were beginning to fill with fluid. We administered antibiotics and put her on a ventilator. We were able to stabilize her, but I chose to have her airlifted to UNM's Medical Center to make sure everything was under control. Her improvement was rapid. In fact, she's being released tomorrow."

"Does she live in Carlsbad?"

"No, she's from Illinois. The family's vacationing in New Mexico. I don't think they had been to the Pueblo, but you might want to interview them. Sometimes survivors can be the key to finding answers. Her name is Amy Bernowich."

"I'll talk to them. Thanks."

Sandy sat a minute and stared at the phone. A survivor. Something they didn't think existed or might even be possible. But what would it mean if a tourist contracted the disease and had never been to the Pueblo? That would seem to blow the theory that it was localized and not very contagious. He'd wait until seven a.m. and give the Bernowiches a call before walking next door to the hospital.

LARRY AND MARILYN BERNOWICH met him at the door to Amy's room. Behind them the three-year-old was playing a board game with her brother when she wasn't shrieking in protest or jumping up and down on the bed in glee.

"Her energy level seems high," Sandy said.

"She's back to normal, but I still can't make myself correct her. She was so sick. I truly believe we almost lost her," Marilyn said.

"We really had a scare," Larry chimed in. "This UARDS thing is deadly—nothing to be messed with. I hate to say this, but I'll be real glad to leave New Mexico."

"I can't blame you. I'd like to ask a few questions—where you visited in New Mexico, what you did, what you had to eat. Could we sit in the hall? It might be quieter." Sandy smiled as he watched the ringlets of blond hair bounce furiously as Amy shook her head "no" before she grabbed the game board and scattered bright colored playing pieces on the floor.

"Dr. Randolph said that Amy was brought to emergency the morning of August 10. That was Sunday. Let's go back to Friday. Can you give me an idea of what you did?"

"Friday we were in Taos. They were having a special dance thing in the plaza downtown. We were staying in Angel Fire and had gone into Taos for the day. In fact, we didn't eat out at all in Taos since we had a condominium. The kids went swimming that afternoon and then we loaded up for Santa Fe. Is that about it, honey?" Larry asked.

"Yes. We spent more time in Santa Fe. We had breakfast and lunch at the McDonalds on the way out of town, I forget the name of the street."

"Did you do any sightseeing? Shopping? Was there anything special that the kids did?" Sandy asked.

"They both went shopping with me. We parked downtown off the Plaza and we shopped under the portal, you know, where the Indians display their crafts on blankets?" Marilyn said.

"Did you buy anything?"

"This bracelet." Marilyn held out her arm.

"And the kids, did they get anything?" Sandy asked.

"Ryan got a rubber-tipped spear, which I'm afraid got left behind in Carlsbad in all the confusion," Larry said.

"And the only time you ate anything—any of you—was at the McDonalds?"

"Yes. No, wait." Larry looked perplexed. "Marilyn, what were those seeds that the Indian lady gave Amy?"

"Pumpkin seeds. Amy took a handful from a basket that the woman offered. I don't think she ate any; it was right before lunch."

"Do you remember the vendor's name? Or where she was from?" Sandy asked.

"No, but I asked her to write her name on the receipt. I thought I might want to get something else from her. I have the receipt in my purse."

Marilyn pulled a half dozen sales slips from her billfold and handed one to Sandy.

"Here it is. The woman was from Tewa. Isn't that the Pueblo where all the people are dying?"

"The illness seems to be limited to people who live in Tewa or have visited recently," Sandy said.

"Let's see, her signature is hard to read, it looks like Mary Toya. Do you know her?" Marilyn handed the slip to Sandy.

"There are a number of Mary Toyas in the Pueblo. But the Governor's secretary is a Mary Toya. It seems like someone told me she sold in Santa Fe on the weekends. I don't suppose you have any of the seeds left?"

"Actually, I made Amy put them in a plastic bag and save them. I have no idea where the bag went. I could go through the laundry at the motel, but I feel certain that we've thrown the seeds away.''

''If you do find them, give me a call. You could put them in an envelope with my name on it and leave them at the receptionist's desk. Now, let's move on to Albuquerque. What did you do here?''

Sandy changed tapes in his recorder and listened to a report of calling Marilyn's aunt when they got to town, visiting with her for an hour then continuing to Carlsbad. Larry and Marilyn were still shaken by their ordeal in Carlsbad, and Sandy cut the interview short.

He wasn't sure that they had been much help. It did, however, establish a link with the Pueblo and keep it localized. Pumpkin seeds. Was there some kind of contamination? Or had this Mary Toya been a carrier? He also needed a full report from the doctors who treated Amy. She was, perhaps, most important to them as the first survivor.

LORENZO'S POCKETS jingled with the clinking of metal bottle caps. Once a week he would go to the one room grocery store by the highway and collect the tops that had been thrown along the side of the store. The summer months always meant a bigger haul. Then some of the men would gather in the shade and swap stories or pull an ailing pickup along side the building and change its oil. An oil change could mean ten to twenty caps and several squashed aluminum cans.

Sometimes the shopkeeper would exchange a handful of bottle caps for a fresh bottle of soda or a package of Twinkies. Today, Lorenzo only found five caps, and three of those had been mashed shut. He thought of throwing them away, but then he thought of how hungry he was. He'd trade them in for a Tootsie-Pop.

He needed the help of the railing to climb the three uneven steps to the store's porch. He paused a moment at the top until his breath returned. Sometimes when his breath left him, he could see the spirit pulling it from his mouth. Pulling and making his lungs burn. He patted his chest. His breath returned, and his soul had not gotten out.

He waved his cane in greeting to the store owner and stepped over the threshold. The store was dark and cool. The tall shelves cast a long shadow down the aisles of food. Lorenzo liked to look at the pictures on the cans and boxes. Sometimes he would poke a sack of flour and watch a white puff escape through the cotton covering. But mostly he liked to open the sliding top of the freezer unit and hold the little frozen sacks of ice cream and popsicles until his hand was numb.

Today, after he traded his bottle caps, he unwrapped his Tootsie-Pop outside. The store owner had given him a pocket comb with a bright metal clip on the side. He held the blue plastic comb up to the sun. Then he held the comb in front of his eyes and saw the world turn color. The house across the road was blue, the highway sign, the gas pump. He clutched the comb tightly and slowly lowered his body one step at a time from the store's porch. This was a treasure that he would put in his hidey-hole. His granddaughter had gone to town today. He would be alone.

He pushed open the solid wooden door to his room, squinted and stood still until he could see clearly, then closed the door against the sun's glare. He liked his room. In one corner was his mother's rocking chair that didn't rock. The curved pieces connected to the four legs were worn flat. The walls were natural adobe and had not been plastered and painted white. Lorenzo liked the rough blocks of terrones that his granddaughter's husband had cut from the river bank. The weeds and grasses made the blocks sturdy and kept them from crumbling. And they had been easy to carve. He had hollowed out a hiding place for his treasures some years ago using a spoon and carrying the dirt outside away from the house so no one would know.

Carefully, using his cane for support, he got to the floor and reaching under the edge of the bed, began to empty his safe. First, he pulled out the ragged Bible, torn and shredded by mice, its cover and spine discolored and moldy; next, three multi-hued marbles that he had found by the playground, then a tattered bundle of feathers, a small wooden cross, a mother-of-pearl rosary, an old coin, a wooden button, and finally a shiny foil packet with a metal zipper-like seal.

He stood and carried the packet to the one small window in his room. The foil was bright and crinkled when he pressed it and smoothed it flat. He thought it glowed in the light. He knew someone who wanted his treasure—someone who had hunted and hunted for it. But Lorenzo had been too quick for him. The little Indian man with tall heels hadn't seen him take it from the Governor's desk. Lorenzo chuckled and hugged his treasure.

THE PLAYING FIELD at Comanche and Pennsylvania in Albuquerque was sparsely covered with grass but had three six-tiered bleachers for fans, which in the case of soccer usually meant parents. The first American Youth Soccer Organization games of the season were always rowdy free-for-alls and judging from the number of sandy spots on the field, this game would leave some skinned arms and legs. Ben Pecos kicked himself for agreeing to take a busload of twelve-year-old girls to an out-of-town meet, and act as chaperon and coach. He wasn't sure this qualified, but IHS workers were encouraged to put in some "community service" time; and he needed a break from collecting data.

He heard enough giggling on the ride in to last until the next century. What could be so funny? He was forever reminding them to stay out of the aisle and keep their seats. Three mothers had come on the bus with them and they hadn't done much better with getting the girls to mind. Too much adrenalin, Ben guessed.

After the game they would stop at a Furr's Cafeteria before heading back. He should probably call ahead so that they'd have enough fried chicken. He smiled. One time the track and field team had cleaned out a Furr's. No fried chicken and no hamburgers. Those were always the favorites. At least the ride back might be quieter and cooler. The wide yellow and black school bus didn't have air-conditioning.

The bus turned into a parking area behind the bleachers and no one listened to his muffled admonishment to exit single-file.

He finally hopped out after the last mother and opened the doors to the luggage compartments. He handed out uniforms and equipment and watched as the group headed for the rest rooms to change.

The summer was gone already. The first week in September and he wasn't any closer to resolving his dilemma. Should he go back to school in January after the internship ran out, or not? It had been easy to get sucked up by the frenzy of the mystery illness. Tomorrow he would start working with Fish and Wildlife. There was going to be a trapping blitz on rodents in and around the Pueblo. And that would further postpone the drug and alcohol support groups that he'd hoped to start.

He jumped as plump arms were thrown around his waist from behind. He pulled free and turned to face a pretty pre-teen with long dark hair pulled to one side on top of her head and the beginnings of a great figure. Jennifer.

"I wish I were older," she said and looked at him expectantly. Ben thought he knew the answer but asked anyway.

"Why?"

"So you would fall in love with me." She had tossed her head to one side and was nibbling on the ends of the ponytail that cascaded to her shoulders.

He smiled at her. This was either some sort of crush or the other members of the team had put her up to it. He looked around but didn't see anybody.

"Why don't I just wait on you? There's probably no need to rush. I have a lot of school ahead if I decide to go back. Let's say we talk about it in five years."

"You're just kidding." The pout made her look older as she caught her lower lip between her teeth and her heavily lashed eyes looked luminous with tears.

"You never know. You'll have to find out. Now, go tell the others we're meeting to discuss strategy in five minutes."

He watched her run back towards the rest rooms, shook his head and then laughed out loud. Well, the summer hadn't dulled his touch. He could still attract the opposite sex. He thought of Julie. The Feast day had turned out to be a bummer. He'd called a couple times since then, but she'd been busy.

And he'd believed her. She was intent on making the most of her "career opportunity" as she called it.

He should have called her this morning and asked her to join them for dinner after the game. He wondered why he hadn't. Was he afraid he might be tempted to get involved? Maybe. One decision at a time. Less complicated that way.

His thoughts were interrupted by his team clamoring for attention. Their opponents, girls in orange tops and white shorts, were lined up across the field. After a short pep talk, he walked over to meet their coach. His team came forward for the coin toss.

The kick-off went without incident and Tewa was the first to score. The three mothers who had come with him yelled loud enough to make up for their lack of fans. Ben made sure everyone got to play and used the three alternates who had made the trip. A half hour of running up and down the sidelines yelling "look behind you" or "get the ball," and Ben was tired. When the referee charged his team with an "off-sides," Ben protested but watched the other team get the ball. At half time Tewa was ahead two zip.

Play had just resumed when Jennifer fell and didn't get up. Ben ran onto the field and made everyone stand back. At first, he thought she had fainted, maybe she had struck her head. But when she didn't respond, he yelled for an ambulance.

Her mother, one of the woman who had come with them, kept screaming "Not my baby, not my baby." Ben had to physically restrain her from trying to drag Jennifer to her feet. A parent from the other team started shouting to get back or they could die of the Indian illness, too. Then it was bedlam. Everyone pushed to get away. Cars spun out sending a cloud of dust over the field. Anglo parents yelled that their lives had been endangered and that the AYSO would hear of this.

Ben cradled Jennifer in his arms and could feel the heat of her body. She was talking incoherently, her arms and head spasmodically jerking. And then she was silent. Her breathing was labored and her chest seemed to collapse with each breath.

The paramedics lifted her onto the gurney and rushed her to the ambulance. Ben asked them to let her mother ride with them and helped the woman climb in back beside Jennifer. The ambulance roared away sirens wailing. He watched it until it was lost in traffic.

Turning back to the group of girls, he realized that most were in shock, some crying, some just standing and staring at the ground.

"Will she be all right?" someone asked.

"I'm going to be honest. I don't know," Ben said.

"Where will they take her?"

"To the Indian Hospital." Ben motioned for one of the mothers to come forward. "I'm going to ask Mrs. Tafoya to take you to eat and then on home. Why don't you get changed and meet her and the driver back by the bus in ten minutes."

Ben noticed a group of Anglo parents standing at the edge of the field. A man left the group and walked toward him.

"You goddamned Indians. You think I'm going to stand around while you endanger the life of my child?"

"No lives are in danger." Ben faced the man close enough now to smell the alcohol on his breath.

"Oh yeah? Says who? Some fucking red-skinned asshole?" He pushed Ben hard with a fist to the chest. Ben regained his balance but didn't answer.

"You tell me my little girl wasn't exposed to your disease out there." The man was six inches from Ben's face and waved a hand toward the field. "You fucking can't, can you? They ought to quarantine your home, rope it off and keep all you in your own filth."

Ben balled his hands into fists but willed them to stay by his sides. To his right, he saw two police cars lurch to a stop on the side street parallel to the field. Two cops were running towards him. He turned back to the man in front of him and didn't have time to duck before he took the full force of a fist to his nose. He knew it was broken before he hit the ground.

"There, you bastard. And there's more where that came from if my little girl gets sick." The cops grabbed the man and pushed him to the ground, slapping the cuffs on his wrists.

"You want to cuff someone?" He struggled to roll over.

"There's the one you want. Get that piece of scum and throw his ass in jail."

RIDING AROUND Albuquerque in the *Channel Nine News* van waiting for something to happen wasn't her idea of an exciting evening. When the radio interceptor picked up a police call to break up a fight at a soccer field, Julie was less than thrilled. But it was more live, on the scene reporting, if the incident proved newsworthy. She sighed. Exposure was everything.

As the van rolled up beside the school bus from the Pueblo, Julie recognized the team banner and saw the soccer team huddled around the driver and two Tewa women. Then she saw Ben on the ground, his face covered with blood. She ran towards him, pushed her way between the two cops and threw herself beside Ben. One cop grabbed her arm and attempted to pull her away.

"You're obstructing an arrest..." he started.

"Julie Conlin, *Channel Nine News*." Julie wrenched her arm free of the cop and gently drew Ben's hair back away from his forehead. "He needs medical attention. Call an ambulance. Now. Or I'll have your badge for failure to provide life-support when needed."

The cop backed away. One of the Tewa women had gone to the rest rooms and brought back two handfuls of wet paper towels. She knelt beside Ben and helped Julie apply the compresses to Ben's nose.

"You pussy-whipped bastards. You going to let some skirt tell you what to do?" The cops had pulled the cuffed man to his feet, and he now turned his anger toward Julie.

"Raymond," Julie called to the cameraman who materialized behind her. "I want full shots of this man and all remarks on tape. I can and will use them in my report tonight on *Channel Nine News*."

"I got everything on film." Raymond moved to the side, his shoulder camcorder focused on the scene before him. Julie rose and stood calmly in front of the man her voice cold and exacting. "In fact, you may want to give us an interview now. Just a few comments to set the record straight. But I must warn you that because of the unprovoked aggression used against this man, this tape could be subpoenaed by the prosecution when this case comes to court.''

"No goddamned fucking Indian is going to take my ass to court.'' The man leaned toward her held back by a cop on either side, but he seemed to be having second thoughts.

"That's enough.'' One cop interjected. "Let's get going. The ambulance is on its way, miss.''

Ben sat up; if it hadn't hurt so much he would have laughed. Julie was something else. He'd rather have her on his side than anyone he could think of. He watched as she turned her attention to getting the bus load of soccer players on their way. She reassured everyone, then double-checked to make sure the driver had directions to the restaurant. The cumbersome vehicle pulled out as an ambulance screeched to a halt.

"I'm going with you to the hospital. I'd hate to have someone botch a nose-job.''

Julie helped him to his feet. As he leaned on her shoulder, he realized the nose still worked as a fresh lemony scent drifted up from her hair. Funny, his nose didn't seem to hurt as much anymore. He was acutely aware of Julie's body pressing into his side as she helped him to the ambulance. It didn't surprise him how much he liked the feel of her leaning into him. It hadn't been in the plan, but maybe this was the kind of complication he needed.

JENNIFER DIED AT 12:01 a.m. Sandy sedated her mother and kept her overnight. She had not left Jennifer's side and refused to accept the fact that she had died of the mystery illness. She insisted that Jennifer had a weak heart and strenuous exercise had caused it to fail. She also insisted that Jennifer had shown no signs of the respiratory illness and had only complained of a headache and scratchy throat that morning.

By the next morning Jennifer had become a number, number ten to the media, and she was headline news. Sandy got a call from Johnson Yepa's office about setting up a community meeting. They wanted him to attend. It was scheduled for Monday evening in the Pueblo. The principal of the high school called shocked at Jennifer's death but wanted to know how contagious she had been and should he worry for his students and take any precautions. The inquiry seemed more self-motivated, Sandy thought.

He didn't know how much new information he'd have for the meeting in Tewa. Hundreds of samples of tissue and blood had been sent to Atlanta. Hundreds more were being scrutinized here. But there was nothing definitive yet. Speculation, but not fact. Theoretical candidates were the viruses that cause internal bleeding, sure-death organisms like Africa's Marburg, Ebola, and Lassa viruses, as well as Asia's Hantaviruses. By the end of the week, they would be attacking the problem from a different angle—dissecting the known carriers of such diseases, the rodents that lived in and around the pueblo.

Portable nitrogen tanks were already in place to hold their remains in the lab behind the hospital. A new floor to ceiling freezer had been installed yesterday. Another bank of computers lined the west wall. The temporary field headquarters had proved invaluable. Not that it looked anything like its counterpart fourteen hundred miles away, it didn't. Here CDC employees wore shorts and jeans in the sometimes stuffy confines of the windowless building. But the swift silent killer was being hunted down by an army of experts, Sandy thought.

The CDC had promised to stay on the scene for as long as it took. Every time Sandy walked back to the lab, he saw new license plates. There were health workers from Arizona, Colorado, Alaska, back East—other labs vacated in order to help solve the mystery. If they could just find answers before this thing escalated.

SEVEN

JOHNSON YEPA WAS beginning to dislike his job being Governor of Tewa. He didn't understand Anglos and didn't want to spend time trying. This mystery illness was a thorn in his side. A festering wound. His people felt they were being pushed around. And they looked to him to make it stop.

He knew it was going to be a bad week when the jar of fermented calves brains and human urine—a concoction that would strip the sinews from the underside of a hide—tipped and spilled in the cab of his truck. He'd had to stop by the side of the road; the fumes were so bad. He offered two grade schoolers a couple bucks each to clean it up, and they had refused. He took the truck back to Albuquerque. It cost him forty bucks at a carwash. And now the smell of minty urine made him gag.

Two nights ago he amorously turned to his wife in bed and with one hand on her breast and his enunciation crisply clear said, "Mollie, let's you and me have some fun." But his wife's name wasn't Mollie. As she had so quickly pointed out. He didn't know how long she stayed locked in the bathroom. He had finally gone to sleep.

Now, to make matters worse, his wife signed them up for marriage counseling with some psychologist at IHS. He had missed one appointment already, but he was thinking he should make the next one. Last night there was no supper on the table when he got home, and this morning his wife left the house without fixing him breakfast.

He stepped out of his office to walk across the parking lot to the community center. He'd have to chase the kids out of the gymnasium and get the chairs set up for the meeting. The sun was beginning to go down earlier, he noticed. It was only seven and there were long shadows reaching behind the parked cars to the center of the lot. Maybe it would be an Indian Summer. Indian Summer. What did that mean? Once in grade school he had looked it up in a dictionary. "A period of mild, dry weather usually accompanied by a hazy atmosphere occurring in the United States and Canada in late autumn or early winter." There wasn't one mention of Indians. Indian corn, Indian file, Indian giving— these he understood; but what did the weather have to do with Indians in the Southwest?

He pushed the bar handle on the door to the community center and felt the blast of rock music coming from the three boomboxes sitting at the edge of the floor. Ten high-school-age jocks were putting in a little basketball time. Johnson regretted having to chase them out. Last year, the Valley team took regionals.

He leaned down to snap off one radio, then moved to the others. Only way to get their attention. Before leaving, the kids dragged folding chairs from the storage room under the bleachers and set them in a U around the portable microphone. One of the kids even got the mike to quit emitting the high decibel shriek that rattled the windows every time Johnson pulled it towards him and said, "testing, testing, 1, 2, 3."

Johnson was ready when the first families arrived. He met them at the door. Mary, his secretary, brought an urn of coffee and plugged it in on the counter that opened to the kitchen. Someone else put out three cellophane-wrapped sacks of cookies, chocolate over marshmallow with a sweet dough bottom. The kind that gave him a toothache.

They would wait until Dr. Black arrived, and then Johnson would open the meeting for questions. In less than half an hour, over one hundred people crowded onto the gym floor. Johnson turned the air-conditioning back on as people climbed the bleachers to find seats and complained of the hot air above the floor. He had not expected so many people.

THE ANGER PRESSED against Sandy as he opened the door. Anger and fear, he thought. He had come alone and immediately wished he hadn't when he realized that he was the only one sitting under the basketball hoop in front of the crowd. He was blindsided by the first question.

"Why did you lie about the death of my daughter?" Jennifer's mother asked amid a chorus of support. "Why did you call it this illness when she had a history of heart trouble and it was clearly heart failure?"

Sandy recalled that this woman could be belligerent and demanding in the best of times. She had chaired a couple Indian rights organizations and had a reputation for not seeing an issue from more than one side. Now, less than a week after her daughter had died, she was like a cornered buffalo ready to charge blindly and hurt anything in her path.

"You've ruined our economy. We have been banned from selling our food and crafts at the Fair this fall." She was standing now, an older daughter on each side steadying her. "An exchange trip of high school students to Northridge, California has been cancelled because they thought they might get 'infected.' This reeks of racism."

Three rows back an older man held up a copy of *USA Today* with the headlines, "The Tewa Flu—Southwest Killer."

"In Albuquerque last week my wife and I ate at a restaurant and saw our plates carefully removed and put in a different pile when we were finished." This from yet another man in the back.

"There were two reporters at my house the day after Peter died," a man yelled out. "Then before they left, two health workers showed up. I don't talk to nobody anymore."

"*Unsolved Mysteries* has called five times." This from Mary, Johnson's secretary. "Then *NBC Dateline, The Wall Street Journal*, and a Paris magazine. But what I liked most were the thirty-four calls from clergy and spiritual healers. A lot of people offered prayers and support."

Thank you Mary, Sandy thought. The crowd was slowed down by the positive side of things. Positive side? What was the positive side? The crowd had turned back to him, now.

"What would you like me to do?" Sandy asked.

"We want you to use accurate information. Don't tell something that isn't so. That construction worker from Pena Blanca helped his family farm. The weekend before he died he used a chemical pesticide to get rid of grasshoppers. Has anyone checked out his exposure to that?"

"And we want people to respect our privacy with our dead."

Sandy saw a lot of affirmative nodding at this.

"Get people to stop discriminating," someone yelled out. Now their expectations were beginning to fall in the miracle category, Sandy thought.

"I'd like to spend my time tonight sharing with you what

needs to be done and why. Then I want your help in telling me how we can accomplish our goals in a way least upsetting to the Pueblo." Sandy spent the next two hours listening and presenting his needs. He tried to explain why they would be trapping rodents in the village and surrounding fields. He sensed skepticism but overall, the meeting had gone well. Before he left, Sandy had a chance to question Mary Toya.

"Mary, do you have a minute? I need to find a Mary Toya who sells at the Governor's Palace in Santa Fe."

"I do sometimes."

"This would have been the weekend of August 8."

"Let me think. Yes. I missed one weekend in August, that was the sixteenth. My sister and I trade off weekends sometimes, but I went to Santa Fe the three other weekends that month."

"A woman from Illinois vacationing with her family bought a bracelet. Her three-year-old daughter took some seeds from a basket. They were pumpkin seeds. Anyway, we think the child was allergic to them and we're trying to find out where she might have gotten them," Sandy lied. But he was too afraid of saying something that might be misinterpreted as an allegation.

"Pumpkin seeds? I keep a basket of pinon or sunflower. I don't have pumpkin seeds with me very often."

"Where do you buy your seeds?"

"Bernies," she said.

"The grocery up by the highway?"

"He buys pumpkin and sunflower seeds in bulk. He almost always has pinon seeds. Are you sure she said pumpkin seeds?"

"Yes. I'll check with Bernie. Thanks," Sandy said.

THE UPS TRUCK lumbered down a dirt road, slowed, stopped, backed up. The driver hopped out, knocked on a door, got back into the truck and turned down another road. The driver had asked directions at the Grocery and still found himself more or less lost. Less, because he knew he was in the right Pueblo and more because every house looked alike. There was a "rush" stamped on the papers clipped to the board on the dash. Some high-priority government delivery that had to get out here today. He swore as he tried another dirt lane and found it a dead end.

The shipment wasn't small. The truck was crammed floor to ceiling with boxes. And something clinked like metal chiming against metal at every bump. And that was more than one a second. He'd be glad to dump this load and be back on the highway. With his wife pregnant and everything, it didn't pay to take chances with this illness thing and hang around the Pueblo more than he absolutely had to.

Ben Pecos saw the truck as it backed out of the dead end by his aunt's house. He waved to the driver and motioned him to stop. The passenger side door was open, and Ben jumped in.

"I'm the one who will sign for these but I need you to take them to the site. Just follow this road back towards the highway and take the last dirt road to the right."

"What's in the cartons?"

"Traps. At least one thousand stainless steel traps."

"What the hell you going to do with those?"

"Catch rodents who might be carrying the key to the mystery illness." Ben had thought the driver was hugging the driver-side door but now he looked plastered to that side of the truck's cab.

"You mean mice and things like that could be the cause?"

"Could be."

"Are they dead or alive when you catch 'em?"

"Alive. It will be up to me to euthanize and send the bodies to Albuquerque."

"Does this pay pretty good?"

"Yeah. But it's pretty seasonal." Ben said.

The driver bumped along in silence. "I'd like to get into something else but UPS pays OK. It's just the hours on the road, and dealing with people who think you're late or miss you all together and get irate about having to set up another delivery time."

"Here." Ben hadn't meant to yell but they almost missed the turn that would lead around the back of the Pueblo. He had set up a tent with some basic equipment for treating his captives about halfway between the edge of the village and the open mesa. He'd keep the traps here and not have to drag them back and forth.

"It's about another mile and a half from here. You'll see a green pop-up tent on your left just past where this road forks. Stay to your left."

"Do any of you folks travel? Or do you pretty much stay put?"

Ben had no idea where these questions were coming from, but he felt the man was honestly curious.

"I lived in California until this summer," Ben said.

"What did you do there?"

"Went to school."

"No shit?" the driver said.

"No shit," Ben said. They continued in silence until the road forked.

"Over there? I think I see your tent." The driver pointed out the window at a hump of green canvas dwarfed by a pinon tree.

"That's it. If you could back up to the tent opening, it would make things easier."

The driver tried three times to line up the wide rear doors with the tent. Swearing, with sweat staining his brown uniform he finally brought the boxey delivery truck to a halt.

"Will this do?" The truck was fairly well lined up but one back tire had run up onto a six inch high boulder and now the back listed badly.

"Yeah." Ben didn't think it would help to point out how lopsided the truck was.

There were fifty cartons of traps. It took the two of them a half hour to empty the truck and stack the cartons under a lean-to beside the tent.

"Hey, are these things any good to eat?" The driver had flopped down under the pinon tree and was holding a handful of pine nuts.

"Sure."

"They could use a little salt, but you're right, they're really good. I always see people selling them along the road and I've wondered.'' He sat munching the tiny brown nuts, breaking their shells with his front teeth. He had found quite a cache at the base of the tree hidden under a blanket of needles.

"Thanks for helping," Ben said.

"No problemo." The driver got to his feet and brushed the twigs and leaves from his uniform. "Not sure I took the allotted time for a break, but the company likes you to keep track of any downtime." He stepped into the truck and reached for another clipboard hanging above his head and made some marks with a pen that was attached by a string. He then gunned the engine, slipped it in gear and the truck bounced off the small boulder and tipped upright. The truck's snub nose dipped up and down as the driver navigated the ruts left by last winter's snow and headed back towards the highway.

Ben dragged the first carton of supplies into the tent and made room in the middle of the floor. Before he got started on the traps, he'd have to inventory the plastic containers, masks, anesthesia, surgical gloves, scissors, tweezers—the full array of lab equipment that was necessary to a successful operation.

The traps would take hours to log in and tag, check the working mechanism, load with bait and stack outside the tent to be picked up later. He would begin to place the traps tonight. There would be a full or partially full moon for the next three nights and he hoped to have all the traps out and operative in that time.

His instructions were specific. Place the traps in a variety of locations; by the river, in the corn fields, along irrigation ditches, on all sides of the village and some within the boundaries between houses by woodpiles and garbage containers. He was supposed to observe rodent activity, take notes and report any aberrant behavior.

It was late afternoon when he finished and he walked the two miles back to his uncle's house to borrow his truck. The Ford 150 longbed would hold most of the traps and solve the problem of transportation. He'd grab a bite to eat at the house and head out at dusk.

The basketball orange moon, kept from being a perfect globe by an imperfect lower right side, cleared the mesa and loomed over the cornfields and river. Ben was already loading the traps into the pickup. He had three searchlight strength battery packs and an electric generator on the truck—enough energy to flood an area with light if needed. He had wanted a spotlight setup in case he encountered larger game. He knew he'd attract the interest of coyotes. It meant checking the traps as often as he could.

He would set traps for six hours, grab some sleep, then check the ones he'd set and put out more, then rest and start the routine over again. Depending on the size of his "catch," the rest of his work could be done during the day. His contract said three weeks work, but in the first few nights he hoped to send a sizable number of rodents to the lab in Albuquerque.

By midnight he had placed two hundred and fifty traps and readjusted his plan. He would have to continue to place traps during the morning tomorrow, get some sleep in the afternoon and then check all or, at least, most of the traps tomorrow night. He had drawn a rough sketch of the Pueblo and outlying area and carefully kept track of where the traps were. It made things easier.

The second night the moon was fully round and seemed suspended in a black sky. Almost a harvest moon, Ben thought, light enough to drive by. The first three hours were successful. Seventy rodents, a mixture of field mice, deer mice, and a ground squirrel had been snared. Ben worked quickly to take them out of the traps, euthanize and drop them into tagged lab containers. He then baited and reset the trap noting time, date and type of quarry on a sticker across its stainless steel back.

Ben peeled off the heavily insulated rubber gloves and pushed up the surgical mask. It would be so much easier to use bare hands and not have something constricting across his nose and mouth. But that was too dangerous. He got back into the truck and pulled up beside the northwest corner of the field and checked his map. He had five traps in a cluster, one row of corn in from the river. He cut the engine and slipped on the gloves.

He could tell the traps didn't look right before he got to them. All the doors had been sprung and the traps thrown back in a heap. All had had some kind of rodent in them judging from the droppings. Who would want trapped mice? Ben had put the word out among the teens in the Pueblo that the traps were not to be touched. Still, it was probably a temptation that was hard to resist. The ground didn't show any evidence of tracks; the mischief could have been done last night.

He reset the traps and turned back towards the truck. The sound of a car drifted across the river. He listened, but the car seemed to have stopped. Could be someone out parking, Ben thought and felt a twinge of envy. This job would be more fun with a little female companionship. He got into the truck and left the lights off as he made his way along the river to the next site. There were seventy-five traps in the rocks and marshes where the river turned and formed a standing pool before twisting closer to the base of the canyon wall.

He would check the traps and then catch a nap. He parked the truck in a strand of poplars and tall grass. He had thrown his sleeping bag into the back with a couple blankets. He worked quickly and had fifty-seven rodents tagged and fifty-seven traps baited and back in place in under two hours. He had earned a nap.

He awoke to pull the blankets closer and zip the bag all the way to the top. The chill air drifted over him from the river and the dampness of the ground seeped through his bedding. He squirmed his body more comfortably into the cocoon and turned on his side.

Cold awakened him again two hours before dawn. Or was it the fact that he had to take a leak? Pushing the warmth from his body, Ben rolled out of the sleeping bag and stood. A muffled clanging caught his attention, metal hitting metal—the sound of the traps being kicked or tossed aside. Suddenly he was fully awake. Someone was raiding the traps. He was twenty-five yards away. Slowly he pulled a high-powered flashlight from the bed of the truck—all the while listening to make sure these were human and not bear sounds.

Then he dropped to a crouch and covered the first fifty feet to the edge of the marsh. Now he could see the intruder. Human and male, but that was about all he could tell. Ben watched him pick up a trap, and finding it empty, drop it. One trap must have held a rodent because the man reached into it and then slipped something into his pocket.

The pre-dawn morning had turned cloudy. The moon high in the sky now offered only pale filtered light. Ben decided to take action. Jumping out of the thicket, he flipped on the flashlight and ran forward.

"Stop."

The figure froze, then drew something from his pocket. A gun. Ben saw the flash of light from the barrel and heard a crash behind him, but he had already hit the ground. He continued to roll towards the safety of the marsh grass even after he knew the intruder had fled. He lay on the ground looking up at the clouds floating over the moon and tried to get his heart to stop pounding.

He didn't think he would ever forget the figure dressed all in Army green—except for the combat boots and the baseball cap pulled down over the ski mask. He wasn't Indian and maybe too slightly built for the average Anglo. And Ben could swear that it wasn't a teenager. But, for some reason that made absolutely no sense, he collected already trapped rodents. Ben was thankful he was a bad shot.

SITTING OUTSIDE the psychologist's office at the Indian hospital, Johnson Yepa studied his wife. She had not said more than five words since breakfast. Now she sat opposite him reading a two-year-old copy of *Redbook*. The feature article was, "How I Can Get a Date with Your Husband" written by a group of "other" women. That's all he needed. He thought of trading her another magazine but all he saw was a dog-eared *Popular Mechanics,* a *Field and Stream,* and a pamphlet on diabetes.

He sighed deeply, filling his chest with air and then exhaled in a rush. He followed through by letting his head fall forward and bob ever so slightly coming to rest on his chest. The man dejected, neglected, spurned. He peeked at his wife through the lashes of his lowered eyes. Nothing. She continued to read, her expression impassive. He sat up straighter and reached for the *Field and Stream.* They had been married a long time, thirty-two years. He thought their problems had started with that Continuing Education course his wife took on relationships. She had spent a lot of time talking about "getting in touch." He had never been able to figure out what that had meant. But he knew that he didn't want to be here today. This could only mean trouble.

The door to the psychologist's office opened and a woman left, a wad of damp Kleenex in her hand. That was a bad sign. Johnson had seen enough crying over the weekend when his wife had called their two daughters. One lived in San Diego, the other in Tuba City, Arizona; both had taken his wife's side.

"Mrs. Yepa? Will you come with me." The psychologist held open the door to his office. Johnson got to his feet.

"Mr. Yepa? I prefer to see you and your wife separately for the first few visits. I'd like to see you next week. You can schedule an appointment with my secretary across the hall."

"Oh, sure Doc, no problem." Johnson looked at his wife. Her head was bowed and turned slightly away from him but he detected the smugness, felt the silent taunt. "I need to talk with Dr. Black about some clinical problems, anyway." He pulled his shoulders back but kept his eyes averted. The Anglo psychologist was wearing soft brown Hushpuppies a little scuffed at the heel. This was not a man who would own a powerboat.

"Mrs. Yepa and I will be finished at four." The psychologist followed Johnson's wife into his office and shut the door.

Johnson replayed the phrase "first few visits." He would have to put a stop to this foolishness. Maybe he'd see the Doc once, but no more. Now he had an hour to kill. He hated the smell of hospitals. He'd sit outside.

He walked towards a cement bench under some pines and had just sat down when a group of white-coated men and women pushed open the door to the old maintenance building and hurried towards the back door of the hospital. They were talking and gesturing, but Johnson was out of earshot. He recognized Dr. Black and Ben Pecos. Seemed like everyone was pretty excited.

Johnson wasn't sure what he expected to find, but he was

curious about the building. It looked different now that he was closer. Lots of shiny duct work on the roof and the one window had been closed, permanently, with cement blocks. And the place had a new coat of white paint. An awful lot of money to house a couple riding lawn mowers and two government pick-ups.

The door was new. Heavy gauge steel about two inches thick. It was propped open with a wedge of wood. Johnson looked back at the hospital and waited to see if he was being watched. All was quiet. He squinted and put one eye to the crack in the door.

He was astounded. There were no lawn mowers or any other kind of maintenance equipment. Within his limited vision were tables lining the wall to his right. Stacks of papers, logs of some sort, were piled on the floor under the tables. Computer cursers blinked. He counted four machines in a cluster at the back. And then he saw them. The clear plastic packets of dead rodents. Hundreds of dead mice and rats and squirrels. Some he recognized only by their fur or tails because the heads were missing.

"Can I help you?" The door jerked open, making Johnson lose his balance. It took him a moment to regain his footing and focus on the speaker, a young woman in cutoffs and a form fitting tee shirt. A surgical mask dangled around her neck.

"I'm the Governor of the Tewa Pueblo. Are you doing research on the mystery illness?" Quick thinking. Johnson congratulated himself when he saw her eyes light up at his title. If he was lucky, she was an Anglo who thought Indians were mystical and wonderful.

"Yes. This is the research lab. I'd be glad to show you around if you have a moment. I'm Nancy Carter, a research specialist from Maryland." She opened the door wider and stood to one side. Her breasts were enormous for her frame, Johnson thought. And her tanned legs were perfect; thighs and calves curved sensuously, tapering to a trim ankle. It was then that he noticed she was a full foot taller than he was. A foot taller, but he could see those legs wrapped around his neck.

"Sir?" She leaned toward him; a floral scent floated between them. He wondered if she dabbed it behind her ears or knees or....

"Thank you." He stepped quickly into the lab and moved as she closed the door. He noticed that it had a combination of locks and the rubber seals were thicker than the ones on his new Kelvinator at home.

"I was just finishing some work over here. Let me show you something." She pointed to a bank of microscopes. Shiny strips of glass glinted under the rows of florescent lights. A centrifuge, some things that looked like microwaves, boxes of slides, two refrigerators and an upright freezer crowded the back wall. He followed her to a backless swivel stool in front of a high counter.

"Have you found what causes the illness?" Johnson asked.

"We are really close. Look here." She slipped off the chair after adjusting the microscope and checking whatever was on the slide. "We're looking for commonality, something all the victims share. We're testing for everything from common microbe cultures to genetic sequence matching. We can even do Polymerase Chain Reaction." She seemed to be waiting for him to say something.

"Really?" He said. "How does that work?" And he knew that she would like nothing better than to tell him. Anglo women scientists were hard to understand. He remembered the anthropologist who wore her shirts tied to expose her naval and short shorts. Spent all summer sifting through dirt and seemed to be orgasmic over pot chards. Women without men could get strange.

"The technique lets scientists try to enhance or magnify unique genetic sequences from blood samples to look for DNA matches with known organisms. But I better get this road kill back in the freezer." She laughed, popped the mask over her face and gathered up an armload of tiny corpses in the lab baggies. "Dr. Black took everyone back to his office for a conference call with the CDC in Atlanta and I promised to clean up."

Johnson nodded, then turned to look through the microscope. At least nothing was moving. One time in biology lab in high school, Bobby Wiebe jerked off in the john and made a slide. When Johnson took his turn at the microscope all the wiggling had made him queasy. He looked back at the slide and let the cool metal circle of the scope push against his eye.

"Well, that's done. Let's see what we have here." She peeled off heavy rubber gloves and leaned toward the microscope. A breast brushed his arm. He felt a blip of life between his legs. He tried to signal the appendage that he affectionately called "Montana." Not now. An erection in tight slacks meant that his penis would be forced down his pants leg and would protrude like a goiter along his inner thigh. Maybe if he thought about baseball.

"We are beginning to get a good idea of what our culprit looks like—it has a protein coat with receptor spikes that hook into the cells it attacks. Internally, it has coiled genetic material allowing it to reproduce while hiding out in host cells." Johnson felt the same feverish excitement that had bothered him in the anthropologist.

"You know, I feel like a real detective, sort of a Wild West deputy riding down a killer." Her giggle seemed out of place. She cleared her throat and regained her composure.

"Here. Look at these lungs." There were two negatives clipped to the twin viewing screens. "These are the lungs of a healthy twelve-year-old. This X-ray taken during her back-to-school physical examination." She pointed to the negative on the left. "Twenty hours later these are the same lungs, this X-ray taken after she died."

Johnson winced. Jennifer. He didn't like looking at someone he knew. Photographs had been outlawed for years by his people because they believed the lens stole your soul. What would his ancestors think of these pictures? Pictures of a person's insides. But it was the young girl's death that bothered him. She had had everything to live for. She shouldn't have died— that weighed heavily on his conscience. He needed to change the subject. He cleared his throat.

"What does this have to do with mice? Our people consider mice to be a vital link to preserving our life in the desert. They gather and spread seeds and guarantee the abundance of food."

Johnson watched Nancy's face register an "oh, you poor dear" expression and felt her hand lightly touch his forearm.

"This must be so difficult for your people," she said.

"Yes," Johnson said simply, but allowed a tortured sigh to escape his lips. He needed to check on the time. And he probably should call Douglas Anderson and tell him about the lab.

"I must leave now." His voice had that "chief of the tribe" resonance. Nancy was beginning to look awestruck.

"Anytime you'd like to drop by the lab, I'll be glad to show you what we're working on."

"Maybe next week," he said.

She opened the door and Johnson stepped out. He had taken a few steps when he saw the feather. Stooping, he picked it up, turned to face Nancy, twirled it between his fingers, his eyes closed, lips moving.

"May your work travel on the wings of the eagle. Be thorough in your hunt; be swift in your flight."

He handed the feather to Nancy and turned to walk back to the hospital. He didn't glance back. He didn't have to. He knew that she stood in the doorway clutching a piece of plumage from the back end of a pigeon and gazed after him mesmerized. He'd make that appointment to see the psychologist next week.

"I'M MAKING A scrapbook." Gloria sat in the chair next to his desk eating her lunch. Sandy found the smells of the Navajo taco distracting.

"A scrapbook? About what?" he asked.

"The deaths and stuff that people are saying. It might be helpful."

"You're right. Good idea."

"I even checked out that Sinclair Lewis book."

"What Sinclair Lewis book?" Sandy was having trouble following this conversation.

"The one about the illness that sounds almost exactly like what's happening now."

Sandy racked his memory, but this was not a day that he'd choose Great Literature as an easy category. "What's the title?"

"*Arrowsmith*. It's all in the book. The tourism problem. How people don't want to talk about an epidemic and scare visitors away. How it's caused because someone fired the ratcatcher."

"Ratcatcher?"

"Umhmmm. The population becomes over run with rats when the person who usually controls them is let go. Local religious beliefs are threatened. It's all there."

"Sounds prophetic."

"It is." Gloria snapped the top on the round Tupperware carrier that had contained her lunch, then handed him the scrapbook. "I like the article on page twenty-seven."

Sandy waited until she had gone back to her office before succumbing to curiosity. Each page of the scrapbook held one to five articles or pictures having to do with the epidemic. Pictures were labeled and all articles had dates and sources. Amazing. The one on page twenty-seven told how a man still talked with his dead aunt every night. She had been one of the very first to die and had foretold her own death. She had warned her nephew that she would be "going on soon" and he should prepare. This was two weeks before she died. Gloria probably believed that someone could forecast the future. Did he? The phone kept him from any further soul-searching.

The message was brief. "He's going to be all right." Great news Sandy thought as he put the phone down. Some unlucky man in the wrong place at the wrong time but, thank god, this time it wasn't fatal. The UPS driver had delivered some traps to Tewa. There was that common link again. Thanks to a concerned wife, he was rushed to the hospital and put on a ventilator at the first signs of illness. The second survivor. He'd get someone over to interview him, but now he needed to fill in on the floor. Lunch hours were never long enough.

"I'll be seeing patients on two." Gloria nodded but continued to talk on the phone. Sandy could see the office's two other lines blinking. He stopped to check with the receptionist and look at the sign-in sheet.

"How are we doing?"

"Not good. I've been telling people to bring a book, bring a library, you'll be here for hours."

Outpatient visits were up fifty percent the last two weeks. The waiting room smelled of dirty diapers and Vicks. Not two of his favorites. Everyone with a runny nose was coming in for X-rays. And they wouldn't be turned away. If the crowds continued, Sandy would ask for Federal reinforcements.

He looked around the room, felt the uneasiness, and thought of the irony. The same day that news of the mystery illness hit the press, it shared space with a budget-cut proposal for Indian health. A thirty-six percent budget-cut from the service that provides medical care to one million American Indians. No one could even estimate how much the epidemic would cost. Fifty dollars per person for lab work, X-rays another twenty dollars. Since Jennifer's death, the waiting room was full even on Saturdays. A small fortune had already been spent on tests.

"How long has the baby been coughing?" Sandy followed the mother holding the feverish baby into the examining room which was now a screened corner at the end of the hall, one of twelve makeshift examining cubicles that lined the hallway.

"One night, maybe two." The mother held the baby tightly. Sandy knew that this was her first child. She had had the baby on the reservation with Twila's help. The little guy must be six months old now.

"Let's keep him overnight for observation." The only problem would be room. With the common cold getting a person X-rays and an overnight, there were cots in offices.

"We may be able to squeeze him into the nursery."

"Will he be okay?" Fear had turned her voice into a whisper.

"We're going to do everything we can." It sounded lame—it was lame. He took the baby from his mother and started towards the door.

"I'll show you where he'll be tonight. Will you be able to stay with him?" Sandy couldn't remember whether she had said she was nursing. He was so tired, he was losing it. He'd have to ask again.

It was three hours before he returned to his desk to catch up on paperwork. In the meantime Gloria had fielded twenty-seven calls.

"Anything important?" Sandy asked.

"A psychic called from Iowa."

"A psychic?"

"Yeah. She said the problem was sheep. She told me to stop eating lamb and make the herd sleep outside."

"What did you say?"

"I told her I didn't like lamb and that she had us confused with the Navajo."

"And?"

"She hung up."

"Any other important calls?" Sandy asked and knew the sarcasm would be lost.

"A senator."

"What did he want?"

"He was upset about this month's *Scientific American*. I got a copy for you. Here's the article. It says the illness is caused by biological warfare. I'll put it in the scrapbook."

"Let me see that. Good God. I suppose we have to cover all our bases. And, Gloria, thanks for getting the magazine. That was really helpful."

Sandy leaned back in his desk chair and read the article. The author was respected in the scientific community. But germ warfare or chemicals? Too preposterous. Next there'd be an Elvis sighting in the Pueblo and the *National Enquirer* would get involved.

EIGHT

JULIE SWITCHED ON her computer and clicked the mouse to open the mystery illness file. Ten deaths. She needed to get out something fresh by tomorrow. She had borrowed copies of the interviews that Ben had conducted with some of the families. She was looking for a human interest angle, something other than how star crossed lovers die before life begins, or thirteen-year-old misses chance to become star soccer player.

The screen was showing "new file." There was no file named "mys.ill." She tried another approach. Same result. How could her file be gone? She checked the electronic program manager. Nothing. The mystery illness file didn't exist. Don't panic. She also had her files on her computer at home. And, thank God, she'd kept that file updated. But to lose everything? She hated to think what would happen if she didn't have a copy at home. All that time and material lost. Maybe, if she looked one more time… Julie electronically traced her steps back through the files and prompts and backup copies. Nothing. It wasn't there. Maybe there'd been a power failure. She walked out to the lobby.

"Anyone complain about problems with his computer?"

The receptionist shook her head.

"Are you sure? I've lost a big chunk of my research on the mystery illness for no apparent reason. It seems strange that I'd be the only one on the network to get dumped."

"No one's said anything to me."

"I'll report it. But let me know if you hear about it happening to anyone else."

"Speaking of the mystery illness, have you heard from Ben Pecos again? After you interviewed him? He is so gorgeous." The receptionist held up a copy of the Journal that featured an article on trapping. Ben was standing beside two uniformed men from Fish and Wildlife.

"A couple times, I guess."

"I knew it. You're blushing. You're dating him, aren't you?"

"I blush if you ask me the time." Julie turned to walk back to her office.

"You're too single. You should be dating someone." The receptionist called after her.

Too single? There would be plenty of time to remedy that after she made anchor. First things first. Now where was the file folder with Ben's interviews? She opened the bottom drawer of her desk and scanned the tabs. No file with the interview copy. Where had she put it? She checked three drawers of the standing file. The folder simply didn't exist. Odd. She'd taken some folders home, but she was certain that wasn't one of them.

Who could want it? There wasn't any competition. Bob had given her the story and seemed pleased with her results. She must have misplaced it. It was already after five. She'd check her apartment. But how could she have dumped her computer files and misplaced the folder more or less on the same day?

"Hot date tonight?" The receptionist asked then rolled her eyes as Julie walked by.

"Sorry to disappoint, but it's just me and a good book this evening. I'll let you know the minute my love life gets interesting." Like hell, Julie added under her breath.

SHE PRESSED THE garage door opener and maneuvered the Miata between two rows of packing crates. Whoever advised throwing out anything not unpacked in six months would have a field day with her. She pushed open the kitchen door, and stifling hot air pushed back. Damn. She'd forgotten to turn on the air-conditioning. Maybe she'd opt for a quick swim before dinner. Part of the allure of this town house was the Olympic-sized pool. Along with the car, the town house had been a graduation present from Mom and Dad.

She pressed the message button on her answering machine, turned up the volume and headed upstairs to change. One thing she was thankful for—Wayne had stopped calling. Probably had hocked the ring and was out lining up the next Mrs. Almost-to-be. None of the messages was urgent. Dentist appointment on Friday. Call her mother. Put out clothes for local charity to pick up in the morning. Pretty dull stuff. Pretty dull life. No. It was the life she wanted. Career first. Speaking of which, she'd better try to find that folder.

It wasn't on top of her desk. She flipped through a stack of marked folders beside the computer. Not there. She didn't lose things. Things could remain packed for awhile, but they weren't lost. She flipped on the computer. Her information file on the mystery illness was intact. She'd print out a hard copy and make another disk backup. She was only out Ben's interviews. She'd decide later whether to ask to copy them again.

She tugged her swimsuit in place. The doorbell. Must be the paperboy to collect for this month.

"Hi. Someone at your office assured me you were home alone." Ben stepped back and Julie felt herself blushing as he took in the swimsuit.

"Wow. My timing is great. You should always wear that color. For that matter, maybe you should always wear that outfit."

"What are you doing here?" Julie tried to sound upset, but it wasn't working.

"Home delivery. Five kinds of Chinese and fortune cookies."

He held open a large sack. "Okay? Can I come in now?"

Julie smiled at him. "Of course. Dining room's that way. Give me a minute to change."

"You don't have to."

"No shirt, no shoes, no service. Isn't that how that goes?"

Ten minutes later Julie sat across from him at the table and watched him pile food on his plate.

"I only have a couple hours before I need to get back."

"How's the trapping going?"

"Okay. I've sent the lab somewhere around 250 critters. I expect another good-sized haul over the next two days."

"Let me go with you." She had said it on impulse. Ben stopped eating and sat looking at her. "Is something wrong?" She asked.

"You may not believe this, but I was shot at the other night."

"Shot at?" Her chop sticks clattered against her plate.

"I reported it to the Fish and Wildlife guys and they seemed to think it might have been a poacher, someone who thought I was trapping beaver or muskrat. But that doesn't make sense. Not this time of year. Pelts would be thin, just beginning to grow thick for winter. And what's really weird, I caught him putting one of the trapped mice in his pocket."

"He kept a mouse?"

"Yeah."

"I don't have a story to top that one, but this afternoon when I got back to the office, my computer file on the mystery illness was gone. Didn't exist. And the folder of interview notes that I'd borrowed from you is missing."

"Does that sort of thing happen often?"

"It never has before."

"Makes you think somebody out there wants to know what we're doing."

"Yes, but why?" Julie asked.

"Maybe someone who wants to find out what's causing the illness so he can publish the results first?"

"But shooting at someone for a Pulitzer?

"Probably worse has been done. Do you still want to spend a night in the woods?"

THERE WAS AN HOUR of light left before the sun would slip behind the mesas. Julie dipped the steel bristled brush into the Lysol mixture and scrubbed and rinsed another trap. They were almost finished. They would set around a hundred and fifty traps, about half of those in new areas, and collect the rodents from the traps set last night.

There was a touch of fall in the air. Tonight would be chilly. Julie brought her thoughts back from thinking about shootings to linger on her surroundings. A pale peach glow was spreading across the sky becoming more intense as the sun sank lower. She could hear frogs, and crickets, slower now with their songs. Sitting on the sandy soil outside Ben's tent, she leaned back and felt the warmth of the desert floor travel up her arms and legs.

"Hey, no slacking off." Ben had walked up behind her, then grinning he squatted down beside her.

"It's beautiful out here," Julie said.

"I know. Come with me. I want to show you something." Ben pulled her to her feet and walked ahead towards the river.

At first, she could only see the pile of jumbled sticks that spread across one end of the pool.

"There. At the far end. There're two of them." Julie felt

Ben's arm around her pointing at something in the shadows. Beaver. Probably a pair. Ben folded his arms around her waist and rested his chin on the top of her head. They watched the two animals swim lazily then dive and disappear.

Ben pulled her tighter against him, and Julie bit back her favorite Mae West line, "You packin' a pistol or just glad to see me?" She liked feeling his excitement. Wanted to feel it. She wanted a physical relationship. She just didn't want one now. She turned to face Ben. The first kiss was gentle, a brush of lips. Then she reached up and with her hands behind his head pulled him towards her and kissed him harder.

When he drew back, he gently pushed her hair away from her face, kissed the corners of her eyes, the tip of her nose, then traced the outline of her open lips with his tongue. He pressed her into him. His mouth covered hers; his tongue teasing, thrusting. At first the sounds didn't register. The crack of a branch. The rustle of leaves. Someone was walking towards them through the underbrush. Ben's reflexes were trigger quick. He pushed her to the ground and whirled to confront the intruder.

"Ben. No. It's Lorenzo." Julie struggled to her feet and hurried towards the old man. "He's cold. He must have lost his blanket. Keep him here. I'll be right back."

Julie ran back to the tent and returned with her new Pendleton poncho.

"You can't give him that."

"Yes, I can. It will keep him warm." She slipped the poncho over Lorenzo's head. The dusk made it difficult to see the brightness of the turquoise and gold pattern, but she watched as he stroked the softness with arthritic fingers.

"He likes it." Julie stepped back, and Lorenzo looked at her. He tried to say something as he continued to push his fingers into the blanket's thickness. He patted the blanket on his chest and over his arms, then turned to walk towards the river.

"You're going to get cold tonight." Ben said.

"Not if you have a spare blanket."

"How about sharing one?" Ben was teasing but the idea appealed to her—very much—more than she wanted to admit.

Think "anchor," Julie admonished herself. You don't want a relationship now, no matter how much you like this man.

"THEY WANT YOU out back." Gloria stood in the doorway to his office. Sandy had asked her once why she didn't use the intercom and she said she needed the exercise. Hard to argue with that, he decided. But it was a little disconcerting to have her make announcements from the doorway.

"In the lab?"

"Umhmm."

"Did they say it was urgent?" Sandy looked at a stack of neglected mail.

"I think they found the bad guys."

"Bad guys?"

"You know, what causes the sickness."

"You're kidding." Sandy was on his feet so quickly that his desk chair toppled over. "Take messages. Don't forward any calls."

"Okay." Gloria said to the empty room.

Seven excited lab techs were clustered in a back corner. "This is it. Us, the CDC, the University of Alabama's mycoplasma expert, UNM—we're all saying the same thing." One man pulled a bottle of champagne from the refrigerator. Another handed out Dixie cups.

"Sure that isn't a little premature?" Sandy asked.

"Not this time. We've nailed this dude." The cork from the champagne bottle ricocheted off of an overhead vent, and a light misting of foam drifted over Sandy's forehead.

"The CDC found antibodies to the Hantaan virus in tissue samples from three of the four people who have died that we've been able to test. We've found 42 of the 257 rodents tested here in the lab to have antibodies indicating that they had been exposed to the Hantavirus. Twelve of the 42 mice were trapped close to the houses of Peter Tenorio and his fiancée. I don't think you can get more conclusive than that." The technician turned back to refilling his Dixie cup and another half dozen held out to him.

"Any particular type of rodent more involved than others?" Sandy asked.

"Deer mice. The real cute ones with the big ears. Forty of them tested positive and only two common field mice."

"So, we have a name. Hantavirus." Sandy said. A virus well known world-wide but not in the United States. But it was bound to happen. World trade. Travel. Sooner or later, few diseases would remain isolated, indigenous to only one part of the world.

He walked back to his office and stopped to tell Gloria the lab's findings. But why wasn't he feeling elated? Something was nagging at his memory. Some question unanswered.

"Is it over now?" Gloria asked.

"You mean people getting sick?"

"Yeah."

"I wish I could say yes," Sandy said.

"So what happens now?"

"It's more important than ever to continue to trap rodents in and around the Pueblo, and throughout New Mexico, for that matter."

"My husband's Navajo. His people predicted this."

"Predicted what?"

"Mice inhabit the night world and the mesas; people inhabit the day world and live in houses. It happens when the pinon nuts are plentiful and there has been abundant snow. It is an old story. When mice come into the world of the people, an ancient illness will happen."

"Gloria, I can't believe this. There's a legend about people dying from mice co-habiting with humans?"

"Umhmm."

"Has it ever happened before?"

"Twice to the Navajo. Once in 1918 and again in 1933."

"Does the legend say how the illness is spread?"

"Mouse urine. The old ones warned the people to keep their hogans clean and keep food in containers. If a mouse touched them, they should burn their clothing."

"I'll be damned." Sandy leaned against the wall and stared at Gloria.

"When there's disharmony among the people and nature, these things happen," she said.

Sandy crossed the hall to his office. Amazing. Folklore and Western medicine both reaching the same conclusion. But there was still something not quite right. Something he should be thinking about. Some missing link.

"Doctor Black?"

"Gloria, you startled me."

"I forgot to give you this. The UNM Medical Center sent it over in the mail."

The white envelope was lumpy. The note on the back flap was signed by Marilyn Bernowich. Bernowich. Amy, of course. One of the survivors. That's the piece that doesn't fit. How could she have been exposed to mouse urine, feces, or salvia from mice around the Pueblo? Her contact was Mary Toya. Hantaviruses were not spread from human to human. Unless… Sandy reached for a pair of tweezers in his drawer. He extracted the plastic bag from the envelope. Pumpkin seeds. They could have traces of mouse droppings. He'd get them to the lab. This might be an important piece to the puzzle.

"THIS WAY, Governor Yepa." The psychologist held open the door to his office. Johnson wished the man didn't look like Bob Newhart, but he followed him inside.

"This must be a very stressful time for you. I'm sure your duties as Governor take you away from your family." The psychologist sat looking at him. Was he supposed to comment? Johnson didn't know. "Your wife shared with me that the two of you seem to be having difficulties. I think that's what we should talk about today. I want to assure you that I listen to both sides and will work with each of you, but I can't rekindle any flames if the fire has gone out." The man looked at him expectantly.

Johnson looked at the floor. Maybe if he acted contrite, concerned, anxious to be helpful. Maybe if he told the truth. Nancy's well-endowed figure blurred his vision. He shook his head. Better. The desk and psychologist were sharply in focus now.

"I'm not sure what my wife has told you...maybe something about another woman?" Johnson waited but the doc was non-committal—not a nod, not a shake of the head, nothing—just that patient waiting.

"Well, Doc, you know how it is. A man needs to keep his blood young."

"I'm not sure I understand."

"The warrior after battle, the hunter after the hunt; there's a need to refuel, to be with a maiden and replenish the source of one's manhood."

The doctor pursed his mouth, frowning slightly as if in thought, then relaxed, never taking his eyes off of Johnson.

"I thought the Pueblo people were farmers," he said.

Johnson paused. He wasn't going to get by with anything. He would have to regroup and try to cut this meeting short.

"You know, doc, I'm probably just wasting your time. My wife and I have talked, and we think she's going to be okay. I would have cancelled today, but I wanted to stop by and say thanks. That meeting with her last week really helped." Johnson stood and moved toward the door. The psychologist remained seated.

"If you change your mind and would like to talk, just make an appointment with my secretary."

Johnson nodded, backed out of the office pulling the door shut after him and bolted for the back door of the hospital. If he was lucky, he'd find Nancy alone in the lab. He wondered how far he could go with her. He could probably work a hand up under her tee shirt and cop a good feel. Maybe even push the cotton fabric up to her neck and bury his face in the scent of floral and warm flesh. The idea was almost too much for him and he reached the door of the lab sticky with perspiration that made his crotch itch.

"Hi. I'm Dave. You're the Gov, right? Nancy said you might drop by. Hey, Nancy, your friend's here."

Johnson followed him into the lab and fought an urge to scratch. Nancy was beaming as she held out her hand.

"I was hoping you'd stop by today. Did you know we've solved the mystery?"

Johnson shook his head, but he was more interested in getting rid of Dave who seemed to be the only one around besides Nancy.

"Come with me." Nancy pointed to the back of the lab.

Johnson noticed the bags of deer mice tagged and stacked in clear plastic containers. Maybe it was just as well Dave was here. It was like trying to think about sex in a morgue. He offered a silent prayer for the souls of the tiny creatures.

"What are you doing with so many deer mice?" he asked.

"We've proved that they are the principal carriers of the Hantavirus, the mystery killer."

"Where did the mice get the virus?" Johnson tried not to think of the investment group.

"Good question. And there are a couple possible answers. One, mice have carried the virus for some time but in numbers too small to impact humans until a couple things happened. Like the mice quadrupled in numbers and came in contact with more humans whose immune systems were less able to combat the virus. Or it has mutated recently to a new deadly form. You know, it just continued to hang around and adapt until it successfully infected a host."

She acted like this was an every day occurrence in nature, not something caused by man in a laboratory. But maybe he should make sure. If the Andersons knew this, they'd feel a lot better about the casino plans, assured that no one suspected....

"How could it mutate?" Johnson asked.

"By exchanging genetic material. Hantaviruses may mutate whenever two invade the same cell at the same time."

Johnson frowned. "I don't think I understand."

"Do you know how influenza epidemics occur? Why every year people have to get shots and aren't immune from one season to the next?"

Johnson shook his head.

"Well, influenza viruses in Asian ducks co-infect with benign human influenza viruses, they swap genetic segments and produce a new strain of flu that the human immune system can't handle. That's why flu epidemics tend to come from Asia.''

Nancy was looking pleased with herself. Johnson noticed the outline of hard nipples pushing at the white cotton stretched tightly across her chest. This woman could get excited over Asian ducks. What would she do with his hand between her legs? More importantly, when was he going to find out? He tried to focus on what she was saying.

''This is probably only theoretically possible for Hantaviruses, but I believe it could happen. For example, we know that this Hantavirus has made one major change. It attacks the respiratory system instead of the kidneys like four other Hantaviruses do. But here I am going on and on, wouldn't you like something cold to drink?''

Johnson watched her go to the fridge in back and admired how the material of her shorts dipped between the halves of her buttocks and pulled above the dark line of her tan when she leaned over.

''Oh no, we're out of sodas. It'll just take a second to get some.'' She was out the door and heading for the hospital basement before he could say he wasn't thirsty. Idly, he sat on one of the stools and twisted around to face the high counter. There were three-ring binders everywhere and note pads scribbled full. An envelope in front of him was from Dr. Black. He picked it up and looked inside and gasped. He slipped off the stool, catching himself by grabbing the edge of the counter. Inside was a plastic bag of seeds. Pumpkin seeds.

An attached note read, ''Mary Toya, Tewa Pueblo, August 9.'' Mary Toya. His secretary Mary Toya? The former Governor's secretary? Had she taken the original packet? Had she brought them here?

His legs had that rubbery feel that followed a good gut punch. He held onto the counter and locked his knees; even his teeth wanted to chatter. He looked around to see if Dave was watching him. No, Dave was at a computer along the back wall with his back to him. Somewhere a compressor was whirring and masked any sound that he might make. Good. Johnson controlled the shaking of his hands and slipped the plastic bag and note into his pocket. He needed to get out of there. He needed to think.

"Uh, tell Nancy that I didn't realize how late it was getting. I have a council meeting at four."

Dave waved and didn't turn from the computer screen.

DOUGLAS ANDERSON, SR. sat at his dining room table, unfolded the newspaper and read the headlines: "Biological Serial Killer Found! Report Shows Hantavirus In Mice Around Since Early 80's." He pushed the pot of coffee towards his son and smiled broadly.

"This couldn't be better." He patted the paper. "Science has triumphed. Half the mice in the state will be killed and it'll be a boon for exterminators, but we'll get back to building that casino."

Douglas, Sr. felt safe and a little smug. They had really only suffered a minor setback. The casino could open by the first of the year. And all this publicity for the virus kept dissenters from paying attention to them. Public hearings last summer brought out protesters but their numbers were dwarfed by the assenting crowds from the Pueblos. It had been the old Tewa Governor who had stood in their way. Luckily Governor Yepa saw the potential in joining a six billion dollar a year industry. Some tribes take in a million dollars a day and funnel much of that money back into tribal projects.

State officials had suggested that they start slow with the lower end Class II gambling, bingo and lottery, but that would have been a waste of energy. No, it had been best to go for the top. Laws were still murky on how much local government intervention there should be. They had gotten in on the ground floor. They would set precedent. They would upgrade the economic status of the Pueblo, and help them overcome an unemployment rate of 30 per cent.

"Are you thinking of sending a crew back into Tewa?" Junior asked.

Doug, Sr. pointed to the paper. "I think it's time. We were only waiting for some answers. In fact, maybe it's time for that hoop-la we couldn't have earlier."

"A party?"

"Why not? Do it up big. The Governor of New Mexico, Legislators, a real who's who of Santa Fe. Nothing spared."

"Sounds great."

"Yes. We could use a little fanfare."

THE TUXEDO SHOP smelled musty. Sort of moth balls and unwashed linen with a heavy scent of Ralph Lauren. A tinny bell attached to the front door announced Johnson's entrance. They rented "dress attire" as the slightly effeminate voice on the phone had said, "for the discriminating." Johnson wasn't sure about that; he was here because it was the only place in Albuquerque that guaranteed the tux, tailoring and all, would be ready by Friday.

He'd had a fight with his wife about buying a tux instead of renting one. He wanted his own. It wasn't just for the Anderson's party; he'd wear it to the casino. Renting was a waste of money, but he had given in. It was bad enough that he wasn't taking her to the party. He started to speak to a gentlemen wearing black tails but realized before he looked foolish that it was a mannequin. Actually, the room was filled with nattily attired molded plastic men arranged to appear to be having intimate conversations. Tea cups and *New York Times* were held by perfectly manicured hands.

Top hats were everywhere. In one circle a dog stood beside its master. The dog looked real. Johnson walked over to put a hand on the dog's head.

"Aren't they wonderful?" Johnson jumped. A slightly built man of indeterminate age glided towards him from the back. "This is Fred. Astaire, of course. And this is Clark. Oh, here's The Duke. Wouldn't he just die, or what, to be sharing a little tête-à-tête with the likes of these?" The man laughed shrilly, a sort of whinny, and flitted among the twenty odd statues arranging a tie here, an ascot there.

"You know they're anatomically correct."

"They're what?" Johnson thought he should say something and not just stare.

"You know, their little dickies are all right there." He patted the crotch of The Duke.

"Why?" It was the only thing Johnson could think of to say.

"To make them look better in swimsuits and underwear. I was a window dresser in New York. I hated the summer months. You can cover up a bad model with clothes but there's nothing you can do with a flat crotch in a bikini brief." He paused to fluff up a pocket hanky. Johnson felt vaguely uncomfortable and thought of leaving.

"You know, one time I had to do an entire window of men in official Olympic swim trunks, the Spandex ones that leave nothing to the imagination, well, let me tell you, they looked awful. Nothing would hang right. If you'll excuse the pun. Of course, I could have stuffed them, but sooner or later the tissue would settle or the socks would shift." He walked closer to Johnson and leaned toward him conspiratorially.

"I bet you can't guess what I did. Clay. Child's Modeling Clay. It was brilliant until the air-conditioning failed."

Johnson let his imagination stray to what that might have looked like, handfuls of clay melting and separating from the host, running down its legs. It wasn't pretty.

"Did you lose your job?"

"Not that time, luckily. But let's see now. You need a little something for Friday night. Correct?"

"Yes." But his reply was lost as the man was already in the back room. Johnson tried not to look at The Duke's crotch.

"You're in luck." He was yelling from behind a curtain that separated the showroom from what must be fitting rooms, Johnson thought. "I even have a delightful maroon that will do just dandy after a few teensy changes."

He emerged with four suits and plopped them over the counter.

"Shall we take a look at that maroon one first?" The man pulled it from the middle of the stack. "Now, of course, you'll want a contrasting cummerbund. But this is such a rich color. Look. Isn't that smart?" He held the suit up in front of Johnson and pointed to the full length mirror. Johnson liked it. It would

do perfectly for meeting the Governor of the State and impress-
ing Mollie.

"I'll take it."

"We'll need to pinch a little here and there." The man stood
in back of Johnson holding the jacket up by one shoulder and
gathering and straightening cloth with the other hand as he
watched the effect in the mirror. Johnson wasn't sure he liked
him standing that close.

"Why don't you just slip the trousers on and let me see the
fit. Dressing rooms are that way." He waved towards the back
behind the curtain.

The dressing room was beautiful. A wine velvet settee filled
one corner, and the walls had some kind of flocked paper that
felt more like fuzzy cloth. Brass cherubs held their arms out to
receive his clothing. Johnson noted that their little legs were
crossed. He felt better.

The back wall was a mirror. Floor to ceiling. Its gilt edges
scrolled towards the center of the frame to hold hearts and more
cherubs. Johnson peered closely at the thick glass. It was an
odd mirror. Then it dawned on him. Two-way. It could be two-
way glass allowing someone to watch him.

"How are we doing in there?" The man sounded like he
was standing next to him.

"Okay. Almost ready." Johnson turned his back on the mirror and struggled out of his clothes. He was glad he had thought
to bring the patent loafers.

"Oh my, my. The color is perrrfect. And the cut of that
jacket...." The man pursed his lips and studied Johnson as he
struggled to walk back into the showroom. The pants legs were
bunched around his ankles, and he had slipped the jacket on
over his tee shirt.

"Have you ever thought of modeling?" Johnson stole a look
at the man to see if he was kidding, then took a sideways peek
in the mirror. The jacket made his shoulders broad before it
narrowed to slim his waist. Not bad. Not bad at all.

"I'll just pin these up." The man knelt with a mouth full of
straight pins after he asked Johnson to stand on a stool in front
of the mirror. "You know, now this is just a suggestion, a band

corset would flatten that little tummy and help accentuate those terrifically slim hips.''

Johnson fleetingly heard his wife laughing. Another thing to keep in the Bronco. But it was something to consider.

THE SPRAWLING ADOBE was nestled in the hills outside Santa Fe. Each window glowed with light that penetrated the surrounding darkness. Pinon smoke wafted upward from multiple fireplaces and disappeared into the night. Cars were parked on both sides of the road leading up to the Andersons' house. Johnson parked a half mile away and could hear laughter of people sitting in the sunken gardens. The end of September and the weather was just now turning cool at night.

A butler opened the heavy oak doors and announced his entrance into the tiled hallway. Tin sconces held beeswax candles that illuminated a nicho containing a Santos de San Isidro. Vigas stained a gray-blue were as big around as his waist and filled the twenty-foot high ceiling of the great room. They were as long as telephone poles. Between the vigas, stripped cedar latillas angled in a chevron pattern and added to the heady wood smells that filled the house.

The fireplace filled a north wall. The raised hearth of white plaster continued around the opening and formed bancos for sitting along the sides. Cushions in blanket plaids had been expertly fitted to line these attached benches. A framed oil of two huge overlapping red poppies dominated the fireplace's plastered flue. Must be by someone famous, Johnson thought, as he noticed the suspended pipe lighting that illuminated it.

The grand piano looked small until Johnson stood next to it. The man at the keyboard pounded out oldies. Johnson stopped to listen to ''Autumn Leaves.'' The white-jacketed server had to ask him twice if he wanted something to drink. Perrier had sounded expensive but tasted like bubbly water.

Douglas Anderson, Sr. waved to him from the other side of the room and then came towards him with the Governor and First Lady of New Mexico in tow.

''Wonderful of you to come, Governor Yepa. Now, if I don't get too confused with two Governors. Have you met Governor

Knight and his lovely wife?" Johnson shook hands. The Governor was saying something about how this was an economic move to release his people from poverty. Sounded like he was rehearsing, Johnson thought. The first lady interrupted once or twice to correct his facts. Finally, Douglas dragged them away to "work the room," as he put it.

Johnson was just trying to decide which corridor might lead to the kitchen when Douglas moved to a microphone beside the piano and asked the crowd of a hundred and fifty or so guests to give him its attention.

"Thank you. Now let me introduce some of our honored guests. The Governor of our fair state, the honorable..."

Johnson tuned out and scanned the room looking for Mollie, and almost missed acknowledging his own introduction. As he moved to the dais and waved to the crowd, he immediately wished he had unbuttoned his jacket when it pulled above the gold cummerbund and caused his pleated shirt to ride up to his bow tie. He resisted tugging it down and stood quietly listening to the Governor extol the virtues of gambling for an impoverished people. A tribe ancient in beliefs and customs. What did he know, Johnson wondered.

Next came Bob Crenshaw, owner of the largest TV station in the Southwest, then ten more State biggies spoke and crowded around him. After that, there was picture-taking. Flash-bulbs winked from around the room. He posed with the Governor and his wife, then Douglas Anderson, Sr. Finally, he was allowed to escape. The pianist struck up a rendition of "Smoke Gets In Your Eyes," followed by "I Left My Heart in San Francisco"; the Governor and his wife two-stepped smoothly in a large circle on the parquet oak floor.

Johnson was getting hungry and wandered over to a canopied table twenty-five feet in length laden with food, some familiar, some suspect. He knew what caviar looked like and avoided that, as well as the smoked salmon, both nestled in greenery at the base of a five foot fountain spurting blue water over its silver sides. He was just reaching for a small triangle of bread with something orange on it—cheese, he hoped—when the lights dimmed.

From his vantage point it looked like half the show girls from Vegas were leaning over the balcony upstairs blowing kisses and shaking their feathered and sequined torsos. Headdresses glittered and waved in the undulating spotlights. Bosoms mounded up and jiggled over the edges of stiff satin cups, and net stockings stretched to their waists. Narrow bands of gold leather kept their stiletto heels on their feet. It was a glorious sight. Johnson almost forgot about Mollie.

Then they descended the curving staircase. The Spotlights highlighted their every step. And all the way down they threw net packets of foil covered chocolate ''money'' and tiny play decks of cards and dice to their adoring audience. Johnson was almost overcome by the sheer magnitude of near-nakedness everywhere he looked.

''They're pretty, but they're going to get cold.'' The soft voice at his elbow sounded familiar.

''Mollie.'' Johnson turned to the small plump Indian woman beside him. Her black and white uniform included a doily-sized hat pinned to her freshly permed hair.

''Anglo 'doings,''' she said. Johnson gathered that she didn't much approve of it all.

''Do you get a break?'' He let his hand stray to her rounded backside. She wiggled away, but laughed.

''Maybe. Why would you be interested?'' Johnson always liked the way she teased him.

''Guess that's for you to find out.'' He pinched her bottom this time.

''In fifteen minutes meet me at the carriage house.''

''Carriage house?''

''It's what they call the garage. Around in back behind the gardens.''

She slipped away just as the lights came up, and the Vegas girls clustered around the piano. Must be going to do a number or two, he thought. He checked the free-form wood burl clock on the wall, twelve more minutes. Maybe he should just leave now so he'd have time to find the place.

The wide driveway in front of the house curved around to the right and disappeared into darkness. Two uniformed valets leaned against a Lincoln and traded jokes. They barely nodded as he walked past. The crunch of the crushed rock echoed and bounced back at him from the walls of the house. He paused to listen to the night sounds. Laughter streamed from the party as a ribald show tune ended. He was alone in the crisp night air filled with the smell of pinon smoke.

The carriage house was really a four door flat roofed adobe building with what looked to be a workroom on one end. The front doors were locked so Johnson moved around to the side. The workroom door was open. He stepped across the threshold and could just make out the shapes of garden tools and a bench along a side wall. Somewhere from the garage beyond, he heard a car door open and saw the interior light blink on in the third car over.

"Here." Mollie's stage whisper carried over the cars.

The first thing he noticed was her uniform carefully folded on the front seat of the Cadillac. Mollie, in a pink shiny slip with toenails to match, lounged in the back seat. He hoped she wasn't wearing underpants.

"Should we close the door?" he asked.

"Nobody will come back here."

He noticed, though, that she was still whispering. He threw his tux jacket on top of her uniform, climbed in beside her and pulled her feet into his lap. He caressed first one foot and then the other before putting a big toe in his mouth to suck noisily. Now here was a woman who knew where to wear perfume, as a cloud of scent circled his head every time she wiggled her toes.

Mollie kneaded his crotch with the toes of her other foot. He watched the bright pink spots push and tickle until Montana was fairly bursting to get out of his confines. Then she sat up and began to unbutton his shirt, struggling with the tiny pearlized buttons in the starched placket.

"Help me with this cummerbund." Johnson's voice was throaty with longing. He first tugged on the band then inched it around his waist so that the hooks and eyes were in front. Now the trousers. But the suspenders, something the man at the shop said would assure him of a perfect fit, were difficult to unfasten. The tiny buttons on the waistband were next. He saw her hesitate when she saw the corset. "Having a little back trouble," he mumbled as the sound of separating Velcro sliced through the silence.

With trousers around his knees, he squirmed out of his shirt after hesitating to unsnap one edge of the bow tie. By now Mollie had encircled Montana with her hand and was busy pumping up and down. He was halfway out of his undershirt when he realized he should have been thinking about baseball. How many times did he have a batter on the way to the plate only to find the batboy had stepped up to hit one out of the park. Too late. Another solo homer.

"You're the only woman who can get me this excited," he said and wished his shorts had been pushed a little lower; their dampness was going to be uncomfortable.

"I better be getting back." Mollie kissed him on the cheek then reached over the seat for her clothes and began to dress. She patted the doily hat in place, kissed him again and disappeared around the back of the car. He heard the workroom door open and close.

He wished she'd stuck around to help him with the cummerbund. He was having second thoughts about dressing this way every night to sit in the casino.

"I THOUGHT MAYBE you'd gone home." The elder Anderson was standing in the front door as Johnson walked up the driveway.

"Just getting some air." He fought an urge to pull the cummerbund down. He'd hoped to get to a bathroom before meeting anyone.

"Did you lose your tie?"

Johnson's hand flew to his neck before he thought of saying he'd just taken it off. Oh, well. Hopefully, it was somewhere outside and not in the back seat of the Cadillac.

"This has been a wonderful evening. This launches an enterprise I've dreamed about all my life." The elder Anderson linked arms with Johnson.

Where did this show of friendliness come from? A little too

much champagne? Johnson had never seen him this mellow. It seemed all was forgiven or, at least, forgotten.

"Will your people appreciate what we've done for them?"

Johnson was being propelled into a room off the entry that looked like an office.

"Some will." That was the truth. Not everyone, but hopefully, a majority. And maybe the others when the money started coming in.

Douglas Anderson had slipped behind a massive desk and now sat feet propped on a bottom drawer leaning back against a maroon leather high-backed chair. "You smoke?" He indicated a humidor on the corner of the desk.

"Don't mind if I do." Johnson pulled the lid to one side and extracted a dark expertly rolled cigar. He admired the tight configuration of its roundness and deep woodsy, yet musky scent. He ran it back and forth under his nose like he'd seen someone in the movies do.

The even snorts and gurgles coming from the chair behind the desk didn't surprise him. The elder Anderson was asleep. He'd dozed off, unlit cigar clenched between fingers, cavernous mouth gaping wide to show the too pink gums of false teeth. Johnson let his eyes search the desk top for a light.

When he didn't find one, he tucked the cigar in his pocket. It had been a good evening—no, a great evening—he amended as he thought of Mollie. Somehow in the quiet of the study with moonlight flooding through a skylight, everything, at last, was all right. He sighed and tiptoed from the room.

PART THREE

NINE

TONY CHANG ADJUSTED the visor with infrared lens, settled the helmet more comfortably on his head, then leaned over the small cage on the work bench. Working in the dark no longer bothered him; he had done it for so long. Carefully, he raised the sliding door on the solid wooden box attached at the back of the wire mesh container. Then he picked up his stop watch and waited.

At first two antennae waved from the opening. "C'mon. Take a step. That's it." Tony often talked to himself, silently encouraging his wards to cross the white line that divided safety and sure death. Next he saw the shiny black head and a tentative front leg. Another member of the family, *Blattidae,* this time *Blatella Orientalis* to be exact, would test a new insecticide.

The black oriental and brown German roach made up most of his collection in the lab. These were the ones common to Albuquerque. And the ones who developed resistance—the steady advancement of tolerance that would keep him in business for a long time. Tony pressed the button on the stopwatch as the cockroach crossed the line. Now the fun began. Sometimes he'd place a little wager with himself as to how fast the poison might work. Under fifteen. He felt today it would be less than a quarter of an hour.

After darting around the cage for a full minute, the roach stopped to clean itself pulling each hind leg through its mouth. At precisely four minutes and seventeen seconds into the experiment, the roach gave a spasmodic twitch but continued to explore its surroundings. At twelve minutes two seconds, it did a shoulder roll onto its side and didn't right itself. Instead, its row of strong legs propelled it in a small, tight circle for another three minutes sixteen seconds.

Then nothing. The roach, still on its side, simply stopped pushing and stiffened. Tony pressed the button on the stop watch. Eighteen seconds. He lost by eighteen seconds. He'd do better next time. Now he needed to tend the incubators containing the thousands of egg capsules—generations of future victims. Or, as Tony liked to call them, "volunteers."

He switched on the lights, hung the helmet on the wall and walked back into the large main room and sat in front of a computer. Lab equipment—test tubes, bunsen burners, glass containers of syringes—neatly displayed down the center of a long metal table reflected the morning sun that streamed in a dozen narrow windows along the top of the east wall.

Another room connected with the large thirty-five by twenty foot main laboratory held a few mice and rats, some rare to the United States like the Bandicoot. Chemicals, stored in barrels, were in a smaller room completely sealed off from the work area. Some were locked within layers of protective covering, steel drums surrounding a dram of killer.

He often wondered what people would think if they knew the contents of his laboratory—in the middle of Albuquerque. He chuckled. The public could be so trusting, so stupid. They were up in arms about storing nuclear waste two hundred miles south or disbanding the arsenal in the Manzano mountains and never thought that there could be things far more dangerous right next door.

He supposed he should tidy up. Douglas Anderson had called insisting on a meeting. Tony didn't like to be ordered around. Who was Douglas Anderson to demand that he drop everything and make himself available for a meeting in half an hour? At his lab, no less. Tony usually made the lab off-limits even to his workers.

But he knew what Douglas wanted—reassurance, now that the virus had somehow reverted to its original state. The newspaper headlines were inciting panic. They had linked it to mice and were doing an all out blitz to warn people what to watch out for. Tony had given it a lot of thought. Actually, nothing better could have happened. This would definitely throw the CDC off track—off track when it came to pinning it on human intervention.

He pushed back from the computer. The monitor and keyboard seen at a side table gave no hint of the hard drive kept in a humidified room protected by alarms and secret codes. A ten by ten room below the floor of the lab. He was careful. He was a scientist. One wall held licenses, permits and plaques of recognition for his work in pest control from countries around the world.

But America was his home. Where else could you become rich overnight? He had been born in San Francisco but moved to Albuquerque when his parents decided to go back to China. Back to China for the retirement that became their graves before the year was out. An unknown virus. His father had shown signs of flu, then broke out with skin hemorrhages. He died from shock. His mother's kidneys stopped working and the waste collected in her bloodstream. Both gone within a month.

Tony became obsessed with their killer. The same hemorrhagic fever had killed one hundred and ninety Americans during the Korean War in the early fifties, the nausea and thirst coupled with small skin hemorrhages that finally led to kidney failure. He had worked to harness the power of that killer to use or to sell as he wanted—worked for years to isolate and change the virus; poured over the volumes written about it by the military labs; tested it on human beings in third world countries where another death was never suspect in the squalor and poverty of everyday life. The search had consumed his life. But the result, the virus that he sold for one million dollars to the investment group, would never be recognized as the one that killed his parents. Virologists would expect the kidneys to collapse first. That was more common. This lung thing would keep them guessing for a while.

It had been somewhat of a fluke that he had even discovered a virus that attacked the lungs. He had toyed with altering Puumala, the virus carried by voles. He had even trapped some voles in Scandinavia where the vole population rises and falls on a four-year cycle. But the carriers were difficult to work with, and he had abandoned the experiment in favor of the Norwegian Brown rat. But it was the Brown rat's cousin, the Bandicoot, who tested positive for a Hantavirus that could be manipulated and changed in form without diluting its virility.

A buzzer sounded and a red glassed globe by the four inch thick steel door blinked a warning and interrupted his thoughts. Douglas must be here. He'd make him meet out front by the insect cages. That would ensure that the meeting would be short.

"Is this place safe?" Douglas Anderson wiped his face with a white handkerchief as he stepped into the lab. Tony thought he let it linger over his nose and mouth.

"Do you mean is the air filtered?" Tony explained the ventilation system that was linked to massive filtration machines that whirred and hummed twenty-four hours a day and pumped fresh air throughout the lab. Because aerosols from the rodents were so deadly, he designed a system that swept them into a hood that kept them separated from air from other parts of the lab. They were filtered by their own smaller system. He had thought of everything. He had been thorough.

"I don't doubt you. I'm just damned upset by this…thing getting loose, spreading like it is. The casino's underway, but nobody's going to gamble out there if they're afraid for their lives. Isn't someone going to suspect the suddenness of its appearance? Wonder where it came from originally?"

"The papers are emphasizing the fact that there's lots of deadly stuff around—stuff the public has no idea exists. Most of it is simply untraceable and lies dormant for centuries, then bingo—half a dozen people die. One researcher called our little flu a 'metaphorical mayfly,' like the insect that lies dormant underwater for years then surfaces and lives only a few days."

"So, what are you saying?" Douglas sounded peeved.

"That no one is pointing a finger at humans as the cause. I've been careful. Don't you believe that?" Tony waited for Douglas's nod.

"Yes, yes, but tell me again why they won't suspect human intervention."

Patiently, Tony reiterated, "I have access to a strain of virus that in its natural state is transmitted by the saliva, urine and feces of the bandicoot.''

''Bandicoot?''

''A very large rat over two feet long.''

''I've never heard of the animal.''

''Comes from India. It has some long-clawed cousins in Australia—insectivorous marsupials from the genus *Nesokia*,'' Tony warmed to his subject, ''They have long snouts and thin closed ears—''

''I don't share your enthusiasm for vermin.''

Douglas interrupted. ''What does this have to do with the virus?''

''In the laboratory I altered the virus so that it was deadly if ingested by someone over fifty. It was no longer a virus but still acted like one. I was able to contaminate foodstuffs, things with shells worked best—that's why we chose pumpkin seeds, something with a hard outer coating, and something the Governor relished.''

''How many did he have to eat?'' Douglas asked.

''Three or four. Not many. He obviously shared them with friends.''

''There's no way that anyone could have gotten sick from just handling them?''

''No. Originally, the people had to eat them but now, it's apparent that a genus related animal ingested seeds from the packet; that animal then became a carrier and reintroduced the virus into its surroundings. I had hoped the Governor would simply eat them, not feed them to chipmunks.'' Tony laughed uproariously.

Douglas seemed pacified. Tony watched as Douglas's eyes roamed the room, taking in the glass-walled homes of thousands of brown and black insects. Some, Tony was proud to point out, measured over four inches in length. The oldest came with a certificate verifying it to be seventy-three years old. And still virile, Tony found out.

''I helped myself to some rodents in the Pueblo area and found two carriers. Now that the CDC has given the virus a name, it'll take steps to stop it,'' Tony said.

"What will they do?" Douglas asked.

"Oh, let's see, continue to trap various animals, especially mice. Now that they've isolated the culprit, they'll go in and trap on a grand scale, educate the public about rodent control and everything should die down."

"This isn't what we had planned. I can't believe this is happening."

Tony watched the agitated elder Anderson pace close to the cages along the side wall.

"Jesus, these things make me nervous. How can you stand to stay cooped up with them all day?" Douglas began to absently scratch under his collar.

"They're quiet," Tony said. He watched Douglas look at him closely, but there was no hint of a smile. "The only way that anyone would be suspicious is if the original seeds were analyzed. But the pouch and the seeds are long gone, right?" Tony asked.

"Right." Douglas said and silently cursed Johnson Yepa. Maybe someone needed to go out there and put the fear of God in him. Face-to-face. Nothing he could misinterpret as witchcraft. He thought he had just the right person for the job—if he could trust that person not to be too rough. But maybe that was called for now. They couldn't afford any slip-ups. Too much was at stake.

THE BUMPY PINK cuticle of his little finger had traces of blood along the nail base. Johnson didn't even know anymore when he was gnawing on his fingers. Nerves. He should be on top of the world. He had only to walk to the door of his office to hear the sounds of all his hopes and dreams coming true. The Andersons had brought the earthmoving equipment back. The party had been a roaring success. His picture had been in the paper. The powerboat would be delivered today. His wife had started fixing him meals again. But there was that little matter of the pumpkin seeds.

How had Dr. Black come to have a small bag of the seeds? Did Mary Toya give them to him? And, if so, why? A film of perspiration broke out on his forehead and upper lip. And then this morning when he took the box of patent loafers out from behind the Bronco's front seat, exactly where he had left them after the party, there had been only one shoe in the box. Only the right shoe nestled untouched in the tissue paper. Someone had taken the left one to cast a spell. Someone who wanted to do him harm? Or just warn him?

"I need your signature on these consultant contracts with Anderson and Anderson Investments, Inc." Mary stood in front of him with a stack of papers. Johnson looked up and then it came to him. Maybe he could find out some answers on his own. Quickly he began opening and closing the drawers in his desk.

"Mary, didn't the Governor keep a sack of pumpkin seeds around here somewhere? I remember he had a basket full on his desk."

"I took them with me after I cleaned the office."

"Do you remember what you did with them?" He looked up. Uh oh. He'd have to back off. He saw Mary's eyes flicker. Did she remember something? Did she wonder why he was asking? She was staring past him fixed on a point over his right shoulder but not seeing.

"I don't know why there's all this fuss. Dr. Black was asking about pumpkin seeds the other night."

"He was?" Johnson feigned surprise and hoped the trickle of sweat that was creeping along in front of his ear wasn't noticeable.

"Some tourist got sick. A little girl from Illinois. Seems she was allergic to them. I'd forgotten that I took some to Santa Fe with me."

"Well," Johnson forced a laugh, "guess I don't want those for my mid-morning snack." He signed the papers and watched Mary leave the room. However Dr. Black had gotten the seeds, he didn't have them anymore. Maybe Johnson's bad luck was really good luck. The spirits directed him to the lab and gave him the evidence. He could feel the anvil-heavy weight rise from his chest. He'd get that trailer hitch put on the Bronco and pick up his boat. And maybe he'd see the medicine man about a cleansing ceremony. A person couldn't be too careful.

"SO WHAT'S THE PLAN? We better get some warnings out in the Pueblo. Tell people what to avoid. How 'bout pamphlets?" The lab tech sat in the front row of the hospital's crowded conference room.

"Limited impact," Sandy said. "We need something more visual and personal."

"Is fresh mouse urine still the number one suspect?" a nurse asked.

"Yes. Aerosols float through the air and can be inhaled," Sandy said.

"We could do a video. All the docs could wear mouseketeer caps and pee on..." The rest of the young physician's sentence was drowned by laughter.

"Sexist. I'm a doc and I'm not going to pee on anything in front of a camera," a woman in the front row yelled. More laughter. Sandy waited until he had their attention again.

"Nothing beats blanketing the earth with good old-fashioned posters." Ben spoke up from where he was sitting on the floor.

"You're probably right. I was also thinking of canvasing the Pueblo—a door-to-door warning—answer any questions at the same time." Sandy saw Twila sitting three rows from the front. "Twila, could you help me organize something like that?"

"We'll have problems making people believe the virus is carried by mouse droppings." This from an Indian aide in the back.

"We've got to make them believe it. Think of the surge in cases this fall when rodents move indoors," Ben said.

"I may have proof that food stuffs contaminated with dried urine caused the virus in a child. Nancy, have you finished testing the pumpkin seeds I gave you?"

"Dr. Black, the, uh, seeds...the packet seems to have been misplaced."

"Misplaced? So, you haven't run any tests?"

Nancy shook her head.

Sloppy. Granted the lab had been chaos lately, but there was no excuse for this. "I expect you to keep looking for it. Let's proceed as if dry feces is a factor." Sandy didn't care if the anger showed in his voice.

"What about getting a list of precautions out to the public?"

"Good idea. Ben, check with Julie," Sandy said.

"What are high risk activities?" a nurse asked.

"Gathering pinon nuts from rodent nests, cleaning out barns, working in the garden…"

"What about camping?" a man in back called out.

"Any sleeping on the ground should be discouraged."

"How close are we to a diagnostic test?" A physician asked.

"Not very. But it has priority. Anything else?" Sandy scanned the group. "Let's keep close tabs on our allergy and asthma patients. Meeting adjourned."

"Mary Toya called." Gloria handed him a stack of phone messages.

"What did she want?"

"Wanted to make sure I told you that she was the one who had given the pumpkin seeds to the little girl."

"Did she say anything else?"

"She got the seeds from the Governor. He had them in the office. After he died, she took them home. She feels terrible that she might have made someone sick."

"It wasn't her fault," Sandy said.

It made an even stronger case for dried mouse droppings being carriers. He'd have to check with Bernie at the grocery. Maybe he didn't keep his bulk merchandise in closed containers. And if he had a mouse problem in his storeroom the combination could be deadly.

"WHAT DO YOU THINK, Mr. Yepa? Isn't she a beauty?" The sales manager wiped his sleeve along a piece of chrome on the bow. "Decided where you're going to keep her?"

"Elephant Butte." Johnson gazed at the gleaming whiteness of the hull interrupted by silver detailing that ran the length of the body, a chain of feathers linked to a webbed circle one foot in diameter on the starboard side. *The Dream Catcher.* The name was done in script and unfurled like a banner above the symbol. The symbol was meticulously painted, every wisp of feather and bit of string was knotted and strung to look like a spider's web. From the center a long twisted rope of eagle feathers fluttered to one side. It looked so real. Johnson reached up and ran his hand over the flat fiberglass surface.

Johnson wasn't happy about using a Plains Indian symbol, but it fit. The symbol and name were right. The legend told of bad dreams that could get caught in the web while good dreams float through freely. He had bad dreams now. People calling to him from the other side. Beckoning him to follow.

"If you'll step this way, Mr. Yepa. We can finalize the papers." Johnson was reluctant to leave the boat, but he followed the man into the showroom.

"Let's see. You put ten thousand dollars down. The special paint job added another four thousand three hundred and change."

The salesman punched the numbers into a calculator and filled in some blanks on a form. "Boy, were you smart to have that paint job done at the factory. Had a friend who towed his boat over to an artist's backyard. Before the guy could even get to it, vandals just about destroyed it. Shame. Don't think it was ever the same. No. You take this baby to the lake and put her under lock and key." The salesman turned the contract towards Johnson. "Looks like you're on your way as soon as I get another fifty-seven thousand, four hundred and thirty-two dollars. I rounded that off so we won't have to worry about the small stuff. Will that be a check or bank draft?"

"Cash," Johnson said. He opened a briefcase and emptied its contents on the table.

"Cash? Weren't you afraid walking around with all that money? You're braver than I am. It's tough out there even in the best neighborhoods. Let me count this, and I'll be right back with your receipt."

THE LAPPING OF the water against the boat's sides was soothing. Johnson stretched out on the decking behind the wheel house and baked in the sun. He had taken off his shirt, rolled up the legs of his jeans to his knees and covered his eyes with a towel. Reflected light from the boat's white surface both blinded and comforted him. Seven feet above the water he was enthroned in blazing whiteness. He relaxed and listened to the shrieks of water skiers. Snatches of conversation from picnicking families drifted over the marina. Number seventy-three. It felt right, *The Dream Catcher*'s new home.

He dozed, letting the gentle motion of the boat pull the tiredness from his muscles. The first drops of rain startled him. Opening one eye, he squinted up at the sky. Blue. Above, to the right, to the left. Not a cloud. Three more splats of water smacked his forehead, chest and crotch. Swiftly, he rolled to the side and stared at the boat tied next to him. Five feet away a grinning ten-year-old stared back, a bazooka water gun at his side.

"Don't bother me," Johnson said. He tried to look mean but thought he hadn't succeeded when the boy didn't budge.

"You got any kids I can play with?"

"No," Johnson said.

"How come you don't go out on the lake?"

"I will later."

But Johnson knew that was a lie. It had never dawned on him that he might need lessons before he could take her out on his own. Two young men had maneuvered *The Dream Catcher* through the tangle of boats docked at the marina and into number seventy-three slip. He wasn't sure how he was going to back her out and steer around the moored boats, not to mention the boats coming in and going out. No, it was a problem he hadn't anticipated.

Johnson looked over the side. The boy with the water gun was gone. Elephant Butte always had big crowds on weekends when the weather was nice. People with families. Maybe he should have chosen Lake Powell or even Navajo Lake. No. The Butte was closer. And he didn't really care if he went out on the water. This was comfortable.

TEN

THE POSTER WAS PLAIN. A large red, barred circle over the caricature of a somewhat startled looking mouse. But the whole thing was two and a half feet by three feet on a black background, big enough to get attention. Ben handed Julie a box of push pins and a roll of masking tape. She was sorting them into groups of four.

"Do you think we have enough posters?" she asked.

"Forty should do it. I vote we go together. That way I know you won't get lost." He noted with a jolt that he had wanted her to smile. But she hadn't. She had been quiet, subdued. Was she angry because he hadn't called? Wasn't this the thing he hated most about relationships? The veiled demands. And he felt himself pulling away—her career, the decision that he had to make about school... The time wasn't right. Or was he just plain afraid he might get too serious and get hurt? They met in the Tewa Community Center to organize the poster campaign before putting anything up around the village. Ben promised to help find some rodent burrows afterwards that could be filmed as part of Julie's series on Hantavirus warnings.

"Julie. I think we need to talk about us." Ben took the posters from her and put them on the table and turned her to face him. But touching her made it difficult to talk to her. He stepped back.

"What is there to talk about?" Her voice was even, unemotional. So far, so good, he thought.

"I've decided to go back to school, on scholarship, part of a pay-back program with IHS."

"How soon?"

"January."

"Do you know where yet?"

"Probably East Coast."

"Psychology?"

"Yes."

"I think that's great. You'll be good." Her smile was genuine, but her voice lacked enthusiasm.

"And you?"

"A year or two at the station here—hopefully as evening anchor—and then probably Los Angeles or Seattle."

"A little tough on romance."

"A lot tough on romance." Julie smiled ruefully. Ben fought an urge to kiss her, hold her, unbutton the blue chambray shirt.

"I'm going to make it, Ben. I have a chance. The Hantavirus has given me the exposure I've needed. I've already had a couple calls offering me spots, but I need more time."

"So, eventually your plans wouldn't include getting stuck in a place like Rosebud, South Dakota? Or Pawnee, Oklahoma?"

Julie shook her head slowly. "You know, I didn't want to be tempted with a relationship. Not quite yet. You're timing is terrible." She laughed, but it sounded half-hearted.

"Is it too late to go back? Start over? Maybe I could be a real shit?" Ben teased but found himself thinking again about kissing her.

"Won't work. We're stuck."

They stood silently. There didn't seem a lot more to say, Ben thought. Their careers weren't exactly compatible. Someone would have to give up something. Sacrifice could come back to haunt a couple.

"Oh no, do you believe this? This guy's ruining my love life." Ben laughed as Lorenzo hobbled across the gym floor his cane thudding against the polished surface.

"We must have disturbed him. He was probably taking a nap in the back." Ben noticed that Julie's poncho was a little dusty.

"I think he remembers you." Ben watched as Lorenzo patted Julie on the arm and pointed to the poncho.

"Yes. I gave that to you." She wondered if he were hard of hearing or if she was yelling too loudly. Lorenzo was gesturing towards the door and pulling on Julie's shirt sleeve.

"He wants you to go somewhere with him," Ben said.

"I think I'll see what he wants. Come with us?" Julie asked.

"I'm no fool. I'm not going to let another man walk away with you." Ben grinned as Julie landed a solid punch on his bicep.

"His house is just two streets over. I think that's where he's going," Ben said and fell in behind Julie who was being careful to let Lorenzo lead the way.

"Yeah. This is it." Ben and Julie waited outside as Lorenzo went into his room.

"Do you have any idea what he wants?" Julie asked.

"No. But he made it clear he wants us to wait here."

Lorenzo appeared in the doorway. The poncho was twisted to one side and flapped up and down as he waved his arms. Garbled sounds were punctuated by a spray of spittle and more arm waving. Finally, he reached into one of the poncho's deep slant pockets and drew out a bright silver packet. As he turned it back and forth, the sun's rays bounced reflected light onto the side of the house. Lorenzo laughed and twisted and turned the packet faster making the spots dance. Then abruptly, he pushed the packet towards Julie.

"He wants you to have it," Ben said. "It's obviously a treasured possession. You gave him the poncho; he'll give something of his back."

"What do you think it is?" Julie took the packet and turned it over, then looked inside. "Looks like some kind of elaborate lab envelope. There are seeds stuck in the creases."

"Let me see." Ben took the packet. "Pumpkin seeds. Funny, Sandy was talking about a packet of pumpkin seeds missing from the hospital lab. Wonder if this could be what he's looking for."

Julie turned to Lorenzo and took his hands in hers and thanked him. She didn't even know how much English he understood but he seemed pleased with the attention. She straightened the poncho and wiped the spittle from the corners of his mouth with a tissue. He stood still then reached out and touched a strand of her hair.

"He likes bright colors," Ben said. "But, then, so do I."

Ben playfully uncoiled a curl and let it spring back into place. "We better get those posters up." Ben folded the foil packet and put it in his pocket. "Don't let me forget to give this to Sandy."

"PRESTON SAMUELS is holding on one for you." Gloria stuck her head in the door.

"Thanks. Pres? Guess you guys are doing a little celebrating out there too?"

"I want everyone to realize that we had answers in ten weeks. That's a record. How are you doing getting the word out? Any resistance? Are people taking you seriously about deer mice being the culprits?"

"The Pound in Albuquerque doesn't have any more cats for adoption. So, some people believe us." Sandy laughed. "But a lot are skeptical. It would be easier for some to point to a uranium spill."

"Easier for us, too. You know, there's something that still bothers me. We've been collecting samples of rodents from across the United States. Places where we know we have carriers for the Hantavirus, and this strain that attacks the lungs appears to be completely isolated. It has only occurred in the Tewa Pueblo in New Mexico."

"Any thoughts on why it's localized?" Sandy asked.

"Not so far. The satellite imagery data is being compared to past aerial weather photographs and other than an unusually lush vegetative growth the last few years, we're not seeing anything out of sync. Of course, when the desert overproduces, so do the rodents."

"How close are you to a vaccine?"

"Hey, we set a record in solving this one; now you want a preventive in another couple weeks? There's never any thanks."

Pres chuckled. "Actually, two researchers at the UNM medical school are pretty close. I'd expect to hear something within a month. They hope to begin testing a vaccine late this fall."

Sandy sat musing after Pres had hung up. There were still a lot of unknowns. At least Ribavirin, an antiviral drug, had worked on the last three suspected victims. There were three people recuperating upstairs right now who probably wouldn't be around without ventilators and Ribivarin.

"Ben Pecos is here." Gloria stood in the doorway her arms filled with troll dolls.

"What are you going to do with those?" Sandy asked.

"Decorations for the bake sale. My daughter's collection. Be sure to buy something before you leave. We have lots of oven bread. The money goes to the Tenorio family.''

Sandy nodded as Ben stepped into the room.

''Is this the packet of pumpkin seeds that was lost?''

Sandy took the foil packet and looked inside. ''Where'd you get this?''

''Tewa. Lorenzo Loretto had it. You know Lorenzo?''

''Everyone knows him. And he could have gotten it anywhere; we'll never know.''

''I take it this isn't the one you lost?'' Ben asked.

''No. But it's an odd packet. Definitely from a lab. Let's get this out back. Let the experts tell us what it is.''

Nancy met them at the door. Sucking up, Ben thought, as she gushed on about how wonderful it was to have them stop by and was there anything that she could do for them. She probably was still beating herself up over losing the first packet. Ben looked over the shoulder of a tech who was getting a package from the stand-up freezer. The results of Ben's trapping were stacked small body to small body, alternating head to toe. Crammed without airspace between, they filled the entire seven foot tall unit. Thousands of cubic inches of dead rodents. Amazing, and all in the name of science, Ben thought. He was beginning to feel sorry for the little guys.

''You're right. This is a foil lab pouch. A new type, expensive, not seen very often.'' Nancy was turning it over in her hands. ''Tell me again where you found it.''

''An old gentleman in the Tewa Pueblo had it stashed.'' Ben stepped over to where Sandy and Nancy were standing. ''We call him the packrat. He's probably close to a hundred by now. Used to be a joke about checking with Lorenzo if you were missing something shiny.''

''There are pumpkin seeds inside,'' Sandy said.

Nancy opened the bag and carefully dumped the four seeds into a glass dish. ''Are you thinking that these came from the same place that the others did?''

''Could be,'' Sandy said. ''If my suspicion about dried rodent droppings also being virus carriers is right, this is our first proof.''

"It seems odd to find seeds in a lab pouch," Nancy said.

"Probably not if you knew Lorenzo. How long until you'll be able to tell us something about them?" Sandy asked.

"Give me a couple days, but I'll start this afternoon."

Good answer, Ben thought. Nancy needed to regain some points lost.

SANDY'S OFFICE PHONE rang once, twice; on the third ring he picked it up. Where was Gloria? Probably another bake sale like yesterday, and she was down the hall arranging troll dolls.

"Black here."

"Dr. Black, could you please come out to the lab right away?"

"Nancy, what's wrong?"

"I don't want to talk about it over the phone. We need to meet. Please. This is very important."

"I'll be right there." Odd, Sandy thought. She sounded genuinely upset. Certainly seemed overly secretive, couldn't talk over the phone, needed him to come out back. He pulled on a sweater and left a note for Gloria.

"Thank you for coming so soon." Nancy looked distraught. "I've discovered something that I think you ought to know about."

"What's that?" Sandy noticed her usually robust skin color was a pasty yellow. Was she ill? He watched her take a deep breath before beginning.

"I've discovered evidence...let me preface this by saying that there is every indication..." Just like the scientist, don't take any chances and make unfounded accusations, Sandy thought. "...that the seeds found in the packet that you left with me yesterday have been tampered with."

"Tampered with?"

Nancy nodded. "All of the seeds exhibit a microscopic hole at the base of the their outer coating. This has permitted someone to inject the contents, in this case the kernel, with a foreign substance."

"Do you have any idea what the substance might be?"

"I need your permission to send the packet and contents to Atlanta, but..." Nancy seemed reluctant to continue.

"You have my permission." Sandy waited for her to go on. She was twisting a silver ring on her finger but seemed oblivious to her actions.

"I know how this is going to sound. And I don't want to upset you unnecessarily..."

"Nancy, what is it, for God's sake?" Sandy was beginning to lose patience.

"What if I told you that I thought the Hantavirus might have been planted?" Nancy blurted out.

"Man-made."

It was more of a statement than a question. Sandy stood looking at Nancy. "Are you sure?"

"I guess I'll go out on a limb and say eighty percent sure. I need the lab in Atlanta to take a look at what I've got."

"We're talking mass murder."

"We're talking very sophisticated, very specialized knowledge and abilities."

"Who would be able to...?" Sandy couldn't finish. Why would someone want to kill people in the Pueblo? Maybe it was a random thing, like the Tylenol tampering. No. There was the lab packet. The seeds were not in any kind of purchased wrapping.

"The person who did this knows infectious diseases, has done research, knows the viral killers," Nancy said.

"Are you suggesting a rogue epidemiologist?" Sandy was immediately sorry he had tried to be funny, but maybe that was the truth, someone disappointed about something.

"What should we do?"

"Follow through with sending the evidence and the results of your findings to Atlanta. We'll hold off alerting the Federal authorities until the CDC confirms our suspicions," Sandy said.

"I'll call ahead and get everything off this afternoon, overnight delivery."

"Good. I don't have to tell you to keep this information confined to the lab. We can't be premature in making any announcements. There are too many people who want to believe that there's a cause they can point a finger at.''

''I understand.''

''And, Nancy, thanks for the good work.''

LORENZO LORETTO shuffled along the road in front of the Mission Church his moccasins sending up small puffs of dust. He paused, then continued towards the river. Stalks of corn towered above his head and made the road seem more like a green tunnel than an artery connecting the village with the flat fertile acres along the river. Harvest time. Water stood in the fields— one of the last thorough soakings of irrigation before the land would be dried so that people and tractors could reap this crop and prepare for the next year.

Lorenzo watched the lazy spinning of delicate dragonflies that skimmed the water at the edge of the field, their transparent wings fastened to iridescent blue bodies. In contrast, fat, yellow-bodied grasshoppers were everywhere. They made the leaves on the corn stalks bend and bounce as they sailed from one plant to another. There were already large half circles chewed from many of the leaves.

The dirt road led to the river's edge. Lorenzo could no longer hear the rapids, but sometimes when he was in his room the river would come to his head and roar in his ears like a flood. He stood on the bank and leaned his cane against a rock. He could see silver minnows bunched together, swimming as one along the shallows.

He was tired. He would rest before walking up river to go to the store by the highway. He didn't need to look long for a place to nap. The four foot thick trunk of the old cottonwood formed a V with its gnarled roots that would cradle his body and help trap his warmth that could be stolen by the wind as he slept. He pulled out long tufts of river grass and lined his bed.

JOHNSON YEPA had more to do than meet with Bob Crenshaw. But when he had gotten to the office that morning, Mary had given him a message that Bob would be there around eleven. He thought of saying he was sick. Things weren't going too well. He didn't know what Bob wanted, but he thought it probably wasn't good. Bob was part of the investors—part of Anderson and Anderson investment team—he knew that much, and when he'd called Douglas Anderson to say that he didn't have time to show Bob around, Douglas cut him off, said he better make time if he knew what was good for him.

It had been two weeks since he'd been to the Butte to spend time on *The Dream Catcher*. He had hoped to go down to Elephant Butte that afternoon and scout the surroundings, maybe spend the night. What good was a dream-come-true if you never got to enjoy it? He reached in his pocket for the roll of Rolaids and chewed two, then swallowed hard. He hated the chalky taste that would coat his teeth.

He couldn't get away even if he wanted to. A group of representatives from Title I was coming at nine thirty. They wanted a tour of the classrooms at the BIA school and the Mission School. He'd ask Mary to take them, but first they would want to meet with him. He hated the meetings. He had to pay attention. And he had to wear a business suit with a white cotton shirt that choked his neck. If he bought a shirt with a comfortable neck, the cuffs would creep out from his coat sleeves and dwarf his wrists finally stopping at his knuckles. He'd asked his wife to shorten the sleeves but then they had been uneven, one side crept out, one side remained neat outlining the edge of the coat sleeve with white just like the pictures in magazines. He wanted both sides to be perfect. His wife said there was a store in Albuquerque where short men could go to find their size. He ignored her and decided to wear a vest and roll up his sleeves.

The Title I people were on time. The meeting took under an hour. They needed to know that Federal monies were being spent correctly and they huddled with the project bookkeeper after they met with Johnson. Everything was in order; everyone was pleased. Afterwards, Mary took them to visit the Pueblo schools. Johnson had walked them to the edge of the parking lot.

He was just thinking of going to his house to change the white shirt when he heard the motorcycle of Bob Crenshaw roar up the highway. Johnson could understand that. A man who liked machines. Big ones. Johnson watched the Harley leave the highway and spin ever so slightly on the gravel incline before Bob goosed it and set it down on a dime right in front of him. Johnson was impressed. Maybe he should get a bike instead of the Cadillac.

"Okay if I leave the bike here?" Bob asked.

"Sure." Johnson watched as he stepped off and tilted the heavy bike onto the stand. It looked even bigger when it was right in front of you, Johnson thought. He liked the way the handle bars curved back with a little flare at the rubber guards on the end. Black leather saddle bags fit neatly behind the rider. These had fringe and silver concho buttons to hide the ordinary snaps. Chrome pipes gleamed and distorted the reflection of Bob's legs.

"Nice," Johnson said.

"Thanks. I'd like to walk down by the casino site. We're better off talking outdoors. I thought you might want to share with me how the seeds got away from the governor."

Johnson looked at the ground. He had been right. This wasn't going to be a good meeting. Then Johnson said something that he wished he hadn't.

"I'm going to take care of the witching." He sort of blurted it out. But he was going to have the curse lifted. That part was the truth. Johnson waited. It wasn't that Bob reacted immediately, he didn't. But the way he walked ahead of Johnson, his back stiff, hands thrust into pockets, he knew. Dumb. Anglos didn't believe in that sort of thing. He'd have to be careful. Maybe, if he talked about the bike. Then, again, maybe he'd just wait to find out what Bob had on his mind.

They walked in silence until they came to the mounds of dirt along the partially leveled road. The now silent roller machine tilted slightly toward the ditch after rain had softened its footing. The foreman had said he'd be back to get it out of there, but it hadn't been touched. Maybe he was afraid after that man had died. It could have evil spirits around it.

The new construction crew just worked around it. And, as always, Johnson's heart jumped when he saw the progress, saw the framed walls, the asphalt spread black and smooth. About a dozen framers were crawling over joists, pulling 2x4s up ladders. Then he noticed the trees. The transplanted saplings at the edge of the drive were wilted, their branches withered and brown. That wasn't a good sign, Johnson thought. That could mean the spirits were displeased. He cleared his throat. He wanted to get this over with.

"You wanted to talk?" Johnson waited, but Bob seemed to be intent on studying the casino. Johnson wouldn't push, that was the Anglo way, badger a person to talk and explain. The Indian way was to wait. The elders told stories of waiting hours for a person to express himself.

Johnson looked past the site to the mountains. The day was becoming overcast and hazy. The purple-gray peaks had blurred edges, their tops blunted by stringy clouds. A large black grackle was poking at something in the freshly turned earth about thirty feet in front of him. Weeds pushed up through the flattened soil at the edge of the asphalt. One rain and the desert bursts into life. Survival, Johnson thought. Seeds could be dormant for years and then spring up even cracking asphalt. That's why his parking lot was six inches thick.

"Let's walk down that way." Bob pointed towards the river. Johnson nodded. He thought Bob was being a little over cautious; no one could hear them now this far from the building, but he kept quiet. It was humid. His white shirt was sticking to his back. Usually, Johnson didn't walk any more than he had to. He hated the film of dust that covered his Ropers. He should have suggested bringing the tribal truck.

They walked in silence but could hear the river now. Johnson knew the water would be cold. It came from the mountains. Snowfall had been good the last few years; the river was running full this fall. He could remember years when it had only been a trickle this time of year. And he could remember floods when the water was brown and churning, tossing boulders along as easily as marbles.

Bob had stopped by the side of the old cottonwood. Even

his black Harley Davidson tee shirt showed a stain of sweat between his shoulder blades. He leaned against the trunk. Johnson stood behind him and waited.

"Douglas Anderson isn't real pleased with all your answers. Like about what happened to the packet."

Johnson had to strain to hear. Bob was facing the river and his words floated above the water and away from him. Johnson walked around Bob to stand beside him. He was almost tempted to find a handful of smooth rocks to skip across the water. But thought better of it. He put his hands in his pocket. Bob seemed to be waiting for him to say something. Johnson looked straight ahead.

"You know you've gotten yourself in the shit, don't you?" Bob said.

Johnson swallowed. He looked away to his left and followed the rising arc of a kestrel with a sparrow in his talons. He felt uncomfortable. Somewhere within, his brain was getting a message that he had to pee. Too much running water. Always happened to him. He knew if he didn't say anything, Bob would continue. Anglos couldn't stand silence in conversations. Johnson stood mute.

"I'd like to hear your side of the story." Bob had squatted by the four foot wide trunk of the cottonwood and stripped a fallen branch of its leaves. Johnson watched and thought of the nun who taught him in fourth grade.

"What do you want to know?" It wouldn't work to act dumb for too long, but he needed to find out what Bob wanted to hear. Tell Anglos what they want to hear and they'll go away.

"Oh, I guess about the pumpkin seeds and what happened to the packet. Maybe how this thing could have gotten out of hand. How there could be ten deaths and maybe more. You know, things like that." Bob continued to squat and watch the river. His voice was soft and flat. Johnson couldn't read it, but the hair on his arms prickled. And, he didn't have an answer. He'd thought about it. The questions would intrude upon his thinking at all the wrong times—in a meeting, in the middle of the night, when his wife was trying to tell him something. How could the deaths be related? What did a handful of pumpkin seeds have to do with the construction worker or Peter Tenorio and his fiancée—or Jennifer? Of all the deaths he hated that one the most, a young beautiful girl....

Johnson didn't see the blow coming. Bob pushed up from a crouch and used his weight to pin Johnson against the tree, his right fist finding Johnson's solar plexus. Johnson crumpled. Something sour spread over his tongue and oozed down his throat.

"You little son of a bitch. You fucking think you can hang us out to dry, don't you?" Bob's voice was a snarl about two inches from Johnson's ear as he dragged Johnson upright by the collar of his shirt. Johnson felt the two plastic pearl buttons on the collar tips pull through the cloth.

"Answer me, you little bastard."

Johnson's tongue seemed to be getting in the way. He sputtered and felt Bob's grip loosen. Maybe if he just tried the truth.

"I don't know what went wrong." The second blow caught him on the ear and the ringing in his head almost closed his eyes.

"Gotta do better than that." Bob's biceps stood out on his arms rock hard from hours in a gym. He was only a head taller than Johnson but seventy pounds heavier. Johnson's feet were sliding and banging against the tree trunk trying to get traction, but Bob held him propped there pinned at the shoulders, his knee between Johnson's legs.

Then, as Johnson would remember the story later, a spirit in the form of Lorenzo Loretto rose from the base of the tree behind them, waving his cane in the air and yelling garbled threats. Bob sucked in his breath, slipped backwards, lost his footing and fell. He released Johnson and the two of them sprawled on their backs in the loose rock.

"Who the fuck is that?" Bob sputtered.

"One of our spiritual leaders. He is close to going to the other side now and isn't with us much in this world." Johnson used his best pious and reverent voice. He could see Bob trying to figure out what to do. Bob struggled to his feet and backed away from Lorenzo who was still yelling; spittle spilling from the corners of his mouth.

"Can you get him to shut up?" Bob asked.

"I can't disturb an elder," Johnson lied but inwardly thanked the spirits for their help. Bob studied Lorenzo and finally decided that he wasn't capable of understanding anything even if he had overheard. He turned to Johnson.

"Let this be a warning. No crap. You don't know anything. You didn't see anything. And that fucking packet of seeds better not show up anywhere. Got that?" Bob was still moving away from Lorenzo and motioned Johnson to follow him.

Johnson looked down at the wet circle that outlined his crotch and then noticed that the knee of Bob's leathers had an identical dark spot. He smiled to himself and followed Bob back up the road.

ELEVEN

BEN WATCHED the blue and gold poncho go bobbing by the open door as Sandy walked into the Tewa clinic. If Julie had wanted to stay on his mind, she couldn't have planned a better way than giving Lorenzo her poncho.

"Are you free now? We need to talk somewhere outside; I don't want to be disturbed," Sandy said.

"Sure." Something's wrong, Ben thought. Sandy looked upset, older, maybe the result of a sleepless night; but his skin looked puffy around his eyes.

"Don't get in the way of any machinery," Mary called after them.

Sandy paused in the doorway. Even a mile away they could hear the roar of earthmoving equipment. "What's going on? They were digging around down there a month ago."

"They're building a casino."

"A casino?" Sandy looked surprised.

"The old governor would never allow it. If he had lived, this wouldn't happen. Gambling's as bad as alcohol," Mary said.

"What kind of gambling? Bingo?" Sandy asked.

"Blackjack, and slot machines, that other stuff. Some of us demonstrated against it, but we lost."

Ben watched Sandy hesitate like he wanted to ask more questions but didn't know what else to say. Something was bothering him, that was for sure. They walked towards the river. Ben remained silent and waited. The day had just a hint of fall. A feel to the air that heralded an unanticipated early coolness. The leaves on the cottonwoods were yellowing and beginning to collect along fences and settle beside the road. Indian Paint Brush was a scarlet splash sprinkled among drying sunflowers. A flock of seedeaters took off in a rush of wings as they neared.

Sandy stopped and pointed to an outcropping of rocks close to the river bank. "Let's sit over there." Ben sat next to him and waited. This has got to be serious, he thought, and not easy for Sandy to talk about.

"What if I told you that preliminary work done on the packet of pumpkin seeds you got from Lorenzo indicates that the original virus might have been man-made?" Sandy stopped and was looking at him. "A virus from another part of the world that was manipulated to act as an untraceable illness that killed quickly. A clever, malicious plot—"

"That's murder," Ben interrupted, then sat there and couldn't think of anything else to say. The word "murder" played over and over in his head. It didn't make sense. "Do you know for sure?"

Sandy sighed. "We're close enough. We need the more sophisticated equipment of the CDC, and we've sent them samples. We'll know something for sure by next week."

"Who would want to kill Pueblo people? My grandmother, Peter Tenorio, Jennifer—is it some racist thing?"

"I don't know. It could be. Do you think there's any chance we could find out where Lorenzo found the packet?"

"That's tough. It's hard to say what he understands and what he doesn't. We could try. He really likes Julie. Maybe she could find out something."

"Great idea. In the meantime I'd like you to do some snooping. I don't know what we're looking for, but I have a feeling it's under our noses. We can't turn anything over to the Feds until we get the official word from Atlanta. You're in a good position to find out what's going on, but be careful."

Ben decided against telling Sandy he'd already been shot at. Could that incident have something to do with this? He'd be careful, but he wanted to know the killer—the person who had killed his grandmother and the others.

"I CAN'T BELIEVE IT." Julie had stopped eating. She sat idly twirling the strands of spaghetti with fork and spoon. "It's murder but more heinous—if that can be possible—because of the ramifications. This could have spread anywhere. There was no way to contain it, at least, that we know of. So, we're talking a mass murderer."

"Maybe that wasn't their first intention. Look at this list. Who on here would seem to be important? Like, politically important?" Ben shoved a napkin towards her with ten names listed. The ten people who had died—nine from the Pueblo and the Hispanic construction worker. At the bottom were the names of survivors. Julie put down the fork and spoon and held the napkin close to the glass container holding a flickering votive candle. So much for a romantic candlelight dinner at Mama Mia's restaurant.

"There's only one possibility. It's easy to see when you look at the list. The Governor." Julie beamed. "Do I get any points?"

"You're right. But he was the sixth victim. So, why didn't it stop there? Or better yet, why wasn't there just that single death?" Ben went back to doodling on a napkin.

"Maybe they covered up their tracks with the other deaths."

"Maybe." Ben didn't sound convinced.

"I think it's a good idea to start with Lorenzo. When can we question him?"

"How 'bout tonight? He's usually in the community center until nine," Ben said.

"Great. Take me by the station to pick up my recorder and drop some copy off."

IT TOOK HER LONGER to find the recorder than she'd planned. Someone had borrowed the one she kept in her office so she went down to check one out of the equipment room.

"Working late, kiddo. What's so hot?" Bob Crenshaw held the door open for her.

"You wouldn't believe it."

"Try me."

"Well," Julie hesitated, but then decided it might be better if her boss knew what she was doing. "There is a possibility that the Hantavirus could have been planted."

"Say that again."

"Someone might have come up with the virus in a lab and sort of turned it loose on the world."

"Why would someone want to do that?"

"I don't know yet. But I'm going to find out."

"Do you have any evidence?"

"It's too much to try to explain now, but let's say that a handful of pumpkin seeds are going to tell us a lot. I'll keep you posted. I may know more after I talk to someone in the Pueblo tonight."

"You going out there alone at night?"

"No. Ben Pecos is with me. He's been a great help with interviews." And don't make judgements about my private life like everyone else around here does, Julie thought.

"Just be careful, kiddo."

BOB'S HANDS LEFT A damp outline as he gripped the edge of his desk. What should he do? Take her out now? Or wait. He could still use her. He'd put a rookie in this job to be useful, so that he'd have an inside track and Julie was still valuable alive. But what if she had the packet? If she did have the packet, who else had seen it? His knuckles burned where he had slammed his fist into the equipment room door. They had been so close. That fuck-up Johnson. Stupid people drove him nuts. Stupid women, stupid men; it made no difference. There should be a test at birth and the flunk-outs drowned.

Bob Crenshaw looked around his office. There wasn't an award worth receiving in the business that wasn't already on display. He had put his life into this station. His life and someone else's money. He let people believe that he had "old family" wealth while the truth was his connections might be upsetting to some.

The one million dollars that the Investment group needed for Tony Chang—needed in order to buy the tainted seeds was easy to get. His friends jumped at a chance to buy into the action. They wanted into reservation gambling in the worst way. Only the Andersons couldn't know. Then after it was too late, the silent partners could become visible. They would buy him out; he'd sell the station and disappear—set for life. Bob leaned back in his chair. Everything, he owed everything to his friends in New York. They had controlled Vegas; they intended to control Indian gambling. They needed this casino. He needed this casino. His cut would buy his independence.

He'd sold his soul for money thirty-five years ago; he'd buy it back the same way. He had been groomed by their money. A juvenile on the way to life in prison who did a big favor for someone high up in the organization. As the years went by, there had been other favors. Some little, some big. They didn't forget. But a screw-up and he'd be dead. He'd always known that. Learned to live with that. This time he'd have company—the Andersons, Tony and Johnson Yepa. But if all went well, he'd spend the rest of his life watching the waves wash up on the shore.

He paced the room, then took his revolver from the bottom drawer and headed toward the parking garage. Just a little scare. If she got hurt, it would slow her down. Keep her from getting the interview tonight. That might be important. He looked at the Harley. It wouldn't be good to take the Hog. Fast, but too easy to recognize. Now, what would blend in out there? What would look like he lived on the reservation? Bob saw the pickup that belonged to the sound tech. Yes. Beat to shit. Dark color. Nothing to distinguish it.

He raced back inside. "Tim, I got a little bike trouble. I need to run home for some tools. Any chance I could take your truck?"

"Yeah. I'll be here a couple hours, so take your time." Tim dug in his pocket for the keys. "Automatic choke farts around sometimes, but it doesn't flood out very often. If it does, just give it a few minutes." Bob caught the keys in mid-air.

"Thanks, Bud. I'll see you later."

The top level of the garage was quiet for this time of evening. Everyone was inside working on something for the ten o'clock news or keeping the network shows going out to most of Albuquerque. Interesting that he, of all people, was a major influence on the lives of others. Ownership had its privileges. Censorship and endorsement were two of them.

Shit. He'd never noticed the rebel flag license plate on the front of Tim's truck. A little mud would obscure that. And might as well do the license plate in back while he was at it. He'd stop on his way out, scoop up a handful of moist dirt from around a recently watered evergreen. Probably should take the gun rack down, too. That would do it. Nondescript to a tee.

He pumped the gas pedal once. The truck roared to life. Needs a muffler but no one would notice that on the highway. Bob shifted into reverse and laid a couple feet of rubber. Not bad for that gear. He just hoped it had something at the top end. He needed to catch up and fast. Julie must have a ten-minute headstart. He wasn't sure what they were driving but they should be easy to spot.

JULIE SAT NEXT TO Ben on the front seat of the pickup, the list on the napkin still in her hand.

"Let's start with the Governor. Who stood to gain from his death," she said, "Johnson Yepa?"

"Not really. He could have been elected Governor in his own right at some other time. And I don't really get the idea that he likes the responsibility much."

"Would there have been a casino if the old Governor had lived? I remember a lot of protests last year and as the Chairperson for the All Indian Pueblo Council, the Tewa Governor was in a position to keep things from going forward,'' Julie said.

"You're right. He was adamant. He thought a casino would ruin the Pueblo way of life. He blocked all debate on the topic.'' They fell silent giving this some thought.

The forty-seven miles from Albuquerque to the Pueblo were flying past. The highway was the darkest stretch in the State on a moonless night. Only one truck had passed them in thirty minutes. Ben saw headlights of an approaching car about two miles ahead. There wasn't a lot of company.

Both of his uncles owned pickups. He'd borrowed the new Dodge Dakota tonight. Ben had told his uncle that he had a date. It worked. Ben had promised not to drive it over seventy, but tonight he was anxious to get home and talk to Lorenzo. Would the old man be able to help? It was hard to say. Could they trust him or would they have to look for clues elsewhere?

"Ben,'' Julie screamed. "He's on the wrong side of the road.''

Ben saw the headlights. A reservation pickup probably with a drunken driver.

"Hang on.'' Ben flashed his lights. Nothing. He pulled closer to the right side of the road. The drunk followed. Then Ben yanked the wheel and swerved left over the center line. As the drunk tried to respond, Ben gunned the Dakota and spun back into the right lane, onto the shoulder and off the highway. The soft dirt caught at the tires as the rear end fought for traction. Julie bounced against the window as the truck freewheeled its way between two fence posts, sideswiped a Juniper and took out a swath of sage and chamisa before it jolted to a stop.

Through the dust Ben listened for the other truck. Silence. Maybe the guy had rolled. Ben threw open his door and slipping and sliding, he scrambled up the sloping embankment. At first he didn't see the other pickup. The swirling dust in the Dakota's headlights distorted his view.

Then he heard the engine turn over. The drunk had stalled his pickup about fifty feet from where Ben had left the highway. Ben swallowed hard hoping to keep a clear head and not let anger make him do something foolish as he sprinted towards the drunk. The first bullet struck the asphalt to his left, the second could have gone anywhere; Ben was already in the ditch on the other side of the road.

He lay there straining to hear sounds of someone coming towards him. But no, the pickup had roared to life and the driver was accelerating towards Albuquerque. This was the second time in a matter of weeks that he'd been shot at. God, people could do stupid things when they were drunk. Sober, the driver of the truck probably wouldn't think of taking a shot at anyone.

"Ben?" Julie sounded panicked.

"Here." Ben quickly crossed the road. Julie had slumped to the ground in front of the Dakota; the headlights making the clotted blood along the right side of her head appear as a black swatch.

"Hit my head." He had to bend down to hear her.

"It'll be okay. We'll get you to the clinic." He picked her up and carried her back to the truck. The cut was just below the hairline and would need stitches. He tightened her seat belt and wadded an old jacket behind her head to act as a pillow. Then he kissed her.

"What are you doing?" She stirred and looked at him.

"Just making it well." He thought she smiled before closing her eyes.

"HOLD STILL. This will just take one more minute." Twila cut a piece of tape and placed it across the bottom of the white square of gauze. "There. Done. I think you two were lucky tonight. That road is treacherous. I don't know what your plans are, but this young woman shouldn't go anywhere for awhile. I think you ought to take her to your house and let her get some rest."

"Good idea," Ben said. He helped Julie down from the examining table and steadied her. He had never seen her this quiet.

"I said rest." Twila looked at Ben accusingly.

"You've got my word." Ben grinned over Julie's head and gave Twila a "scouts honor" salute.

He left Julie wrapped in a blanket on the living room sofa, her blood-stained blouse soaking in the bathroom sink and went back outside to inspect the pickup. There was remarkably little damage compared to what might have happened. The front bumper was pulled away from the body of the truck and a fist full of underbrush wedged between. A few scratches on the right side. He could get by with having that side painted. His uncle would be mad but understanding.

Ben leaned against the tailgate. He didn't feel lucky, but something told him that's what he had been—lucky that the drunk hadn't hit them, lucky that the man was a poor shot. If he was going to be a target, better to be one for amateurs. Amateurs. The word jolted him. That was exactly what they weren't working with. Amateurs didn't target a particular population with a sophisticated virus. But it could have been coincidence that he'd been shot at twice recently—once over the traps and now.

Or did someone think they knew too much? Someone here? On the reservation? Or outside? What happened could have been a warning. But only someone from Tewa would have recognized his uncle's truck. And who knew what time to intercept them? It made no sense. The evening's events must have been an accident unrelated to the mystery illness. Ben sighed. He'd check on Julie then take the truck back to his uncle.

JULIE AWOKE at seven according to the travel clock on the night stand. She was in a strange bed, in a strange house, and couldn't remember how she had gotten there. Her head throbbed if she moved. So, she didn't move but raised a hand to touch the bandage on her forehead. The drunk driver. They'd run off the road. She struggled to sit up. Her head seemed too heavy for her shoulders. She had Advil in her purse, wherever it was.

"Hot tea, toast, and orange juice." Ben stood in the doorway.

"Smells good, but I'm not sure I'm hungry. How about a glass of water and finding my purse with the Advil?"

"What do you want to do today?" Ben asked. Julie seemed

to perk up after the pain relievers, even took a couple bites of toast.

"Find Lorenzo."

"Sure you're up to it?"

"Yes. I think he may be able to help."

BEN DECIDED THAT they should drive. Their first stop was Lorenzo's house. The door to his room was open. Ben hopped out to check inside, but the room was empty.

"Do you know where he likes to go?" Julie asked.

"All over. He has a couple favorite nap spots, but he could be anywhere. Let's start at the church and work our way back towards the community center."

It was easy to spot the bright poncho coming out of the fire station. Ben waved at Lorenzo but was quick to see that Lorenzo only had eyes for Julie. She hugged him then pulled a piece of foil gum wrapper from her purse. In pantomime she pointed to the bright foil and then mimed putting something in an envelope, then pointed to the foil again. She held her hands, fingers extended, to show an object about the size of the packet then pointed to him and to the poncho. Lorenzo looked confused then began waving his arms and "talking."

"No use. We just can't get through." Ben patted the old man on the arm.

"I hate to give up. I'm not being clear," she said. "Have you ever tried to mime a foil package?"

"Sounds like a killer charade."

"Wait. Look. What do you think he's doing now?" Julie asked.

Lorenzo, using the tip of his cane, drew two circles in the sand. Then he carefully connected the circles with a straight line through the center.

"Owl eyes? Glasses?" Ben stood behind Lorenzo to get a better look. Lorenzo then drew two lines, short and slanted like a V on its side on top of the first circle.

"Handlebars. It's a bicycle." Julie mimed riding a bike, and it was clear that she had guessed correctly. Then, methodically, Lorenzo began tracing the same pattern on the front of his shirt.

"Now what's he doing?"

"I think it's an insignia, you know, a bike on the front of a tee shirt. Maybe a motorcycle, like a Harley-Davidson emblem, something a tourist might wear."

"God knows where he might have seen someone on a motorcycle. I can't think of anyone who owns a bike in the village," Ben said.

"I don't know whether this will work but it's worth a try. Just don't laugh." Julie picked up a sharp pointed rock and drew a stick-figure rider on the bike. "Lorenzo, who is this?" She pointed to the rider. Lorenzo stood quietly and then slowly put his two index fingers to the sides of his head, one above each eye pointed outward like tiny horns.

"The devil?" Ben said. "The devil now rides around the country on a Harley?"

Julie patted Lorenzo's arm. So close, but he just didn't stay in reality long enough to make sense. She didn't know what she had hoped to accomplish, a ninety-six-year-old man would not make a good witness. But there was something about a man on a bike. A man who looked like the devil? Acted like the devil? There was no way of knowing. But it seemed safe to say that the man had upset him.

BOB CRENSHAW WAS waiting for her when she got to the office.

"Grab a cup of coffee and tell me how your evening went."

"Could have been better." Julie pointed to the wide Band-Aid that covered the hairline crease above her eye. "Be there in a minute."

She grabbed her coffee mug that had BOSS—Better Off Single, Stupid—in red block letters on the side and stopped to fill it.

"Guess you better close the door. I think this calls for a little privacy." Bob motioned to an overstuffed chair across the desk from him and waited until she was comfortable. "Shall we start with the Band-Aid. What happened?"

"A drunk on the reservation was driving on the wrong side of the road."

"You were lucky."

"I know."

"So, tell me, how did the interview go? Weren't you seeing someone who was going to tell you something about the virus? About it being, did you use the word 'planted'?"

"Yes. But the witness has turned out to be, well, unreliable."

"Uncooperative?"

"No. Simply unable to remember anything that might be helpful." She didn't want to say too much about Lorenzo. She didn't want his name to get out and have people hound him for information, scare him to death.

"Who is this witness?"

"No fair, Bob. I need to protect this witness. At least, for the time being."

"I don't think I need to be reminded about witness protection, Julie."

"Sorry, I'm just not comfortable giving the person a name just yet." The silence felt awkward. It was tough turning down her boss, but he should know better than to ask. "What I can tell you is that this all started with a packet of pumpkin seeds."

"I suppose this prize witness had them?"

"Yes. The witness found the packet and now we're waiting for the CDC to come up with some answers."

"What do you expect them to find?"

"The lab here thinks the seeds were doctored in some laboratory to give the victims, those eating them or possibly just handling them, the virus. We're just waiting on the CDC to confirm that."

"Who could kill ten people?" Bob leaned back in his chair and propped his feet up on the edge of the desk. "I never understood the mind of a serial killer. So, what happens next?"

Julie ignored the reference to a serial killer. But that guess was as good as any she had had. "Depends, of course, on the results. But I suppose the FBI will get involved."

"When will you hear something?"

"In about five days."

"If I can help in any way, let me know." Bob turned to pick up a pile of papers from the credenza in back of his desk.

Meeting's over, Julie thought. Then she saw the insignia on

the back of his tee shirt. A motorcycle with the Harley emblem. She could see how something like that might impress Lorenzo. But instead of assuming that's what he saw, she should make sure. It would be an easy thing to check.

"There is something you can do. Would you let me borrow one of your tee shirts? One like that one with a picture of a Harley on the back?"

"What for?" Bob had grown still and peered at her, his eyes squinted almost shut. Julie was immediately sorry she had said anything. He probably thought she was passing judgement on his clothes.

"It might help one witness, a young boy, who thought he saw someone tampering with the rodent traps. He had difficulty explaining the clothing that the man had on." She lied. Bob continued to stare at her. God, please, don't let me blush.

"I suppose I could bring one tomorrow."

"Thanks." Julie hoped she didn't appear too eager to get away as she opened the office door and escaped into the hall.

JULIE HAD LEFT a message for Ben at the clinic, but when he didn't call back, she decided to drive out to the Pueblo anyway. She had the tee shirt in her purse. It was black with the Harley insignia in orange and silver. It probably wasn't going to prove anything. But she needed to assure Lorenzo that he had communicated. Somehow that was important. If, in fact, he would even remember describing the shirt the other day. His memory seemed so unpredictable.

She told Twila that she was going to be in the village looking for Lorenzo and to tell Ben when he came back. She left the Miata in front of the Community Center and walked towards the center of the village, by the church and past the plaza, then back towards the highway and stopped at the grocery store.

"I'm looking for Lorenzo."

"You're the one who gave him that blanket-coat. Ben Pecos's girlfriend." The elderly Anglo man behind the counter leaned forward to look at her and smiled widely enough to show a row of missing molars on the upper right.

"Yes." Julie laughed. There seemed to be an active grapevine in the village.

"Well, you just missed him. He took his orange juice and went out the door not five minutes ago. Sometimes he sits on the steps for awhile, but I guess not today."

"Thanks."

Julie used the store's high front porch as a lookout and thought she saw a bright spot of blue and gold disappear around the corner of a house about two blocks away. When she got to the spot, she almost fell over Lorenzo sitting in the shade leaning back against the cool adobe. She squatted beside him and tugged the poncho forward so that it wouldn't rub on his throat. He smiled and patted her arm.

"Lorenzo, look." She pulled the tee shirt from her purse and spread it on the ground between them. "Is this like the shirt you saw?" He looked at it then traced the wheels on the motorcycle with a bent finger. Julie watched him. He seemed to recognize it; he was tracing the same pattern that he had drawn on the ground. Then he put his fingers to his head to form horns and turned to look at her. Yes. That was it. He remembered or, at least, he had given consistent information twice this week.

This next part was a long shot. Julie knelt over her purse and lifted out the heavy aluminum foil look-alike packet she had made that morning in her kitchen. Either a brilliant idea or just another dead-end, it was difficult to predict which. He would notice that it wasn't the same, but he might tell her something about the one he had given her if she could jog his memory.

"Lorenzo. Where did you get the packet like this one." He probably didn't understand a word she was saying, but he took the packet and seemed to be talking to himself. "Where?" Julie touched his arm, pointed to the packet and then pointed in a circular motion around the village.

"Did you find it here?" Julie took the packet back and placed it under a nearby rock and mimed turning the rock over and finding it.

Lorenzo made a noise that sounded like a laugh and then shook his head. He began waving his cane then stuck the tip in the loose dirt. With one hand braced against the house and the other grasping the head of the cane, he struggled to his feet.

He motioned with his head for her to follow him. Julie scrambled up and stayed a few steps behind as they headed along the road leading to the community center. When they got to the Tribal Office, Julie held the heavy door for Lorenzo to enter. Mary must have stepped out, Julie thought, as she looked around the reception area. Lorenzo had paused, too. Then quickly he lurched onward and through the door leading to the governor's office.

Julie saw the outline of a man hunched forward with his head on the desk. Suddenly waving his cane and shouting gibberish, Lorenzo loomed over the still figure. Johnson Yepa sprang upright then stumbled to his feet. The poor man must have been asleep, the desk blotter had left a crease along his cheek.

"What do you want?" Johnson's speech was thick. He rubbed his eyes and blinked repeatedly as if trying to focus.

Before Julie could answer, Lorenzo grabbed the foil packet from her hand and put it on the corner of Johnson's desk. The gibberish now was almost deafening in the small room as he pointed triumphantly to what he had done.

Julie wasn't sure what happened next. Johnson Yepa started screaming, then he pointed to the packet, jumped backwards and in his scrambling tipped over his desk chair. The chair wobbled, then crashed heavily into the glass-fronted bookcase. Each pane burst into a thousand glittering fragments spraying the carpet with dots of light. But her attention was glued on Johnson. His back against the wall, he began to slide, his legs no longer holding him up, to sit bug-eyed and unseeing, his mouth slack, his hands pressing into broken glass.

"What's going on in here?" Mary stood in the doorway.

"Get help. I think Governor Yepa might have had a stroke."

Julie lifted his hands from the glass-filled carpet. His blood stained the white cuffs of his shirt and dripped onto his slacks.

Julie extracted two large slivers from his right palm and talked reassuringly but knew that he couldn't hear her. The paramedics arrived, stopped the bleeding and put temporary bandages on Johnson's cuts. Where was Lorenzo? Gone. And so was the make-believe foil packet. She smiled. This was the second time he had taken a packet from this office. At least, she knew that much.

She stood aside as the paramedics wheeled Johnson out. He was ashen and still in shock. He looked like he had seen a ghost. She knew that many of the Tewa believed in spirits from the other world. Had Lorenzo frightened him so badly? He had been asleep. But he also had reacted to the packet. He seemed to recognize it. She was sure of it. He was surprised by Lorenzo but went into shock over the packet.

"Where are they taking him?" Julie stood by Mary's desk and watched the paramedics load Johnson into the ambulance.

"Albuquerque. I'm going to run over to his house and tell his wife. Could you answer phones while I'm gone?"

THE PINPOINT of light seared his pupils as it wandered back and forth. First, one eye and then the other. Someone pulling up his eye lids and looking into his soul.

"Aghhhh." Johnson sat bolt upright. The intern's penlight clattered to the floor. Johnson looked around. The startled doctor had jumped back from the examining table and was hovering about three feet away.

"Governor Yepa, how are you feeling?"

Johnson tried to rub his eyes but hit himself in the nose with a ball of gauze. His hands were taped and wrapped. Boy, if his hands were this bad after the fight, think of the other guy.

Only, Johnson didn't remember a fight. There was something in the back of his memory trying to move up into his consciousness. He strained but couldn't quite reach it. Couldn't quite....

"No. No. No. No." Johnson scooted to the bottom edge of the table; the hospital gown, open in the back, caught on one of two metal triangles that jutted out from the base. He hopped off trailing a strip of ragged blue-checked cotton. He didn't see his clothes. He needed to get out of there.

"Nurse." The Intern had moved to block the door and was yelling over his shoulder into the hallway.

"Where are my clothes?"

"Governor, you've been injured. We need to finish the examination. I'm suggesting you stay with us overnight just for observation."

"Can't do that." Johnson now saw the packet clearly, on the edge of his desk where Lorenzo had placed it. Of course, Lorenzo had stolen it in the first place. Why hadn't he thought of that? And now that girl knew about the packet. Knew something about the packet. How much did she know? He needed to think. He couldn't stay here.

"I'm reluctant to release you without running some more tests. You've lost some blood. You appeared to be in shock when you came in."

"His wife is here." A nurse poked her head in the door.

"She'll take me home." Johnson looked around the room again trying to see his clothes.

"I won't hold you against your will, but I want you to promise to rest. Take it easy a couple days and call us if any of the symptoms return. Nurse, get Governor Yepa's clothes."

TWELVE

"WHAT DO YOU MEAN you never thought it would come to this? We all knew it was possible. Not very probable, but possible." The elder Anderson was pacing in front of the window that framed the Sangre de Cristos mountains. There was already a dusting of early autumn snow on the peaks. He felt strangely confident. No, relieved. Perhaps, it was his need for control. Whatever. The deaths of two more people were necessary. The sooner the better. Johnson Yepa had proved himself to be unreliable. And Tony's lab held the answers to all the CDC's questions.

"What about the reporter?" Bob Crenshaw asked. "Do you think I should worry that she asked for one of my tee shirts?"

"Why'd she do that?" Junior asked.

"Something about a kid seeing someone raid the traps. Kid thought he recognized a Harley emblem."

"Would Tony try to implicate you? We know he helped himself to some rodents. Maybe he wore a Harley tee shirt to be funny," Junior said.

"I wouldn't put it past the little fuck to put the screws to us," Bob said.

"Doesn't sound like this reporter has much. Anyway, let's not worry about her just yet. Isn't she our best insider at the moment? Won't she keep you informed?" Douglas Anderson, Sr. waited until Bob nodded before going on. "I think we know who needs to be removed. We can't risk their sharing what they know."

Douglas barely acknowledged their nods as he turned his back to the room to stare at the mountains again. This view was his salvation. A glass encased valium for the spirit. He had built this office building and kept the corner office with the 180 degree view for himself. The burnt-orange leather couch, love-seat and ottoman were the only man-made attempts at decoration. Not very good ones even taking into consideration the Peter Hurd oil on the back wall.

No, he needed to commune with nature, God's handiwork. He felt strong looking at ten thousand feet of solid rock. The Aspens were turning. Blocks of gold edged long sweeps of green that defined the upper slopes. Deciduous trees whose glory was two weeks long once a year. Nature shooting its wad and waiting twelve months to do it again.

"Dad? What's our time frame for what has to be done?"

"Quickly. I don't think we have much time."

"WE HAVE PRETTY SOLID proof that the original lab packet was taken from the governor's office," Julie said. "I also think it was the fake lab packet that made Johnson react like he did."

"What are you saying? That Johnson might have been involved? Might have known what the packet contained?" Sandy had asked Ben for an update on the poster campaign but welcomed a chance to question Julie about Johnson Yepa's "spell." It had unnerved the new intern who had treated him.

"Yes. I want to investigate Johnson. It might answer some questions."

"What will you do?" Ben asked.

"Interview people, do a police check, credit check—those kinds of things. Has he been doing anything out of the ordinary, been seen with people who might have a motive; it might lead somewhere."

"You know when I called the Tribal Office today, Mary said that Johnson was recuperating at Elephant Butte. I thought it was so strange that I questioned her." Sandy paused. "She said he had a boat on the lake. Not that he had rented one but that he owned one."

"I never knew he owned a boat. What Pueblo Indian would have a boat? Must be something recent. Maybe I'll check around. There aren't many boat shops in Albuquerque." Ben reached for the phone book. He'd jot down a couple addresses and then drop in to talk with the salespeople. They might not be very open over the phone.

Ben didn't know what he was looking for, but Marineland seemed a good place to start. He had parked in the drive and hadn't crossed the lot before a salesman accosted him.

"How can I help you today?" The salesman's plaid jacket was expensive but tasteless, Ben thought.

"A friend of mine bought a boat here recently. Keeps it at the Butte. I'd like some information about buying one like it."

Ben thought the man almost licked his lips. It was certain that he could hardly contain his excitement.

"Would this friend be an Indian gentleman?"

"Yes. Governor of the Tewa Pueblo. Johnson Yepa."

"Oh yes. I worked personally with Mr. Yepa, but he knew exactly what he wanted. Twin engines. Plenty of power. And the insignia. How do you like that emblem?"

"Emblem?" Ben asked.

"Yeah. The Flycatcher. No, that's not quite it. Big net thing with feathers. You know, right underneath the name."

"A dream catcher?"

"Yes. Had that symbol done special for him at the factory. It turned out perfect—silver and white with a touch of turquoise."

"Must have set him back a paycheck or two," Ben said.

The salesman laughed nervously. "I was led to believe that Mr. Yepa was independently wealthy. But come with me; let's look at the catalogs and talk about what you want."

"Can you show me the model that Johnson has?"

"Right here." The salesman spread a four-color foldout across the desk. "Now the detailing was extra. I think he ended up paying about four thousand for that. And he chose a custom engine job."

"So how much is this going to cost me?"

"Well, maybe I can work a discount on this model." The salesman feverishly pressed his calculator's keys. "Give or take a few hundred—maybe you'll want some additional gear—it should come in at around seventy thousand."

Ben was glad he was sitting. Seventy-thousand. Where did Johnson get that kind of money?

"How long will it take to get one in?" Ben asked.

"Without the special paint job about two and a half weeks."

"I'll let you know." Ben rose to go.

"Listen. It will be a pleasure doing business with you, but do me one favor. Don't do like your friend did and carry all that cash around with you. It's just too dangerous. Ask someone to help you open a bank account. That's safer."

"Thanks for the tip." Ben said.

JUNIOR ANDERSON waited masked by the shadows of the alley. Finally, Tony's secretary left the building, slipped behind the wheel of the blue Ford Escort and pulled out onto Montgomery Blvd. He had parked his Toyota 4x4 and ridden his mountain bike down the paved access driveway behind the lab. He lucked into finding a party in full swing just two blocks over. One car more or less wouldn't be noticed. He shifted the heavy backpack to rest higher on his shoulders.

Leaning the bike against the back wall, Junior stood in the shadows and listened. An air compressor of some kind roared on, the main unit enclosed in chain link not two feet from the back door. He'd called ahead. Said he'd be by at nine. It was Tony who had suggested coming in the back. Did he suspect something? Hard to tell with him.

Junior needed enough time to case the lab, decide where to place the incendiary bomb, kill Tony and get out of there. He took a gulp of the chilly night air and began a series of relaxation exercises he used to ward off migraines. He felt the stress melt from his forearms dissipating through his neck and shoulders making him feel lightheaded. He slumped against the wall but the heavy backpack almost toppled him. A little before nine. It was time to get going.

Junior pressed the button by the door. He wasn't sure it worked. The place was tight and soundproof. That was good. Tony answered before he could press the buzzer a second time. He followed Tony through a darkened room to the center part of the lab and dropped the backpack on a nearby table. A rat-like animal with enlarged canines was in a cage on Tony's desk.

"So what's the occasion? Need more reassurance?"

"You could say that," Junior said.

Tony was fussing with the rat which seemed to be in an ill humor. "You know after I handed over the packet, my part was finished. If you guys couldn't control…"

Junior's fist slammed down on the desk; the startled rat crashed against the top of his cage, eyes wild.

"Dump and run. Is that it? Let me tell you something—" He leaned across the desk but pulled back, dragging his hand across a fist-sized granite paperweight. What the hell? Tony was swinging the rat by the tail. So much for strangling him. Without thinking, Junior grabbed the paperweight and swung at Tony, the blow grazing his right temple.

With one flick of Tony's wrist, the rat came flying through the air clawing and slashing the front of Junior's down vest on the way to his neck. Junior felt its teeth sink into his thumb as he struck at it then unzipped the vest dropping rat and goose feathers to the floor. He drop-kicked the writhing bundle against the wall. The rat was either dead or stunned, but it didn't move.

He turned back to Tony. Only he was gone. Junior spun in a circle. Where...?

Then he saw Tony wiggling on the floor pulling himself toward some sort of trap door under a heavy table. Tony pulled the door open and disappeared head first into blackness. Junior lunged and caught the edge of the door before it clicked into place. He had just inched forward for better leverage when he felt the rat crawl up his pantsleg.

"God damn it." Junior jumped to his feet stamping the floor as he unbuckled his belt and dropped his Levi's. This time he grabbed the rat by the tail and bashed it against the wall. It went limp, and he tossed it on Tony's desk. Junior rearranged his clothing. He didn't need to try the trap door. By now, it was secured from the inside. He took a moment to steady himself.

Maybe this was better. He'd block the trapdoor with something heavy, set the bomb for twelve minutes, ride to the Toyota and be out of the neighborhood before the lab went up. It would appear that Tony had been trapped. Not killed. Trapped. Junior started to whistle. By the second bar of "Some Enchanted Evening," two rows of caged rats had roused themselves to stare at him.

JULIE HAD PROMISED to cover the "live from the street" portion of the ten o'clock news for a reporter who had gone home ill. Julie was hoping the evening would be slow and she'd have a chance to do some Johnson research. But no, just her luck that there was a four alarm fire in the Heights.

The news van pulled up across the street and slipped past the police barricades before the area was cordoned off. The fire was burning rapidly. Flames leaped twenty to thirty feet and illuminated the night sky.

"What kind of store is it?" Julie couldn't remember what had been there and the sign across the front of the building had melted and slipped to the sidewalk.

"Bug place. You know, exterminator stuff. Probably why it's going up so quickly. Lots of chemicals." The cameraman finished dragging equipment from the van.

"I've never seen anything burn like this. Will they let us get closer?" Julie asked.

"Not much closer for awhile. Guess we'll just have to wait this one out. At least the structure is cement block." He began getting shots of the fire and surrounding shopping center.

"I'll try to interview some of the other shop owners. I'll meet you back here in thirty minutes." Julie walked towards a health club where an assortment of people in sweats and leotards clustered on the sidewalk.

"How did the fire start? Did you see anything?" She questioned the woman nearest the door.

"It wasn't a matter of seeing. It's what we heard."

"Loudest explosion I've ever experienced. Sonic boom stuff. Enough to rattle the windows." People recognized Julie and crowded around hoping for an on-camera interview. This always happens, she thought.

"What did you see?" Julie turned to another bystander.

"The fire just rolled out of the top of the roof."

"Yeah. I didn't see nobody leave, either," someone said.

"Is there reason to believe that people may have been trapped in the building?" Julie asked.

"Could be. Mr. Chang and his secretary are usually the only ones who stay late. I didn't see them leave tonight."

"Mr. Chang?" Julie asked.

"Anthony Chang of Bugs No More."

"Do you know Mr. Chang?"

"Not really. I've worked here at the Center for three years and I've seen him a few times. Keeps to himself."

"Thank you. Will you be here later if I want an on-camera interview?" The woman shrugged and didn't seem too interested in being televised.

The firemen used foam to smother the flames then water to soak the perimeter of the building. Julie waited with the cameraman until the rubble was reduced to a smoldering mass. While firemen still poured water on the interior, Julie saw two firemen in protective clothing go into the building. She walked over to the fire chief.

"Do you know if anyone was inside?"

"We have reason to believe that the owner was working late this evening. That car has been identified as his." He pointed to a late model Buick sedan at the edge of the parking lot.

"Any speculation on how the fire might have started?"

"Not at this time. There's no doubt that it was a chemical fire, but it's my understanding that Mr. Chang kept a wide assortment of chemicals here at his place of business; so I'm not suggesting arson. Our specialists will get on it right away. Now, if you'll excuse me."

Julie watched as the chief joined a firemen not far from what had been the front entrance of the building. The fireman appeared agitated and pointed to the ground. Then suddenly both men began to stomp their feet and hop backward. Julie moved forward to get a better view.

"Get back." The chief was screaming at her and pointing at the ground.

At first Julie couldn't see why they seemed so upset. The water ran in streams and blackened debris littered the parking lot. Steam rose from smoldering piles of beams from the roof. Hoses crisscrossed; some had been discarded in a tangle beside one of the trucks. Someone had thrown a black tarp the size of a queen-sized blanket over something by the door.

Then all on its own, the tarp began to move. Up over the pile of hoses, down around a pile of soaked insulation. Little ripples would stretch the tarp out then it would bunch up again and move on in another direction. It looks alive, Julie thought.

Oh God, it is alive. She, too, jumped and ran towards the lead firetruck. Cockroaches. Hundreds. Thousands, maybe more. A few strays were scuttling along the perimeter of the building before shooting across the parking lot into darkness.

"Get the Orkin people." The chief was now back in control standing on the running board. "Hose that area. Keep 'em contained if you can. That's right, push 'em back."

The chief turned to Julie. "You know, you do this sort of thing long enough and you think you've seen it all. This is my twenty-fifth year, retirement scheduled for December 1, and then along comes another surprise. Who the hell would collect those suckers? Let alone keep 'em alive. What do you think he fed them?''

Julie was saved dwelling on the care and housing of cockroaches by a yell from a fireman.

"I need some help over here." The fireman had emerged from the building and was standing by what had once been a door. "There's some kind of basement under the floor in the main room. I don't think it's too big, but we're going to need a pump to get the water out."

"Anyone trapped down there?"

"Don't think so. But it's hard to tell. We're not going to know until we get it emptied."

Julie watched as three men rigged a generator and pump, pulling hoses towards the interior shell of the building. Soon the water from the room was gushing from a hose through a sophisticated set of filters back into a large holding tank on the back of a truck.

"Evidence. We keep everything if we think it might help," the chief explained. "And, believe me, you never know."

Most bystanders had left the scene after the cockroach episode. A few hardy souls watched from across the street, but even those were asked to move when the Orkin personnel arrived. Two men in bright yellow rubber suits and matching helmets pulled hoses from their truck, then checked with the chief before fanning out, nozzles in hand, to spray the parking lot.

"Will you be able to get all of them?" Julie asked the man closest to her.

"We'll use chlorpyrifos. It should do the trick."

Julie watched as the lethal mist settled into crevices, and those of the black insects who had not reached freedom suddenly flipped on their backs, legs wiggling in the air.

The chief had left the truck to walk back towards the building. Two firemen struggled to lift an awkward bundle wrapped in canvas over the threshold before putting it down in the parking lot. A body, Julie thought. She motioned to the cameraman, but he was already getting footage from his vantage point beside the Orkin truck.

"Has there been an identification?" Julie asked the chief when he returned.

"The owner, Anthony Chang."

"Cause of death?" She thought he hesitated.

"This is speculative. I'll say I never said it if you quote me, but the victim suffered a blow on the head and that could have—"

"Intentional?"

"Now you're asking questions the coroner will have to answer."

"But he died from a blow on the head?"

"I didn't say 'died' from the blow. In all probability, he drowned. He was floating in that underground room we found."

"GOOD LUCK or good planning?" Douglas Anderson stood in front of Bob Crenshaw's desk.

"A lot of good luck. Did you know he had a computer room below ground?"

"Not a clue."

"It could have worked against us. We were fucking lucky." Bob said.

"Are the coroner's findings complete now? Death by drowning after suffering a blow on the head more than likely caused by the explosion of lab chemicals?"

"Yeah. As far as I know. Sit down. Let me check with Julie Conlin. She's been on the story from the start." Bob pressed Julie's extension and flipped the conference call button.

"Julie. Anything new on that fire story? Or is everyone satisfied that Mr. Chang was the victim of his own lab's volatility?"

"That was the last word I got. There was a report in this morning's *Journal* about the neighborhood being up in arms over the roaches. Hopefully, you have stock in Orkin," Julie said.

Bob laughed. "I'll check with my broker. Thanks." Bob switched the phone off. "Satisfied?"

"We squeaked by this time. My God, that could have been a disaster," Douglas said.

"Don't dwell on it. Our lives are charmed. A year from now we'll be laughing…"

"Yeah, yeah, all the way to the proverbial bank," Douglas finished.

"Don't knock it. I haven't seen you turn down money recently."

"I just hope to hell you're right," Douglas said.

Both men turned at the two short knocks before the door opened, and Julie walked in.

"Oh. I'm sorry. I didn't know there was anyone with you. I just wanted to leave a copy of the transcript of my interview with the coroner. Thought it might be helpful."

"Thanks. I'll be tied up awhile, but I'll catch you later."

"Of course. My apologies for interrupting." Julie smiled at Bob and the older man in the meticulously pressed pin-stripe suit then closed the door behind her.

THE OLD MAN sat leaning against the mud wall of the hut, his legs crossed in front of him and stared at Johnson. Johnson didn't have a good feeling. He found the missing patent loafer that morning stuck in the chimney of his wood stove. But not until after he had smoked the house up by lighting a fire. He didn't believe that it had gotten there as a prank. Plus, he had begun to hear voices. So here he was making arrangements with the medicine man to get rid of the spell—cast out the witches from his life.

Johnson sat in front of the man on the ground. The dampness and cold began to make him uncomfortable. His dress slacks started to feel clammy and stick to his backside. He shifted his weight. He knew the old healer would take his time. Think about the ceremony that he would need to perform and then set a date. This was just the first step.

For the cure the old man would put two tail-feathers of the red-tailed hawk on his upper lip. This enabled the medicine man to see witches even in darkness and swoop down upon them with the speed of the hawk. He would wear a bear paw complete with claws on his right arm. No witch could survive his power. These men were known as *tsiwi* or "those of the sweeping eyes." They saw all.

"In ten moons." The old man spoke. Johnson wondered what date that was. Ten nights from today.

"Follow the ways of your people. Pray to the *Po wa ha* to guide you. Let the *akon gein* stand guard."

Why should he let dogs stand guard? Was it that bad? His life was in danger. But, hadn't he known that?

"There will be one more death before the dying ends, before death's house is full. But know, my son, not all death is due to cowardice or accident or anger; some are valiant in death— leaders remembered by all."

Johnson waited but there wouldn't be anything more. The old man made a motion to dismiss him. Johnson stumbled when he tried to stand. One of his legs was completely numb. He hobbled towards the door and out into the gray, overcast day and walked back up the road to his office.

Mary had put a copy of the *Journal* on his desk. But he pushed it aside. He couldn't stand to read about Tony Chang another time. The victim of an accident. Maybe Johnson knew differently. Somewhere deep down he knew that Tony had known too much. Had been a threat. Had been taken care of.

Johnson walked to the bookcase, now without the protective glass doors, and pulled out a dictionary. Flattened between the pages in the middle was the packet of pumpkin seeds he had taken from the hospital lab. Maybe it was time to put his plan into operation. His insurance plan. He sat at his desk, picked up a pen and began a note.

"SAY THAT AGAIN. Did I hear seventy thousand dollars?" Sandy sat forward elbows on his desk.

"Here's the brochure." Ben pointed to a picture of a boat like Johnson's.

"Nice."

"Somehow I can't see Johnson bucking the waves at the Butte in that or anything else."

"I know. Me, either."

"Julie thinks the money had to have come from some deal involving the casino."

"What do you think?"

"I'm going to find out, but I'm not too sure I'm comfortable going after the Governor of the Pueblo. One of these days I'll be able to start that alcohol program in the community. He could make my life miserable if we're wrong."

"I see what you mean."

"I guess I'm relying on Julie to do most of the work."

"Preston Samuels is holding on one." Gloria waved hello to Ben from the doorway.

"Thanks Gloria." Sandy picked up the receiver. "Ben, stick around. This could be interesting.

"Pres, what's the good news?"

"Well, I think it falls more in the category of bad and maybe not so bad."

"Great choice. What have you found?" Sandy asked.

"Let me just say that I wished I had this person on my side. I could use someone with expertise like this. I don't suppose you have any idea who might be behind it?"

"Not so far. Sounds like you think we're looking for a specialist."

"He or she would have to be. For instance, the kernels of the four pumpkin seeds that you sent me had been treated with minute particles of an altered viral agent known to be most threatening to people over forty years of age. For the elderly, it acts suddenly and lethally."

"A synthetic?" Sandy asked.

"Not entirely. Here at the CDC we've been in possession of Hantavirus strains from samples taken in Japan, China, Scandinavia, India and even New Orleans. This particular strain's origin was the Korean striped field mouse. As a rule it carries Hemorrhagic fever. Outbreaks are almost always in adults. Especially those 40 years of age or more. Children seem almost immune."

"We lost around two hundred soldiers in the Korean war to the virus, right?"

"Right. And because your virus was attacking lungs and not

kidneys, we didn't suspect a Haantan at first. It was only after we found evidence of a Hantavirus in rodents from the area that we were sure. Then, of course, it also started showing up in human tissue and blood samples.''

"Let's go back a bit. You think someone altered the virus to attack the lungs?''

"We're sure of it. The chemical makeup of the saliva from the Korean striped field mouse is alike in type with that found in the bandicoot—''

"Bandicoot?''

"Large rat like the brown wharf rat but is found in India. We've had rats in our coastal towns in the US test positive for Hantaviruses for some time now.''

"Comforting,'' Sandy said.

"One of the things that made us suspect human intervention is the use of saliva from the bandicoot. If they'd just stayed with the domestic brown rat, we might still be stuck. But the bandicoot saliva gave it away. That's definitely an import.''

"How was it done?''

"I can tell you what we think happened but it may be years before we unravel the biochemistry behind it. Remember New Mexico's L-tryptophan scare in '89? We discovered the agent, an impurity from a Japanese lab, but we're still working on why the contamination worked the way it did.''

"I can live with a guess,'' Sandy said.

"I hate educated guesses but, frankly, that's all we may have for awhile. We're probably working with a bacteriophage virus. A virus that preys only on bacteria cells.''

"Complete with little spike-like feet that act as receptors,'' Sandy said.

"You're getting the picture. As you know a bacteriophage injects its own DNA into the cell and converts the cell's reproductive machinery into a virus factory.''

"And if the virus acquires bits of the cell's own DNA in the process, the virus can mutate and evolve into a new form very quickly.''

"Exactly. Take the bandicoot, a carrier of a Hantavirus that no specific illness has been associated with yet and cross its genetic material with that of the Korean striped field mouse, known to carry a virus deadly to older adults; you have a new virus, in this case one which attacks the lungs of older people.''

"Amazing. Wonder how long it took someone to come up with this?'' Sandy asked.

"I doubt if the person had the good luck to marry these two right out of the chute and get what he wanted. More than likely, we're looking at years of research and possibly some trial and error using human guinea pigs.''

"You're not exactly painting the picture of a humanitarian.''

"No, I'm not.''

"Any explanation for why it stopped preying on the elderly and started attacking younger people?''

"Another alteration. We're running tests now, but we think initially the pumpkin seeds could infect a host, in this case human, through their ingesting the seeds; then, the originally doctored seeds were eaten by a genus-related species, in this case deer mice, and the virus, now altered once again, reverted to a pattern of indiscriminate infection no longer bound by its DNA to attack primarily one age group. The mice had become a reservoir allowing the new-type virus to jump to other animal species like humans.''

"Simple case of genetic and evolutionary modification in response to opportunities in their environment,'' Sandy said.

"Certainly answers the question of why it remained localized.''

"Exactly. I might add we found traces of mouse droppings in the aluminum packet. Wherever it was kept, mice had access to it. So, at least, that part of the mystery is solved.''

"Now what?''

"Our findings have been turned over to the Feds. There may be someone in the files whose MO matches what's happened. Who knows. I'm just glad our part has been so productive.''

"And we continue to trap rodents in the pueblo area?'' Sandy said.

"Absolutely. Trap and test. We'll expand our operation to include all of New Mexico and spot-test areas close by in Colorado and Arizona.''

"Let us know if anything changes," Sandy said.

"You do the same." Sandy hung up the phone.

"Did you follow most of that?" Sandy asked Ben.

"I think so. It's difficult to think my grandmother was the innocent victim of some plot—that she just sort of accidentally got in the way."

"I know. Ten innocent people died and another half dozen came close."

The two men sat in silence. Ben thought of how his grandmother had died; how he had been cheated of spending time with her, living with her in the village, learning the ways of his people. Did she know that he had decided to work in Indian health?

"I want to catch the murderer," Ben said.

"Listen, I think we just leave everything in the hands of the feds. You could get in the way of their investigation—"

"Or help. I know the reservation. If Johnson Yepa is involved then they need to know. Julie can help. It's important for me to do this."

"I understand but I wish I could talk you out of it. You're valuable to us here, alive and well."

"Thanks. But I have to find out."

"Be careful. It wasn't a bunch of born-yesterday cream puffs who came up with this plan."

"I know," Ben said.

"The evidence is conclusive? There really is someone out there who committed mass murder?" Julie asked.

"Yeah. Sobering thought, isn't it? Why the Pueblo was targeted, we don't know. I'm sure it wasn't an accident."

"I keep coming back to Johnson Yepa's seventy thousand dollar boat. Someone paid him to do something. They must have," Julie said.

"He could have gotten some kind of kickback for allowing the casino on Tewa land."

"Is that illegal?" Julie asked.

"Probably not. There could be a problem if the tribe knew. Lining his own pockets possibly at the expense of others. But the feeling around the pueblo is that the casino will bring in jobs. Most people honestly support it. So if Johnson made something for bringing industry in, they'd probably look the other way."

"I could interview him about the casino and just see what he says." Julie sat facing him. "That would be a good place to start. Just feel him out about what he hopes to do for the tribe by bringing this kind of industry to the pueblo."

"I suppose you should keep it low-key. You don't want to scare him off. And, he may be perfectly innocent."

"You have to remember that I saw Johnson's face when Lorenzo put the fake lab packet on his desk. He was traumatized. My gut feeling says he's in it up to his gooey hairline."

"And we both know that Lorenzo can't testify. So, what do we have?"

"Not a lot." Julie smiled ruefully. "Okay, back to square one. Are there any other leads besides Johnson? Anything we've overlooked?"

Ben had borrowed Gloria's scrapbook and moved to sit beside Julie on her couch. "Maybe if we look at the newspaper clippings." Ben began to turn the pages.

"Wait." Julie reached out to turn back a page.

"I'd almost forgotten about the little girl from Illinois. Wasn't she the first survivor?"

"Yeah. And more damning evidence for Johnson. The seeds that made her sick came from the Governor's office. I wish that packet hadn't gotten lost."

Ben fell silent and closed the scrapbook. Finally, he walked to the fireplace.

"What if I started a fire?" he asked.

"Are you setting the stage for some big romantic evening at home?"

"Sounds good to me."

"You forget I'm a working girl and it's after eleven. If I'm going to meet you in Tewa at nine tomorrow morning, I need to get some rest."

"Parentheses reads 'I'm not ready to be alone with man I'm attracted to.' Right?"

"I think we decided that this relationship would have trouble working," Julie said.

"Maybe you decided."

"I'm pretty sure it was a shared decision."

"Okay. I'll take a raincheck on the fire and romantic evening and a raincheck on a discussion of this relationship thing. See you in the morning." He kept his voice light. He wasn't sure that he didn't agree with her—one thing was for certain, Ben didn't trust himself to kiss her. And they both probably knew it wouldn't stop there. Julie stayed on the couch as he let himself out.

THIRTEEN

THE ELM WAS a survivor probably because its roots had found the septic tank. Shading the west side of his grandmother's house, the tree had exacted a price from anyone who climbed it. Skinned knees and one broken wrist had been a part of the summers Ben had spent here.

The piece of twisted sisal that hung from a thick branch had rotted and gave way easily when he tugged on it. He would use nylon rope this time, safer and longer lasting. Ben didn't see the Miata pull up across the road from his house.

"What are you doing?" Julie was almost beside him before he saw her.

"Tire swing repair. One of those things I promised myself that I'd do before I left again." He saw Julie look away. He wanted to say "You could come with me," but didn't. Instead, he tried to focus on the morning ahead of them.

"Nervous?" He asked.

"A little. I worked on a list of questions. I'll keep things general. See what happens. I don't want to risk sending him to the hospital again. Is the appointment still on for nine-thirty?"

"Mary put it on his calendar."

"Guess I better get going. I'll meet you back here in an hour," Julie said.

"Can I count on you to give this contraption a trial run?"

Ben held up a shiny new black rubber tire. "It'll be done by the time you get back."

"Sure. Why not?"

Ben liked to hear her laugh.

JULIE SAT IN the reception area and watched two repairmen carrying oblong panes of glass into the governor's office.

"It'll be a couple more minutes," Mary said. "They're fixing the bookcases. Could I get you some coffee?"

"No, thanks. I'm fine." Julie hesitated, then turned to Mary. "Mary, did you support the building of a casino on Indian land?"

"No. I hate the idea. Too much change. Outsiders will crowd into our village everyday soon, not just at feast days."

"Who wanted the casino?"

"People who would get money for it."

Julie was about to ask another question when Johnson appeared in the doorway to his office and nodded to Mary.

"You can go in now," she said.

"Thank you for agreeing to see me." Julie took a chair across the desk from Johnson. The workmen were gathering their tools. One man plugged in a dustbuster and vacuumed the area. Johnson and Julie waited. The new glass doors reflected a tree, almost without leaves now and wisps of high cirrus clouds—the view from a west window, the only one in the office.

"Governor Yepa," Julie began as the workmen left the room, "I would like to ask a few questions about the new casino being built here in Tewa." She acknowledged his nod before going on.

"What made you decide to go with Class III gambling and not start with Class II like other tribes?"

"The opportunity was made available for my people to benefit greatly from high stakes gambling. We have, I believe you say, 'on the drawing board' three major projects. An eight-bed hospital and clinic, a library, and an elementary school. These will all employ our local people, as will the casino.''

Julie thought his answer sounded rehearsed. Johnson was leaning back in his chair and towered a good two inches above her. She fought the urge to peek under the desk to see if his feet touched the floor. Could they be resting on a footstool or box? He must have that chair cranked up as far as it would go.

''What safeguards do you have in place to protect your interests from being taken over by organized crime?'' Julie thought Johnson looked surprised. She wasn't sure where this line of questioning would take her, but it was an important consideration. One of national concern lately.

''I don't understand.''

''Let me quote from the Treasury Secretary, 'Indian casinos are an attractive target for money laundering and other criminal endeavors.' Two weeks ago, Ted Turner announced that he didn't think there was any casino on Indian land that didn't have mafia ties.''

''We've used a local investment group as consultants on our project. There is no hint of any wrongdoing. The group is very well established and quite close to the Governor of New Mexico.''

''What is the name of the group?'' Julie asked as she watched Johnson begin to rummage through a stack of envelopes and papers.

''Anderson and Anderson, Inc. Here.'' Johnson emptied a manila envelope onto the desk spilling out several 8x10 glossy photos. ''There's the governor and yours truly.''

Johnson seemed pleased at his celebrity status. Julie leaned forward and held the picture to the light. A smiling Johnson in a Tuxedo stood between New Mexico's Governor and his wife.

''Here's a picture of Mr. Anderson.'' Johnson slid the photo towards Julie.

Again, there was Johnson standing next to a man with one arm around Johnson and the other around the shoulders of Bob Crenshaw. Julie looked closer. That was the same man who had been in Bob's office last week. What part did Bob have in all this? He could be an investor. Or just a friend of this Anderson person.

"Where were these pictures taken?"

"At Douglas Anderson's house in Santa Fe. It was a celebration for the opening of the casino."

Julie looked briefly at pictures of a euphoric Johnson flanked by long-legged chorus girls, their breasts touching his head as they leaned in to frame the shot. Another photo showed laughing people around a piano, then there was one of the Governor of the State dancing with his wife, and one last photo showing Douglas Anderson, Bob Crenshaw and State legislators piling food on their plates from a buffet table with a fountain centerpiece.

"Do you know this man?" Julie pointed to Bob.

"Yes." Julie thought Johnson seemed reluctant to elaborate.

"Is he a member of the investment group?"

Johnson shrugged his shoulders. "I guess so." Julie waited but he didn't offer further comment.

"Had you met this man before the night of the party?"

Johnson started to say something and then nodded. Julie noticed that sweat, caught in his hairline, was about to trickle down his forehead.

"Has Mr. Crenshaw ever visited the Pueblo?" Julie thought Johnson tried to conceal a look of terror as his glance darted from her face back to the pictures on the desk. He's scared to death of Bob, Julie thought. How odd.

"I think he came once to see the building progress." Johnson abruptly stood or rather hopped down from his perch, Julie noted. "You must excuse me now. My council is meeting at ten o'clock."

"YOU'RE BACK EARLY." Ben was waiting by the tire swing.

"Interesting. I found out the name of the investment group acting as consultants for the casino, Anderson and Anderson, Inc. of Santa Fe. Bob Crenshaw is also a member of the investment group. Or, at least, I think he is."

"Your boss?"

"Yes. The really interesting thing is Johnson seemed scared to death of him."

"Any reason?"

"There was nothing apparent. He cut the interview short after I questioned him about Bob." Julie paused. "You know I haven't seen the casino site for awhile. Could we take a look?"

"As long as we stay out of the way of workmen. You'll be surprised. It's coming along quickly," Ben said.

Two eighteen wheelers parked across from one another squeezed the dirt road down to one lane just before a sweep of asphalt widened to connect with the parking lot. Julie gazed at the unmarked black expanse broken by large aluminum stumps, electrical outlets, holding capped wires coiled in their centers. Eventually, stork-like poles would tower overhead.

"How many lights will there be?" Julie thought she had counted twenty-four oval breaks in the paving.

"Enough to light this sucker up for miles," Ben said.

"Would it be all right to take a closer look?"

"Probably, somebody will tell us if it isn't."

Two hundred cars could fit easily on this lot, Julie thought, as they walked up the long driveway that curved around the building to the back. Other open areas, four and five feet across in irregular shapes, had been curbed and slightly elevated. Must be for trees or shrubs. They would dot the otherwise sterile surface with life. As they neared the front, the massive height of the entrance now only framed and covered with plywood loomed up and outward hinting of a thirties look to come.

"What do you think that is?" Julie pointed to a twenty-four foot wide basin dug out and lined with plastic.

"I think someone said a fountain. This is some sort of holding-pool base."

"Unbelievable." Julie moved towards the double wide opening that would be the door. "Look at the size of this. Everything seems so grandiose."

She moved on into an open area with electric outlets stubbed in coming up through the cement slab in three foot intervals.

"Slot machines?" she asked.

"Probably. Looks like there will be five rows of ten to a row."

Other areas of the room would be raised above the main floor. Other kinds of gaming would go on there, she guessed.

As she wandered towards the back, she looked up at the high ceilings. Now only a suggestion of grandeur as beams and braces domed upward into the clear blue sky.

"There is nothing small about any of this, is there?"

"And nothing cheap," Ben said.

At the back Julie found the kitchen. And to the right a room that looked like it would be closed off to form a dining area.

"Did you know there was going to be a restaurant?"

"No. But nothing surprises me." Ben inspected an area that would eventually be rest rooms and a lounge.

"I'm going to take a look out back." Ben followed Julie through the kitchen and back to a curve of asphalt that led to a cupola topped small building on the side.

"What do think that is? It looks like some kind of gazebo."

Julie thought its architecture a little garish. But then, it would probably blend in just fine.

"Valet station, I think."

"Is there anything they've missed?" Julie walked around it and looked inside. She stood for a minute looking first at the framed structure with its valet station like a side-kick then past the construction and paved-over field to the river and mountains. Nothing had ever seemed so out of place. The building's rambling largeness appeared awkward, gangly, a self-conscious effort at beauty but knowing it had already lost.

"Seen enough?" Ben asked.

"Yes. I need to be getting back."

"Another raincheck on testing the tire swing?" He was grinning. "I'm amassing a stack of those." He fell in beside her as they walked back across the immense parking lot.

"What's our next move?"

"I'll try to get some information on Anderson and Anderson. And maybe I'll follow up with a piece warning New Mexico about how a casino like this could be a sitting duck for organized crime. It was apparent that Johnson had never given it a thought."

"THIS IS IRRESPONSIBLE journalism. And goddamn lies."

Bob Crenshaw was pacing up and back in front of his desk waving a few pages of copy wadded tightly in his fist.

"Nothing in that is presented as fact. At best it's a warning. Copy based on conjecture but with real possibilities." Julie sat at the conference table. "It wouldn't be the first time that organized crime has moved in to take over an unsuspecting group. Johnson Yepa looked absolutely blank when I asked him how the tribe would safeguard themselves against something like that happening."

"Johnson Yepa is a stupid little man who couldn't find his ass with both hands."

"How do you know Johnson?" Julie watched Bob check his pacing and pull up a chair across from her.

"Some business dealings." A muscle in Bob's cheek twitched, spasmodically jerked half a dozen times, then subsided.

"That would include the current casino under construction, right?"

"And if it did?"

"Then, I'm talking to the right person. Casinos, as cash-intensive businesses, offer all kinds of opportunities for money laundering. Indian Gaming is producing annual revenues of almost six billion dollars now."

"You have nothing to base these accusations on." Bob appeared to be fighting to control his temper. His jaw was clamped tight as if to stop the tic which was twitching the muscle in front of his ear.

"I'm not accusing. I'm offering a warning. A wake-up call to the legislators in Santa Fe that if they're not on their toes, potentially the biggest money-maker in the state could become corrupt. And before they even know it. It took Nevada forty years to weed out organized crime from their casinos."

"That won't happen here. You must be aware of the Federal Indian Gaming Commission?"

Julie ignored his snideness.

"That's another good point. The Commission is understaffed and wouldn't know a godson of Vito Genovese's if he walked up to shake hands. They're babes in the woods." Julie paused and decided to appeal to his instinct for timeliness. "Besides, the hearings of the House Native American Affairs subcommittee on legalized gambling on Indian land are beginning this week. We should have some comment." Julie waited while Bob stared at the table. When he looked up, she caught her breath and reflexively moved her chair back. His face was contorted with anger. Red splotches highlighted his cheeks; his lips pulled tight against his teeth.

"You're a fool. A green, two-bit, hot shot journalist who looks good on camera. A fucking dime a dozen." He leaned closer. "Don't forget who made you. I gave you your chance. Gave you the Hantavirus story. I can give and I can take away."

Julie prayed that her knees wouldn't buckle as she stood.

"Is that a threat?" She hoped her voice sounded coolly detached.

"Yeah, you might say so." He seemed to master his anger and draped a leg over the side of the chair. "Don't overstep your boundaries, kiddo."

She gathered the crumpled copies of her story and started to pick them up. Bob's fist came down hard on her hand pinning it to the table.

"I think those are mine." He picked up the papers and moved to the trash basket by his desk. "This is where this story belongs, and this is where it's going to stay."

All Julie could think of was getting out of Bob's office. No wonder Johnson had seemed afraid of him. He could be a monster. Heads turned towards her, then quickly away as she walked back to her cubicle. They must have heard the shouting. She grabbed her purse, put on some lipstick then continued down the hall to the elevators. She'd take a drive, get some lunch, think. She'd struck a chord. Why had Bob reacted so violently?

The heavy basement door to the underground parking stuck

and took her leaning a shoulder into it and pushing before it released. The Miata was around the corner in a space for compacts. Fumbling for her keys, Julie didn't see Bob Crenshaw leaning against the trunk until she was almost on top of him.

"It's okay, Kiddo, I didn't mean to startle you. I was off base upstairs. I shouldn't attack your journalism. It's just that the station's a couple points down in the ratings this month and I don't want to take any chances with something that might get people in an uproar. Scare 'em. Get everyone running around yelling mafia. Guess you might say I'm just a little over zealous in protecting my investment. Can you understand that?"

Julie didn't say anything.

"Hey, let's be friends. You know I think you're one of the biggest talents in Albuquerque." Bob opened the car door for her. "The next anchor spot is yours. Cross my heart, just for you, it already has your name on it."

Julie was trying to sort through her feelings. Distrust topped the list. This schizoid who was yelling at her five minutes ago now wanted to patch things up. Bribe her to forget his outburst. Somewhere inside, her instincts were telling her to go along.

"All right. I can accept an apology."

"I knew you had some smarts besides those good looks. You're back on the team; hell, you'll soon be leading the team. How's that?"

Julie nodded, tossed her purse into the convertible and slipped behind the wheel. She didn't watch Bob leave but felt relieved when she heard the basement door thud shut.

ELEPHANT BUTTE WAS one of those lakes that spread for miles along the highway, sending inquisitive fingers of water exploring along stretches of flat land, poking at its edges into places where it shouldn't be. The lake was full for this time of year. The marshes that followed the outer boundaries of moisture were closer to the highway. Cattails, now brittle and bursting, trailed puffs of white seeds as they gently tossed and bounced off one another in the wind.

Johnson stopped at the bait shop for supplies and ice. He had come down for the weekend. Maybe the last nice weekend before a cold snap. If you could believe TV weather people, there would be a barometric dip on Monday. He pulled a shopping basket from the stack by the door and started down the first aisle.

Five bags of Cheetos, a loaf of white Wonder bread, Velveeta, Vienna sausages, mayonnaise, two packages of spice cupcakes and a liter of Seven-Up. What had he forgotten? Plastic utensils and plates. Johnson moved to a picnic display in the corner. He chose red and white checked plates with cups and napkins to match. Festive. Cheerful. He needed cheering up.

His world was pushing in on him. Even the casino didn't thrill him anymore. He had dreams where enormous talking pumpkin seeds chased him, yelling curses. In one dream the seeds tackled a medicine man and trampled him while trying to get to Johnson.

His wife asked him to sleep on the spare bed in the sewing room. His outbursts and nightly sweats scared her. But he refused to see a doctor. He knew what it was. He had angered the spirits.

He had never meant the plan to get out of hand. He thought the spirits would have excused him killing an old man who stood in the way of helping so many. But when Peter Tenorio and his fiancée died, and Jennifer, he knew his days would be numbered.

He had expected the warnings. The cleansing rite had not been strong enough to stop them from coming for him. The ritual had been too late. He heard the old man's voice chanting "Some can be valiant in death; leaders remembered for their bravery." Was he hinting that Johnson already knew what he had to do? Take the necessary action to fill the cemetery once and for all? Sacrifice his own life—

"Is that all?" The clerk behind the counter was staring at him. Must have asked twice, Johnson decided. Lately, he could just drift off, leave the real world, sometimes forget where he was.

"Yes. And add a bag of ice."

He loaded everything into the back of the Bronco and

stopped a moment to admire the white deck chair folded behind the seat. He had ordered it from a catalog. One of what seemed to be hundreds that came to his post office box in the Pueblo every other week. He wondered how he could stop this mail. He knew the post office employees were enjoying it. Sometimes he'd find ads circled or pages with their corners turned down. Sometimes the items were jaunty mariner's caps or nautically striped tee shirts, once an ad for red and blue boxer shorts had been marked with a lewd comment penciled in the margin just below the small mast of the sail boat motif that decorated the waistband.

The deck chair had come unassembled. Johnson was proud of the way he had put it together, using neatly capped wood screws and painting the pieces a glossy white. Across the back he had stenciled "The Dream Catcher," in a marine blue with silver feathers hanging from the "D." His wife complimented his work and wanted him to make another one for the back yard. Along with laying sod and building flower boxes. But she didn't know that he wouldn't see the spring. She didn't know that he would need to go with the spirits soon.

They were everywhere. Sometimes, like tonight, their eyes would peek out from behind parked cars, follow him, peer over his shoulder. Lately, he had begun to hear them talk. Just mummers, but loud enough to block out the voice of someone talking to him, someone in the same room. At first, he tried to answer back. Explain. Make them see why he did what he did. What he had to do. He was the leader of his people.

He parked on the strip of paving to the right of the marina office. His was only one of four cars. He had missed the crowds of late summer—the families taking advantage of Labor day weekend to enjoy time together before returning to school or jobs. Late October wasn't exactly the height of the season. But the lake was beautiful this time of year. Beautiful in its quietness.

He picked up the deck chair and decided that he'd have to come back for the groceries. No use risking a nick to save time. Now that was an Anglo thought. Johnson paused to consider, then stepped up onto the floating walkway that led to slip seventy-three.

The Dream Catcher was outlined against the autumn sky. A fiery sunset spread behind her, warming the paleness of the blue backdrop and tinting everything in its path with a blush of pink-gold. Johnson slung the folded chair over his shoulder and maneuvered the dangling ladder with one hand. He hoisted the deck chair over the side first, then followed. He stood on the deck and watched the sun set before going back for the groceries. Suddenly his stomach rumbled. He needed to fix something to eat. He rolled two slices of white bread around chunks of Velveeta, opened a bag of Cheetos and poured a glass of Seven-Up.

He carefully sponged the counter, put what needed to be kept cool in the small bar fridge next to the gas cook stove, and climbed back on deck with his dinner.

The now gray-pink light lasted a long time. Johnson watched a slice of moon pop up from under the horizon like it had sprung from the water to climb above the semi-circle of hills. The black night sky started to twinkle with tiny points of light. Johnson shivered. It had gotten cold. The chill seemed to lift off the surface of the water and drift across the deck settling under the chair. He went below and came back with a blanket and another sweatshirt.

He liked to muse on the origins of his people and the ceremonies that made them strong. He even recounted the mistakes he had made. During the last winter solstice, when the sun deity reported to the others on what had happened during the year, he had been marked for death. And Johnson had chosen to ignore the warning. Even animals who will die during the up-coming year are marked in some way, a bird is missing a feather or two from its tail, a deer has a slit in its ear.

Even then there was a chance he could have averted death. He could have put pine gum on his forehead, under his arms, and on his elbows and knees. But he didn't. And because he didn't, he couldn't attach himself to the sun's rays. He couldn't stay in the light, among the living.

Johnson sighed. So much had happened. He heard the short

haunting hoot of an owl from the wooded area behind the rental cabins. The gentle rocking of the boat was soothing. He dozed fitfully then awoke thinking he had heard voices. He listened. Nothing, only night sounds. He wrapped the blanket tighter around him and turned in the chair so that his arm cradled his head.

He dreamed of skimming the water in *The Dream Catcher*. When others would try to follow, they would get caught in a giant net and he would slip through. When the head of the turtle-man appeared at the front of the boat, he wasn't surprised. Johnson waved him to come forward, then rose to embrace this deity throwing open his blanket as the turtle-man climbed aboard.

"I welcome you, turtle-man, as my guest. Please, enter my humble house above your water-home. You do me great honor."

The turtle-man didn't answer but his great glassy eyes watched Johnson. His black slippery skin shed water. Leaving a puddle on the deck, he sidled forward on flippered feet slipping under the weight of the yellow shell humped behind his neck. When the turtle-man held out his hand, Johnson took it wondering at its rubbery feel. The turtle-man led him to the side of the boat and motioned towards the water.

"You do me an even greater honor by inviting me to your home at the bottom of the lake," Johnson said.

The turtle-man reached out to steady Johnson. Friendly, reassuring. Then he motioned Johnson to step up beside him on the edge of *The Dream Catcher*. Johnson did so and gazed out across the water. He sighed.

"I will go with you now," he said.

In slow motion, poised, hand in hand, Johnson and the turtle-man jumped, pushing upward and outward, gracefully curving in the air before tumbling beneath the surface of the water. Johnson watched the bubbles swirl around and around caressing the turtle-man, then tickling him as he sank in the turtle-man's home. Johnson breathed in letting the water fill his lungs until all he could see was a blinding patch of white light that stretched into a path filled with deities beckoning him to follow.

"WHAT IS IT, Gloria?" Sandy looked up from his desk.

"Has Johnson Yepa been admitted to the hospital?"

"Johnson? No. I don't think so. Why?"

"He didn't come home last night. His wife is worried. He was gone all weekend."

"Where'd he go?"

"She thinks he might have gone to Elephant Butte. But she's not sure."

"Maybe she should call authorities at the lake."

"That's what I told her." Gloria turned to go back across the hall.

Sandy adjusted his reading glasses and looked at the numbers on his computer screen. No wonder he always had a stiff neck. He needed new glasses. But maybe he was finding it difficult to do the cost-accounting because he hated to "crunch" numbers. Follow-up reports were always tedious. Sandy hated the paperwork that went with program management.

"Dr. Black?" Gloria was in the doorway.

"What now?" He tried not to sound exasperated but knew that he'd failed.

"It's about Johnson Yepa."

"Again? Don't tell me, he just showed up at his office."

"No. He's dead."

Sandy pushed back from his desk and turned to look at Gloria. "Dead? How did it happen?"

"He drowned."

"A boating accident?"

"They don't know. But it doesn't look like it."

"Foul play?"

"They don't think so."

Sandy turned back to his desk. Stunned. No, more like paralyzing shock. But maybe they were the same thing. He couldn't think straight. He needed to contact Ben. He wondered if Ben or Julie had found out anything. It seemed impossible that Johnson was dead. And suspect that he would drown, unassisted.

"WHAT DO YOU MEAN, he took your hand and just jumped over the side?" Douglas Anderson, Sr. poured another cup of coffee.

"You had to be there. No lie, he took my hand, all the while calling me the turtle-man and saying how he wanted to visit my home, and he just followed me to the side of the boat and then jumped." Junior lavishly spread an onion bagel with cream cheese.

"Was he on something?"

"Don't think so." Junior's words were muffled by a mouthful of bagel. A trickle of butter dropped to the neck of his sweatshirt and left a dark stain.

"How can you eat at a time like this? You killed someone. And now you're eating like a pig."

"What's wrong with you? Haven't you been listening to me? I didn't kill anyone." Junior put the bagel on his plate. "We have the extraordinary good luck of having an intended murder victim help us out by committing suicide, and you're pissed."

"I don't like it that you left the body. Didn't we agree that you'd dispose of the body?" Douglas knew he was sounding peevish. Everything seemed to upset him lately.

"But I didn't have anything to cover up. I didn't have to strangle him or bash his head in. I just went swimming with him. And watched as he chose to drown. He never even fought for air."

"If you're lying to me…"

"Dad, why would I lie? I'm in this as deeply as you are. I thought you'd be happy that I'd been spared having to physically do away with someone. This whole thing is making you jumpy."

"Bob Crenshaw thinks we have to get rid of the reporter."

"That girl?"

"Yeah. Seems she's been a little too snoopy. Bob thinks she may be on to something. May go to the feds with a lot of questions, put them on our trail."

"So, what's he going to do?"

"He says not to worry. Says he'll take care of it."

Douglas pushed back from the table. How could he condone another death? Was there no stopping who would have to be killed? He was too old for all this dying. He'd talk to Bob. Maybe he was overreacting. Could be the girl wouldn't have to be killed. She was such a pretty thing. Her whole life was ahead of her.

FOURTEEN

JULIE LEANED BACK in her office chair and stared at a blank monitor. Ben had left a message for her this morning on her voice mail. "Johnson Yepa is dead. Some sort of accident at the Butte or could be suicide. I'll come by this evening. I don't want to miss that home-cooked meal you promised. We can talk then."

Johnson Yepa would not have committed suicide. But did she know that? No, just instinct. And what good was instinct? Nothing she could go to the Feds with. She had contacted the coroner. There was no evidence, or as he had emphatically put it, "Not a snowball's chance that anyone helped him drown." So what was bothering her?

Anderson and Anderson, Inc. seemed to be on the up and up. No history of bilking the public. In fact, just the opposite. Douglas, Sr. was known for his philanthropy. He'd made millions in real estate in Santa Fe. She had put a call in to the State Gaming Commission. She'd check on the casino backers, find out who the principal investors were. In addition, she'd get a list of any consultants or contractors. Somewhere there might be a clue, some tie that might be damning. If there were no surprises, she'd have to admit her sixth sense was failing her.

She was discouraged. She wanted to nail the killer or killers. The one who had killed Ben's grandmother. To boost her standings as an investigative reporter? Or to help Ben? Probably the latter. It was painful to think that he would be leaving in a couple months. She had to make some decisions. Unhurried ones made with a clear head. The phone interrupted.

"I've got someone from the Commission for Gaming on one."

Julie reached for a pad and pencil. This better be good. If the casino wasn't the common denominator, she'd be fresh out of ideas. She picked up the phone.

"Julie Conlin? Ed Tafoya, State Gaming Commission. How can I help you?"

"I'm gathering material on the Tewa casino. At this point, just doing some background on the principle investors, contractors, any contacts that the tribe might have had in getting this thing off the ground."

"I can probably help you. That's all public record. Let's see. Anderson and Anderson, Inc. are listed as consultants.

"Romero Construction got the original bid for building, but reneged about two weeks into the job. They were followed by James, Inc. out of Albuquerque. To the best of my knowledge, they're still on the job."

"Do you have a list of names—those behind Anderson and Anderson, Inc.?"

"Well, there are two corporations. One is the original real estate company based in Santa Fe. The other is an investment company. Which one do you want? Wait a minute, looks like both did consulting with the pueblo."

"Let's take the real estate company first."

"Principals are the two Andersons, Douglas, Jr. and Sr. Then someone named Evelyn Coffer, an Edward Martinez, Walker Smith, that's the former Governor, P. Walker Smith, Andrew Wellington and Martin Sawyer. Got those?"

"Yes. Reads like a who's who of Santa Fe, doesn't it?"

"Got that right. Here goes with the investment company. First, the list of members includes three from the list I just gave you, Wellington, Smith and Sawyer; but add Augustine Chavez, Mr. and Mrs. Walter Monroe, and Albert Dunhill, that's State Senator Dunhill."

"And the principals are the same? The two Andersons?"

"Yeah. No wait, add a couple names to that list, too. Robert Crenshaw and Anthony Chang."

"Let me read these back." Julie checked each name after it was verified.

"I have the names of the surveyors. That contract was subbed to a company out of Arizona."

"Okay. Might as well get as much as I can."

"The Wilson Brothers, Surveyors and Appraisers, Tucson, Arizona. They look like the only out of state company involved. I guess they tried to keep jobs local."

"I'm assuming everything's in order with their permits? A Class III met with everyone's approval?"

"Not at first. But Douglas Anderson is persuasive. Of course, he has the Governor in his hip pocket. But I'll deny it if you say you heard it here." Julie waited for the nervous laughter to subside. There it was again, cronyism. If it could be bottled and exported...New Mexico wouldn't have a worry.

"Your boss's no slouch when it comes to getting what he wants, either. Bob Crenshaw must have lobbied just as hard as Douglas Anderson. The two of them spent months at it. Too bad that illness thing almost ruined it for them."

Or made it all possible, she thought, as she ran down the list of names again.

And there it was. It might as well have been flashing neon. The link. Thank God, her sixth sense was still intact.

"Listen, Ed, I'm sorry to cut this short, but I'm being paged. Thanks for all the information. You've been a great help."

Yes, a very great help. Now to contact the Fire Chief. Probably better to just run by. She grabbed her purse and stuffed the two pages of yellow legal tablet inside. She couldn't leave the list here. A laptop and her recorder, the in-the-field paraphernalia of the working reporter and that should do it. She quickly thrust both into a canvas briefcase.

"I'll be out this afternoon. I've got a couple interviews. I may or may not be back before five. If not, see you in the morning."

The receptionist nodded, picked up an erasable marker and

drew a line beside Julie's name on the large white schedule board.

THE FIRE CHIEF was in. Now, if she could be just as lucky in another way. She needed information—the most damning evidence so far. She quickly crossed her fingers.

"He'll see you now." His secretary pointed down the hall. "Second door on your left."

The fire chief got up immediately to shake hands.

"Yes. I do remember you. Spent an evening on a fire truck together not long back. You're a reporter with Channel Nine." He laughed and pointed to a chair in front of his desk. "But you can't be here about that, that fire's old news by now."

Julie only hesitated for a second. There was no reason not to just get to the point.

"If you're a Channel Nine fan, you must know that I've been reporting the Hantavirus story, heading up the investigation for the station."

The fire chief nodded frowning.

"I understand that there were several hundred cages of rodents in the Chang lab. Do you know what happened to them?"

Silence. She thought he recognized where her questioning was leading as she watched him chew the inside of his jaw so she pushed on.

"If Mr. Chang trapped locally, there's every possibility that rodents in his lab carried the deadly Hantavirus. I was hoping that you'd had any survivors—in whatever condition—checked. I'm just tying up some loose ends to my story on the virus. It's important to investigate any link to rodents."

"I'm not sure I'm at liberty to say what was done with the lab contents." She thought he looked worried.

"If, and this is just hypothesis, the rodents or any parts that you might have recovered have not been tested for the virus—"

"Yes, yes." The Fire Chief got up from behind his desk and walked to a window. "That was a pretty intense fire, if you remember. Chemical fires always are."

"I doubt that any live rodents were saved, but what if some had been frozen, preserved in some kind of chemical tanks. I noticed tanks in the back of the building.'' She waited. She had him thinking and weighing the implications of a sloppy reporting job, not being careful with human lives. There was enough hysteria in the community over the virus as it was, if word leaked out that there had been a potentially dangerous situation in the North East Heights of Albuquerque...something that could have spread....

"If there were any survivors, carcasses—and I'm not saying there were—they survived because they were away from the center of the fire and have already been admitted as evidence,'' he said. "Arson isn't suspected but heat intensity, center of blast—those things need to be determined. The contents of the lab, the rats, help us get a picture of what happened—it's just routine.''

"What would that entail?''

"Shipping them off to the State lab.'' The chief pulled a log from the top desk drawer.

"But you're not sure that happened?''

"I'll tell you in a minute.'' He turned a few pages before he found what he was looking for, then he checked several entries before looking up. "A number of parcels were sent to Santa Fe, but I'm not at liberty to say exactly what was contained in those samples.''

Or someone wasn't very accurate in his reporting. There was no doubt that the chief wasn't above a little behind-chewing. And "storm cloud'' didn't do justice to his expression. She certainly had his attention on this.

"I'd like you to do something for me.'' Julie was busy writing on the back of her business card. "If the rodents are still intact, send a sample to IHS, Dr. Sanford Black, Clinical Director. The CDC still has a lab set up here in Albuquerque at the Indian hospital. Right now, they're primarily doing rodent testing. This could be important.''

The chief looked relieved, probably felt she was cutting him some slack by not mentioning using the information in a story.

"I'll tell Dr. Black that he'll be hearing from you in the next couple days. Is that sufficient time?''

"Yes. I'll have Santa Fe contact him directly. We may be

able to get him something by noon tomorrow." He took the card, then rose to walk her to the door. "Miss Conlin, I'm sure every precaution was taken in handling any evidence."

Julie smiled. "I sincerely hope so."

DID SHE HAVE a lot to tell Ben. They could decide what to do when he came by tonight. But, it was probably time to let the authorities know everything they suspected. There weren't any definitive answers yet; no one had come forward with a confession and a lot did depend on whether Tony Chang's collection of rodents held any clues. But the coincidences were overwhelming. Tony Chang dies; Johnson Yepa dies. Both apparently of accidents; both players in the casino deal, probably key players. One in a position to come up with the killer in his laboratory, the other in a position to take the pumpkin seeds to the pueblo. Give them to the governor.

Julie pushed the garage door opener, and pulled in between the packing crates. She'd go back out for groceries after she called Sandy so there wasn't any reason to close it again. It was only five fifteen; she should be able to catch him at the office.

Then, time for a shower, start the pasta, bring some wood in for a fire; Julie laughed, it was beginning to sound like a fun evening. She fumbled for her keys and then realized that the back door was open. Standing open about an inch. Thank God, for garage doors. She must have forgotten to close it after she'd taken the garbage out.

She tossed her purse on the kitchen counter. Talaveras tile in a mixture of terra cotta, yellow and blue covered the counters and bordered the Saltillo tile on the floor. She reached in the Fridge for the pitcher of apple juice and carried it to the kitchen table, a glass and rough wood beam thing with matching chairs. The gift from her always trend-conscious mother had actually fit right in.

She punched the message button on her answering machine and grabbed a glass from a rough pine cupboard above the sink. Her dry cleaning was ready; Ben would be there by six fifteen and would she like to see a movie; a girl at work reminding her of the baby shower for the receptionist; then the whirring of the machine before someone hung up. People still had a problem with leaving messages. She waited. There was one more message.

The voice wasn't familiar, could have been altered in some way. It was male. Possibly an older man. But it was the message that made Julie brace herself against the sink.

"Get out while you can. They're going to kill you. You know too much. Leave Albuquerque. Don't treat this as some joke. Your life is in danger."

Was someone trying to scare her? He was doing a good job. Her knees felt like rubber. What should she do? Give the tape to the police for starters. Just another thing to talk to Ben about. She couldn't just stand there; she was starting to run late if she was going to have everything ready by six thirty. She took a deep breath and walked to the drawer under the phone, and got a new tape. But before she messed with a tape, she should call the hospital. It wasn't like she'd forget to tell Ben about the threat. Could be a prank, but it could be for real.

She dialed the hospital. Gloria said that Sandy was upstairs, did she want to leave a message?

"Tell him to expect some rodents from the State lab, no, that may not be true. Just tell him that I'll call back in the morning."

The arm came around her suddenly, pinning her arms to her sides, another hand around her mouth. She struggled, kicking backwards and up but not connecting with anything solid. She was being lifted off the floor. It was the last thing she remembered.

JULIE'S CAR WAS GONE when he got there, but the garage door was up and the back door open. She'd probably gone to get something for dinner. She'd offered to cook and he had enthusiastically accepted the invitation. Maybe tonight they could talk about the two of them.

The apple juice on the table was cool so it hadn't been sitting out since breakfast. It seemed odd that she hadn't even started dinner yet. He checked his watch. Six twenty. Well, maybe she'd worked late. So much for the movie idea. They'd just have to figure out something else to do. He smiled. He'd finally made up his mind to force the issue; tell her exactly how he felt and suggest a couple ways that they could work things out after he left. Do the long-distance thing for a year or so. But he couldn't walk away without an understanding. An understanding about their future together.

He walked towards the dining room; the table wasn't set. In fact, other than the door being open and the juice out, it looked like she hadn't been there. He turned back to the kitchen and automatically straightened a throw rug that was wadded under the phone stand. The plastic lid to the answering machine's tapedeck was up. Maybe she had gotten some message and had to leave. He looked around for a note. Nothing on the table, nothing pinned to the fridge with a magnet. He toyed with playing her phone messages. It wasn't like he was opening her mail. But it was a little snoopy. He'd wait. She should be back any minute. He flopped down on the couch.

BEN SAT UP and tried to get oriented. Long shadows invaded the room, broken by the twinkling lights of the city below. The view through the French doors leading to the deck captured the best of Albuquerque. Or, at least, it was a reason to live in the foothills of the Sandias. The furnace coming on had awakened him. The blower from the forced-air unit was the only sound in the town house. Julie. He was at Julie's. And she wasn't here. A feeling of panic rose from somewhere and threatened to squeeze the air from his chest.

They were supposed to have dinner. What time was it? He fumbled with the switch on the table lamp and checked his watch. Oh, God. It was seven o'clock. Something was wrong. Very wrong. He could feel it. She would have called, not just stood him up. Hadn't she left the door open for him? He stood, walked to a floor lamp and turned it on, next, the hanging lamp over the dining room table. The light wasn't reassuring. It didn't help to quell the rising feeling of dread. It just kept him busy for half a minute.

What if there had been an accident? He'd check the hospitals.

She could have gone to the store and was hit by a car. He walked to the phone. Stay calm. You don't know anything for sure, yet. Talking to himself wasn't very reassuring, either. He opened the drawer to find a phone book.

Maybe he should just replay her messages. She, or someone, had already listened to them—if there were any. Or, maybe she'd erased them. He rewound the tape. He'd just replay the last three or four. It couldn't hurt to check.

He was almost ready to say it had been a bad idea when the last message began. A death threat. He played it once, twice. By the third time he knew that he didn't recognize the voice. He'd take it to the police. But then they'd just assume that she had run. Panicked and bolted. He knew better. But, did he? Yes. She would not have gone anywhere without telling him. What would she have done after hearing that message?

Maybe the neighbors had seen something. He grabbed a spare key off the peg board by the back door, locked up, and ran across the narrow expanse of Bermuda grass that separated the two dwellings.

An elderly woman answered the door and kept it as a shield between them as she peered at him closely.

"I'm a friend of Julie Conlin. Ben Pecos. We were supposed to meet at her house tonight. She left the back door open for me but hasn't come back. Did you see her leave earlier?"

The woman studied him. "Well, she borrowed my eight quart kettle. Told me about cooking dinner for someone. Sounded like that someone was special." The woman smiled coquettishly.

"But did you see her leave?"

"You know, now that I think of it, I did, earlier. Just a minute, let me ask Harold. We were just getting back from playing golf." She started to go back into the house. "Oh my, I'm forgetting my manners. Step inside. This will only take a minute."

It seemed like hours before the woman came back.

"Harold says her garage door was up when we got home. He says he saw her little red car parked inside. What I remember was the big white van in the driveway. You know, like the van from the studio. She sometimes drives it home.''

"Did it have the Channel Nine insignia on the side?''

"Oh dear. I can't say that it did or didn't.''

"Did you see either one of the cars leave?''

"Yes. Both of them. Someone was driving the van and it followed Julie in her car.''

"So, Julie was driving the Miata?''

"Well, I couldn't swear to it. I just assumed that it was Julie. I had stopped for a few groceries and was taking the things out of the trunk of our car.'' The woman paused. "No, I didn't actually see her. I waved. I remember doing that.''

"What time was this?''

"Early. About five-thirty.''

He thanked her and ran back to Julie's. Should he go back inside and wait? Call the station? It was seven fifteen. No. He'd go to the station. Maybe, just maybe, there was some emergency and she had been called in to work late on a story. It sounded good, but he didn't believe it.

UNNECESSARY ROUGHNESS, abduction, life-threatening…but you had to be alive to make those kinds of charges and Julie knew that if she didn't come up with something fast, that was the one thing she wasn't going to be. Her head ached. She remembered passing out after someone put pressure on her neck. She had just called Sandy; what else was she doing…Ben. He'd be there by now looking for her. Would he stay or would he leave, thinking she'd had to work?

She eased an elbow out to the right to brace herself from hitting the side of the van as it turned a corner. Whoever was driving was a maniac. The voice in her kitchen that told him to put her in the back of the van and follow him was all too familiar. Even semi-conscious, she recognized Bob Crenshaw. Then after the van doors were slammed shut, she'd heard the Miata start. Bob must be driving it.

The ropes at her wrists pulled and itched. At least the ropes at her ankles didn't chafe through thick socks. But it was the tape—heavy, wide and metallic gray—wound double thickness around her mouth that was the most uncomfortable.

She was stretched out flat in the back of a van. It was one from the station. That much she was sure of. The driver was someone she'd never seen before. Odd man. Didn't seem comfortable with his role as heavy. In fact, he didn't seem a menacing type at all. More like an accountant who lifted weights and bit his fingernails. He had the hands of someone who sat at a desk. And the nervous mannerisms of someone unsure of himself.

So, who would kill her? There it was. She put it into words. It was the truth. Either the man driving or Bob Crenshaw would get rid of her. She wasn't in the back of the van trussed up like a wild animal unless she was going to slaughter. This certainly corroborated what her sixth sense had been screaming— she had been right. Isn't that what the phone message had warned her about—knowing too much? She had reached that expendable level.

She just wished she knew where they were going. How much time would she have to react? Would someone open the doors of the van and shoot her? Too messy. They'd probably drag her out at some point, then what?

The van turned another corner then bounced over two speed bumps and angled downward before it suddenly stopped. Where were they? Bob opened the passenger side door and said something about "when he got back…" then the door slammed shut and the driver turned up the radio at which point the door opened again and Bob growled about not attracting attention. The radio went dead. They must be in a public place.

The station. The underground parking at the station. Her hearing was distorted by the tape but the van door had made that echoing sound of a parking garage when Bob slammed it. Now what? They wouldn't kill her here. Somehow it didn't make her feel better.

Julie had never been good about telling time without a watch, but it seemed like she'd been there over an hour before she heard another sound. A car door slamming shut next to the van. She had a feeling it was the Miata. The springs in the bucket seat creaked under the weight of the van's driver pushing back away from the steering wheel. Must not want to be seen.

Julie lifted her legs together high above her head and brought the heels of her shoes down hard on the floorboards; ''ouch,'' not enough noise, quickly twisting onto her side, she banged her feet against the side of the van before the driver yanked a handful of her hair pulling her a foot in the air.

''More of that, and I won't wait for Bob.''

He dropped her back but leaned over her, his hand still holding a fistful of her hair. The pressure brought tears to her eyes. So much for his being a softy. And, so much for trying to attract attention; no one had heard her. The man slipped into the passenger's seat but turned back to keep an eye on her. Then as an after thought, he climbed beside her and unrolled a canvas tarp tucking it snugly around her arms and legs and pulling it up to her chin.

''Now, try to throw yourself around.''

Julie hated the confinement. But she had watched his face as he covered her. There wasn't one part of her body that he hadn't looked at. He hadn't touched, just looked and lusted after. Maybe she could use his wanting to her advantage. But how? There were two of them.

There was still a chance that Ben would have sensed something was wrong and…and what? He would have gone to her house expecting dinner. Did he know her well enough to know she'd never have reneged on a dinner invite? No he probably didn't. He could have just given up and gone home. It was difficult to keep the tears back. How could she have been so stupid? Not seen Bob for what he was? Not been more careful.

BEN PARKED to the west of the building, number One Broadcast Plaza, in a visitor's space. He thought Julie usually left her car underground in the area reserved for employees. It wouldn't hurt to check on his way in. The garage was a two floor, spacious cement attachment to the back of Julie's office building. The ramp leading to the underground level curved to the right. All the signs and large sweeping arrows looked freshly painted but the florescent lighting bled them of color, leaving little contrast between pillars, floor and the light tan ceiling.

Ben jogged down the ramp and checked a row marked "compact cars only" along the north wall. Halfway down the row, a quick look told him no red Miatas. He headed toward the elevator. Better yet, he'd take the stairs. He wondered if anyone was ever "on duty," some guard who spent the night walking up and down the ramps, maybe lapping the building once or twice. He didn't see any evidence of human existence. The elevators were enclosed in a glassed-in box, obviously heated and cooled and provided with a sand filled canister for cigarette butts. The building was posted "no smoking"; the metal sign had been tagged with graffiti.

The stairs were behind the elevators near a large closet area marked "Maintenance." Beside the room, six spaces were reserved for "Maintenance vehicles only." And there it was.

Between two white vans. Ben checked the passenger-side door. Open. He looked inside, then got into the car. Nothing out of place. Didn't look like the glove compartment had been touched recently. No remnants of torn clothing or blood stains on seats or floor. Not that he was looking for something like that, but he was relieved when he didn't find it. With her car here, she just might be upstairs working.

He leaned toward the driver's seat and struck his knee on the gear shift. It had been left in neutral. The emergency brake was on—yanked to its limit by someone stronger than Julie, Ben thought. But not leaving the car in reverse was a dead giveaway that Julie hadn't parked her car. Nor had she pushed the driverside seat back four inches.

He eased out of the car and looked around. No sign of life. Closing the car door echoed among the pillars, but no one appeared to ask him what he was doing. He'd check upstairs and see if anyone knew where she was. Something told him to go back to the front entrance and not let anyone know that he'd seen Julie's car.

The evening receptionist was busy answering phones and whispered for him to wait. Ben looked around. Only about half the room full of cubicles that stretched behind the information desk were lighted. Ben saw four people still in front of computers.

"Are you looking for someone?" The switchboard operator paused, answered another line, talked a moment and looked back at him. "Another one of those stupid giveaways. Do you believe that people burn up the phone lines to try to win a calendar with our weatherman's picture on it?"

"Is Julie Conlin here?"

"I haven't seen her. I start at six, and she wasn't here then. Looks like she signed out at three-thirty." She pointed at the schedule board on the wall. Under destination it said "interview," time back had a question mark.

"Can I help you?"

Ben turned to face a middle aged man in tee shirt, jeans and a fleece-lined leather jacket. Bob Crenshaw. It must be.

"I'm Ben Pecos. I'm here to meet Julie Conlin."

"Julie was here about six." The man was brusque.

"I didn't see her, Mr. Crenshaw." The receptionist interrupted. Ben saw a jaw muscle twitch in front of the man's ear. Edgy, Ben thought, but why?

"Of course you didn't. I saw her downstairs. She was leaving her car. Said she was meeting a friend for dinner. I assumed this person was picking her up in front." A thin forced smile, anything but friendly.

"Thanks. I'm sorry I missed her." Ben kept his voice even.

"Wanna leave a message?" The receptionist held up a pencil and note pad.

Bob had slouched against the counter and was watching him. Making certain that he left? Ben couldn't tell but didn't get a good feeling. Something Julie's neighbor had said...a white van, she had assumed it was from the station, had been parked in the drive, left when the Miata pulled out. There was a white van next to the Miata downstairs.

"No. I'll run by her house."

Actually, I'll run as far as the parking lot, get in the truck, park on a side street and wait for Bob Crenshaw to leave, Ben thought. He had a jacket on; he must have been on his way out. Following him might be my only chance. Bob Crenshaw had lied. If Julie had been in the parking lot downstairs, she hadn't driven her car there. And she didn't tell Bob she was meeting someone for dinner—not when that someone was waiting at her town house across town. Put that together with the neighbor's information, and it looked a little suspect for the boss. Ben would swear that Bob Crenshaw knew a whole lot more than he was letting on.

FIFTEEN

LORENZO WON the argument. But not before he grabbed the poncho to him and held it tight, sticking his arms out of the sleeve slits and locking them across his chest. His granddaughter wanted to take it off. Take off the poncho and his shirt and underthings. A basin of warm water, a washcloth and bar of soap sat on the edge of the dresser. She pulled; he pulled. Exasperated, she left him, yelling over her shoulder that he needed to wear a clean shirt and underwear. He needed to use the bar of soap and washcloth. What would the doctor think? That she couldn't take care of her own grandfather. That's what. Then the nurses would see. They would see the holes and the gray stains under the arms. She would be humiliated. She'd never take him anywhere again. He could just get his flu shot at the clinic and not have a physical by the nice doctor at the Albuquerque hospital ever again.

Lorenzo waited until she had stomped from the room. He marveled that sometimes his hearing was crystal clear when it was something he didn't want to hear. But maybe he had just heard it all before, knew what she always said when she brought a pan of water into his room and a bar of soap.

He knew that they would go for a car ride. A long one. The same one that they took every year when the sky turned a watery blue and the clouds thinned to strips that stretched above the horizon. He had watched two crows swoop down to pick the corn fields this morning. The great black birds of winter were back.

One had called to him before it flew towards the mountains. Did it want him to follow? He should go to the mountain. He had made a promise to the spirits this summer. He would visit one of the four sacred mountains of his people. *Oku pin,* turtle mountain, loomed over Albuquerque. Maybe this trip was meant to be. Yes. The spirits were showing him the way. Showing him the way to come to them in prayer and homage.

Lorenzo knelt by the corner of his bed and reached into his hidey hole. He had found three shiny quarters in the pay phone at the community center and he pulled them out, then two bottle caps, a piece of green glass and two feathers from the tail of a hawk. He would offer a present to the spirits at the earth navel on *Oku pin.*

He peeked out the window. His granddaughter put the heels of her hands onto the middle of the car's steering wheel and pressed forward all the time looking expectantly at the house. She was mad. He looked around his room. Did he have everything for his journey? A blanket. *Oku pin* was cold. One time as a young boy, he had run from his home to the base of the mountain and then up to the top. He almost froze and had to dance to keep warm.

His granddaughter slid from beneath the steering wheel and opened the back door of the car when she saw him in the doorway. Lorenzo got in and clutched the blanket thinking she might try to take that, too. But she didn't pay attention to what he was wearing. She just snapped the buttons down on all the doors and got back behind the wheel.

Lorenzo watched *Oku pin* get bigger and bigger as they got closer to the city. High, high up, white patches clung to the rocks. He would climb as high as the snow tonight and sleep among the trees that smelled of freshness and stayed green under their white blanket.

He tried to blink as fast as the telephone poles were whizzing past, but it made him feel sick. He pressed his face to the cool window and searched the side of the road for something shiny, but everything moved too quickly. Riding in cars always made him sleepy so he pulled the hood of the poncho up, pushed his head to the back and closed his eyes.

It startled him when his granddaughter reached around from the front seat to pull the button up on his door. Then she stepped out, smoothed her dress in place and opened the door for Lorenzo. They were at the hospital.

He stopped to draw the tip of his cane through some oil on the parking lot but his granddaughter tugged on his arm. She always seemed to be in a hurry. They would only sit upstairs. They always had to wait. And he would wait until the time was right to continue on his journey to *Oku pin.*

He balked at the elevator, then stepped inside when he saw the blinking lights. When the floor fell away and his knees struggled to push him upright again, he laughed and pounded the floor with his cane.

"He likes elevators." Lorenzo watched his granddaughter say something to a man who stood in the swaying box with them. Then the doors opened onto a room of chairs and people. Lorenzo wrapped his blanket tighter around him. His granddaughter walked to a desk and spoke to someone sitting behind it, then steered him towards two chairs by the window.

"*Oku pin.*" He said and pointed at the Sandias.

His granddaughter looked at him in surprise and then nodded as she leaned close. "I'm going to the rest room. You stay right here. Don't move."

Lorenzo watched her go, then picked up his cane, waved to the young woman behind the desk and shuffled towards the elevators.

There was no one inside the box when the doors flew open. He stepped across the crack in the floor, and missed being squashed as they flashed together behind him. Then just as suddenly, after barely a jiggle, they opened again and Lorenzo saw the dry brown lawn out in front of the hospital. Before he got out, he pushed all the buttons clustered together along the side panel and stared as a light came on behind each. Then he stepped forward and walked slowly out the front door into the sunlight. At last, he was free to visit *Oku pin.*

He walked to the corner of Lomas and Girard and paused to stare at the mountain. A group of people crowded around him. Young people with books. A girl smiled at him. She took his arm when the giant car with windows everywhere jolted to a stop in front of him. She helped him up the steps. He watched as she offered coins to the man behind a great wheel.

Lorenzo dug into his pocket and pulled out two shiny coins and a bottle cap and held them out. The driver looked at him closely.

"Where are you going?"

The man had asked him something. Lorenzo wasn't sure but pointed out the huge front windows at the mountains.

"Oku pin."

"What'd he say?" The bus driver turned to the girl.

"I don't know. But I think he wants to go to the mountains."

The bus driver looked back to Lorenzo then carefully took the bottle cap and folded Lorenzo's fingers back over the two shiny quarters.

"There you go, Pops. Move it along."

The girl motioned for him to follow her and pointed to a seat by the window. She sat across from him but got off after three stops. She smiled and waved to him from the ground and Lorenzo watched her become smaller and smaller as the bus pulled away.

Lorenzo was excited. The spirits would be happy to see him. He would rest with them, maybe have something to eat. He watched the driver eat a sandwich, his reflection clear in the moon-large mirror above his head. Lorenzo looked away when the driver's eyes stared back at him. At the next stop the driver walked back and gave him half of his sandwich.

The bus stopped many times but the mountain got bigger and bigger. Finally, the bus stopped and the driver said something to him. He waited. The driver walked back and squatted down and pointed at the mountains through the window. Lorenzo nodded and let the man help him down the aisle and out the door. When the bus left, Lorenzo stood a moment before he stepped onto the pavement, crossed the street and continued out onto the open mesa.

The sun would be setting behind him soon. Already, *Oku pin* was red purple with streaks of rose across the top. He didn't feel the harshness of the sandy desert floor, his moccasins tied close at his ankles kept pebbles from pushing between his toes. Once a branching clump of chollo caught at his outer blanket but he continued, a piece of the stickery cactus swinging along beside him.

This night was glorious. Lorenzo paused to watch a jackrabbit leap and twist, running from a neighborhood dog. Finally it stopped to wash its ears knowing that the dog, long spent, was ambling back to civilization. He was higher than the street now and could see car lights rush past one another in the approaching darkness. But he was not alone. The night slipped around him like yet another blanket and the moon rose, full and golden, to turn the green-brown of the desert into a silver filigree of shadows.

"GLORIA, CALM DOWN. How can a ninety-six-year-old man be caught in an elevator between first and second floor?" Sandy followed Gloria up the stairs and the two of them joined a small group of onlookers in front of the elevator doors.

"Where's maintenance?"

"In here, Doc." The muffled voice came from the shaft.

Sandy stepped up to converse without yelling.

"What happened?"

"An electrical failure. Probably a short. Someone jammed the circuit board."

"Are we to believe that Lorenzo Loretto is in there?"

"It was the last time anyone saw him. Getting on the elevator. I've looked everywhere. He's got to be trapped in there." At this, Lorenzo's granddaughter began sobbing loudly.

"Gloria…" Sandy started to ask her to stay with the woman, but Gloria was already at her side with a box of Kleenex.

"Can you see if anyone is inside?" Sandy asked.

"Not yet. Still working on getting this plate off the top."

"How long has he been in there?" Sandy asked.

"Over forty-five minutes now, maybe closer to an hour."

"He should be okay. Air supply is fine." But Sandy knew that he wasn't being very reassuring.

"What if he's had a stroke?" Now, the granddaughter's imagination had kicked in, Sandy thought.

"Let's not speculate until we can see for ourselves. It should be just a few more minutes." Sandy hoped he was right.

"Why don't you take Ms. Loretto down to the lounge, Gloria. I'm sure a soft drink or a cup of coffee might taste good about now."

"How can you suggest such a thing? How can I leave my grandfather?" Fresh wailing. This time Gloria gave him a disapproving look.

The crowd was about four people deep. Sandy noted a couple hospital gowns among the watchers. A ninety-six-year-old man gets stuck in an elevator, and it becomes a bed-emptying experience. Sandy wished everyone would just calm down and stop blocking the hall.

"Any progress?" Sandy stepped back to the elevator's closed doors.

"It's still going to be another fifteen or twenty minutes. The electrical is a mess. Do you want me to continue to try to get into the box itself? That plate just doesn't want to budge."

Sandy counted to ten. What had the man been doing? Of course, he needed to try to reach Lorenzo. Sandy even found himself beginning to feel pressured. Surely, the old man should be yelling by now. What if he was in need of medical help? What if he had had a stroke?

"Dr. Black. Telephone. I transferred the call to your office. They're holding on three." Sandy thanked the receptionist and went back upstairs.

"Black, here."

"Are you the one in charge of the Indian hospital?"

"Yes. How can I help you?"

"Well, this may not be anything, but the more I thought about it, the more worried I got. So, when I got home, my wife thought I should call to make sure everything was all right with the old man."

"I'm not following you. Who did you say you were?"

"Oh, gosh, I'm sorry, John Romero, I drive a city bus. I picked up an old man at the corner of Lomas and Girard. One of your people. Real nice old guy, but I don't think he spoke any English. Anyway, he wanted to go to the mountains. It was my last run before coming in."

"When was this?"

"About four-thirty."

Sandy checked his watch. An hour and ten minutes ago. It was already beginning to get dark.

"Where did you let the man off?"

"As I said, he wanted to go to the mountains. He rode until the last stop, above Tramway at Menaul."

"Did you see where he went?"

"Just took off across the street and into the foothills. I guess that's when I sorta thought something might be wrong."

"Could you describe this man?" Better be on the safe side, Sandy thought, but he knew it was Lorenzo.

"Real old. There wasn't any skin that didn't have a pucker in it, if you know what I mean. Wore a blanket over something that looked like another blanket. Seemed to be bundled up real good."

That's a relief, Sandy thought. At least, they wouldn't be treating hypothermia when they found him. If they found him soon enough. It was even more likely that they wouldn't find him at all. Every year someone got lost hiking in the mountains. There weren't always happy endings. Sometimes the mountain only gave up its secrets after a spring thaw.

Sandy thanked the man, got his name and address then tried to gather his thoughts before he called the police. No doubt they would organize a search party and comb the area but what chance was there that a ninety-six-year-old man could survive for long in the cold? Blankets or no blankets.

Sandy didn't relish having to tell his granddaughter that instead of being inside the elevator, her grandfather was cavorting among the foothills of the Sandias. But he couldn't help grinning. The sly old fox had given her the slip. Ninety-six and wily. He should be in such good shape at ninety-six. Sandy grabbed his coat. After he called the police and told the group upstairs, he'd head out to Menaul and Tramway. Maybe he could be of some help.

"WAS SHE ANY TROUBLE?" Bob Crenshaw glanced in the back of the van. There was no movement under the khaki-green tarp. "I see you had to cover her."

"Yeah. She got smart. Tried to attract attention. I thought I might have to ice that guy who came snooping around a few minutes ago."

"Yeah. Close. He was asking for her upstairs. He might have suspected something. Hard to say. I think I got rid of him. I just don't want her killed here. Plenty of time when we get to the mesa. We just needed to wait until after dark."

"How come the mesa?"

"There's a body a month uncovered out there. This will just be one more."

Bob Crenshaw backed the van out of the parking space next to the red Miata and goosed it a little going up the ramp. Piece of cake. He could trust his biker buddy, who owed him one anyway, to take the fifty thousand and disappear. Go back to southern California and keep his mouth shut. And it was time. Time to get rid of Miss Anchor Material and get on with the casino.

Traffic was light. For once I-25 was accident free. He moved the van through the Big-I interchange and on north keeping an eye out for Paseo Del Norte. Bob would take Paseo east past Tramway, parking the unmarked van beyond the residential area in the rolling foothills of the Sandias. There wouldn't be any joggers at eight o'clock in the evening.

He had thought of everything. Using the maintenance van, white, no distinguishing marks, not taking the message tape out of her machine so that anyone who heard it would think she'd run; it was vaguely disturbing that it sounded like Douglas Anderson, maybe he should have taken it. No, instinct told him he was okay. He had worked late, then ate dinner at home with a friend. A sack of Powdrells barbecue behind his seat filled the cab with the heavy scent of hickory and spiced tomato sauce and attested to an iron-clad alibi.

He slowed the van and drove quietly through the pricey neighborhood of rambling adobes, two story mediterraneans and a few ranch style homes. All was quiet. He continued on the dirt road that bordered the Elena Gallegos Land Grant. Open space. Miles of it stretched before him at the base of the mountain.

He pulled off the road and up and over a sandy ridge, finally cutting the engine when he was in a gully and couldn't be seen.

BEN WATCHED the white van lurch to the top of the ramp, pause, then roar out of the station's parking lot turning west towards Lomas. He couldn't see the driver, but guessed that it was Bob Crenshaw. Suddenly he didn't feel so certain anymore, about anything. He was taking a chance. What if he was just wasting time? But what else was there? Ben Crenshaw had lied. He must have something to hide. Maybe that was good enough.

He eased into traffic and followed a couple blocks behind. Whoever was driving was intent on getting someplace. Not speeding but pushing the limit. The van got onto I-25 off of Lomas and headed north. Ben almost lost the van on the freeway but caught the flash of white as it turned off onto Paseo Del Norte. What a laugh if Bob was just going home. They climbed past Louisiana, past Wyoming, past Eubank and Tramway. Ben thought he might be right when Bob, at last, turned down a residential street. But then he watched as the van just cruised around.

Ben cut his lights and followed the white van through the residential area, giving the driver a head start when he headed out onto the mesa. When the tail lights disappeared, he quickly parked, locked the truck and started out on foot using the brightly lighted radio tower on the mountain as a marker. The van couldn't be more than a mile away. But there was no way of knowing where it had parked. Ben felt a terrible urgency. If Julie was in the back of the van like he thought....

"Please, dear God, don't let her be dead."

His breath burned his lungs as he ran in the cold night air dodging the rocks and cacti.

THE MOON WAS higher now. Its golden surface bleached white revealing the gray pockmarking that marred its face. Lorenzo was tired. The mountain beckoned in the distance. Several spirit guides had joined him and he had stopped often to talk with them and rest. His feet were cold.

Oku pin played games with him, skipping away as he got near and sliding farther back out of reach. He had waved his cane at the mountain and thought he heard it laugh. He wouldn't steal its secrets. He asked it to let him enter, let him climb to the stones heaped in a mound, to the earth's navel. He must make an offering to the spirits.

He slipped down the sides of the arroyo and waited until the spirits gave him his breath back. He looked around him. The arroyos carried water down from the mountain. The spirits had shown him the way.

They had placed him in the dry water-path that would lead to *Oku pin*.

He pulled himself upright and shouted a prayer to the moon, to the spirit guides and lastly to *Oku pin*. His heart fluttered in his chest at his happiness. He dug his cane into the soft sand and shuffled forward.

"DID YOU HEAR something?"

Bob's friend had pulled Julie from the van and propped her against the back tire. Julie had heard it too and it didn't sound human. She shifted her weight. She could taste blood on her tongue where the electrical tape had pushed her upper lip against her teeth.

"Yeah. Coyotes probably. They come down into the foothills and stalk domestic cats."

"You're kidding." The friend sounded incredulous.

Bob laughed. "Hey, this is the wilds. A few years ago the city was invaded by black bears. Thirty or forty of them raiding garbage cans and scaring everyone to death."

"Let's get going. This place gives me the creeps." Bob's friend looked nervously around.

"Take it easy. Cut the ropes at her ankles but leave her hands tied." Bob handed the man a hunting knife. "Walk her about twenty yards up the arroyo and leave the body exposed. Less to identify later on.''

''Jesus, are you saying wild animals will eat on the body?''

''C'mon. You knew this wouldn't be a drive-by shooting. Just get going.''

Julie watched Bob climb back in the van. The interior light blinked before he closed the door. The muffled sounds of a local rock station intruded on the desert silence. Bob was just going to stay out of sight, sit tight until it was all over. The friend was hired help. Must be making a bundle for this little favor. Julie looked up at her soon-to-be assassin. He was sweating in the cold night air. Should she be elated that there would only be one of them to contend with? Now, at the end.

She couldn't stop thinking about Ben. Had he been at the station? Had he been the one looking in her car? Asking questions in the office? He had to be. Did he suspect foul play? Would he notify the police?

Julie ached from lying in one position under the heavy tarp for what must have been two hours. She watched the man kneel at her ankles and slice through the rope that was beginning to cut off circulation. Her knees buckled when the man dragged her to her feet, and he had to catch her and hold her to keep her upright.

This was her chance. She had to keep panic from pushing anything rational from her consciousness. Thank God, Bob didn't want to get his hands dirty. She caught the man's eye. Then watched as his gaze wandered down the front of her open blouse. She had seen the way he had looked at her earlier. Maybe, just maybe, she could prolong the inevitable by seduction. Long enough to give her a chance to escape. Unless he was into necrophilia.

She slid a knee up his inner thigh, slowly, barely touching the fabric of his jeans, maintaining eye contact. His hands tightened on her shoulders. He was thinking of it. Just a little rape before he had to earn his money.

She leaned forward and let the fingers of her trussed hands seek the bulge of his crotch. Her hair brushed his chin as she played with the zipper in his slacks, pausing to caress a growing fullness between his legs. He had the idea. He was breathing harder now as he roughly turned her away from him and then supporting her with an arm around her shoulders, started to walk into the shadows. Wispy clouds obscured the moon, then floated on, leaving the silver light unobstructed.

He thrust a hand inside her blouse, kneading a breast, then he began to hurry, pushing and pulling her around a bend in the arroyo and out of sight of the van. No use letting your benefactor see you take advantage of a fringe benefit, Julie thought.

Someone had discarded a mattress at the side of the deep ditch about a hundred feet from the van; he pulled her towards it and pushed her down onto her back. He ripped her blouse to the waist, yanked her bra up and reaching under her skirt, tore the elastic band of the silk briefs.

He arched over her, taking a nipple in his mouth, sucking and biting while his hands fumbled with his fly. He pushed himself back to his knees and pulled his jeans and shorts down, exposing his erect penis. Julie sat up and took it in her hands, running a thumb over the head and squeezing and pulling on the shank. He moaned, shuddered, then grabbed her by the hair, reached for the hunting knife and in one movement cut the tape behind her ear. He wrenched one side free to expose her mouth, then forced her head forward and down.

Suddenly he froze. She felt his body tense.

"Bear. A fucking bear."

The words were a strangled whisper. Julie felt the fist that had held her head immobile let loose of her hair and go slack as he pulled out of her mouth, pushed backward and tried to stand. Hobbled by his underwear, he fell hard, bare buttocks and tailbone crunching against a jutting piece of granite imbedded in the arroyo floor and surrounded by chollo cactus. But his scream of pain was drowned by the grunts coming from the animal that ambled toward them.

Julie grabbed the hunting knife and scrambled away and up the side of the arroyo before she turned to take a good look. The creature's large head and bulky body kept it from moving quickly. For all its size, it was balanced upright on spindly legs. Legs wrapped in leather, its feet in moccasins.

"Oh, my God."

The light of the moon danced over the plaid hood of the poncho, illuminating the large checked pattern before ducking back behind a cloud. "Lorenzo." Julie started to move forward when a hand closed around her ankle. Bob. She whirled and brought the knife above her head to bury it in his neck, just as her feet were pulled out from under her, and she felt herself sliding down the embankment on her back, the knife clattering to one side.

"Julie. It's me. Ben." He picked up the knife, cut the ropes at her wrists and pulled her to her feet. "Grab Lorenzo. Get him out of the way. I'll take care of the guy on the ground."

Then he was gone, back over the lip of the arroyo and across the sand and rocks. Julie rushed to Lorenzo, hugged him and assured him that he was safe, then led him to a clump of pinon. The next time she looked, Ben had the man's arm twisted behind his back, the knife at his throat. The man's slacks were still around his ankles.

In the distance a car started. The van. Bob was getting away. But, did it matter? He probably wouldn't get far. Lights were coming down the arroyo. The first two policemen to reach them were on horseback and after talking with Ben, quickly radioed for backup and put an all points out on the van. Then Sandy and a search party on foot joined them.

"Other than being hungry, this guy's in great shape." Sandy finished checking Lorenzo and handed him a granola bar. "Now, what about you?" He turned to Julie. "Looks like the rope took a little skin off of your wrists. And let me see that tape burn." Sandy turned her head to the side and held a flashlight up to her cheek.

"I'll live. That might be the one who's injured the most." She pointed to the man held by the two policemen.

"If you've got a minute, doc, this guy's got some nasty looking puncture wounds to the glutes."

Julie stood huddled in Ben's jacket, trying to keep her teeth from chattering. Shock or cold, she didn't know which. She just knew that Ben hadn't stopped holding her since the police had come. His arms felt good and kept her from thinking about what had almost happened.

"Let's get everyone into the patrol cars." A young officer nodded to Ben and Julie. "I'd like to get your statements tonight. It shouldn't take more than an hour or so." As they walked back to the road, Julie kept Ben's arm around her.

SIXTEEN

WHEN IT DAWNED ON Bob that his pal just might take time for a piece of ass, he'd thought of going after them, making certain that she was killed quickly. But then he thought, why not? She deserved to get screwed, and his pal had never been one to turn down a little nooky. Fifty thousand and a fuck wasn't bad pay.

He heard the scream above the radio and rolled down the window. Why the fuck had he untaped her mouth? He turned to get the revolver out of the glove compartment and saw the twinkling lights moving toward him just above ground level. A search party about a hundred yards away. The lights dipped and scattered, then merged for a few moments before fanning out some twenty across.

He didn't even realize he was beating his fists against the steering wheel. He had thought something like this might happen.

Something might go wrong. That's why he had placed a call to his sponsors—they had always liked to be called that—back East. And now the plan they suggested would be put into place. He turned the key in the ignition, gunned the engine, and rabbit-hopped over two low mounds of dirt and cacti before climbing up the side of the arroyo. He couldn't risk his lights until he was back on the street. The van had amazing traction and tractability for something so big and bulky; it slid down an embankment and crashed over the curbing, spinning out as the tires fought to take hold of the sand covered pavement. He'd go back to Paseo Del Norte but get on the access road that paralleled the freeway.

He reached for the portable phone and dialed the number on the yellow sticky stuck to its side. A quick call and a pilot would meet him at Coronado Airstrip. He felt the wad of thousand dollar bills push into his groin as he pressed the gas pedal. He'd thought of everything. By the time anyone came looking, he'd be in Mexico. Then on to South America.

The pilot would be in the second hangar to the left. Bob pulled the van around back, sticking to the shadows behind the huge rounded structures. There. A white BMW was parked at an angle just beyond a door at the back. Bob pulled the van alongside.

The cavernous building was dimly lighted. It took Bob a minute to get his bearings.

"We're gassed and ready to go." The voice was just above a whisper, emotionless, with a hint of urgency.

"You startled me." Bob had not seen the tall man in dark clothing until he'd been almost on top of him.

"This way."

The pilot walked briskly ahead of him to the front of the hangar. A single-engine plane sat facing north. Single-engine. Not that he'd expected a Lear Jet, but this? This looked like a stunt plane—or maybe a cropduster. It had to be a relic from the fifties.

"What's the problem? 'Fraid it can't fly?"

"No. No. I'm just not crazy about flying in general."

"I suggest we get going." The pilot was already up the steps and ducking into the cockpit.

Bob scrambled up the ladder pulling it into the plane after him. The door seemed solid but a little tinny. He took one of the two seats behind the pilot and tried to concentrate on the gauges and not on the fact that the engine seemed to be missing out. Finally, it caught, held and whirred into motion.

"We're off."

They taxied the length of the runway, turned, wobbled, the

engine stuttering one last time before the small craft lurched forward, and gaining speed, lifted into the air.

Ahead of them loomed the Sandias. The pilot was looping to the Northeast. Bob watched the mountain grow large. He could almost count the trees on the crest. He looked down into the thickly forested slopes broken only by long slashes of cleared land. Ski runs.

"I hope your trip is pleasant."

Bob jerked back from the window. The pilot was pointing a 9MM at his head. In one fluid motion the pilot hit the door with his boot, crouched and jumped backwards pushing away from the plane, his parachute only grazing the gaping opening in the plane's side. Then he was enveloped in blackness, the roar of the wind and sputtering engine punctuated his retreat.

DOUGLAS ANDERSON SAT smoking in his study. He'd start the cigar before dinner and finish it with coffee and a little B&B afterward. He rolled it between his fingers. This particular cigar was one of a dozen individually wrapped in its own plastic humidor all neatly lined up side by side in his desk drawer. One of life's little pleasures that he allowed himself—thanks to close friends who traveled.

He had a call in to Bob Crenshaw but was only vaguely worried that he hadn't heard back. He'd been contacted by the foreman of the construction crew working on the casino. They were ready to lower the glass domed ceiling into place in the morning. The grand opening would be January fifteenth. No set-backs. They were right on schedule. Even the new Tewa Governor was supportive.

"Dinner's ready." Mollie had rapped lightly on the door before stepping into the room.

"Where's Junior?"

"He's already at the table, Mr. Douglas."

"I'll just be a minute. Tell him not to start without me, Mollie. And take that bottle of white wine out of the fridge."

"Yes, sir." Mollie retreated into the wide hallway closing the door behind her.

Douglas took two last puffs on the cigar before carefully

tapping it out and dropping it back into its case. Junior could just wait on him. Age had some privileges. At one time he had considered booting Junior out, not letting him come home to live after his divorce. But the house was empty. Too big for one person now that his wife was dead. And he could get lonely. No, it had been a good idea to let Junior come back.

He walked across the great room to the dining area off the kitchen. The hand-thrown pottery dinnerware and matching serving pieces gleamed in the candlelight. He always dined by candlelight. It was civilized and made almost any food look appetizing. Not that he had to worry about unappealing food. Mollie was a jewel. All his friends tried to steal her away.

Junior folded the evening newspaper and placed it on the table as Douglas pulled his chair out and sat down. No reading at the table. That had been a rule since Junior was a child. Mollie placed plates of leafy greens covered with croutons and an aromatic dressing in front of each of them, then passed a covered basket of toasted parmesan bread to Douglas.

"What's for dinner? Something Italian?" Junior asked.

"Umhmm. Pesto and Linguini. One of your favorites, Mr. Anderson."

Neither one of them seemed talkative, Douglas thought as he passed the wine to Junior. Of course, neither wanted to say too much in front of Mollie. Douglas helped himself to seconds on the pesto sauce. Mollie had outdone herself. The pesto was perfect. Maybe another raise was in order. He couldn't afford to lose her.

MOLLIE WATCHED from the kitchen, filling dishes or running in to carry away dirty plates. Dessert was a sour cream apple torte with toasted almonds, but it was the pesto that she was most proud of. She slipped the note from her apron pocket and smoothed it out on the counter. She had kept it hidden, but Monday she knew it was time.

"If anything happens to me—if I should die or end up missing—use these seeds and make something for the Andersons to eat."

It was simply signed, Johnson. She struck a match on the

grout between the hand painted tiles around the sink and held the flame to one corner of the note. It caught quickly; the corner curling and falling away to ash as Mollie dropped the remnant into the stainless steel basin. There, that was done. Next, she turned on the disposal, aimed a stream of cold water at the drain and scraped the last of the pesto and linguini into the center of the swirling mass.

She didn't know for sure what would happen, but she could guess. Something terrible. She didn't care. She missed Johnson. And, she could always find another job. Mollie was humming as she carried the coffee carafe into the dining room.

"Mollie, you've outdone yourself. The pesto was superb."

Douglas was leaning back in his chair. "Was that a new recipe?"

"No. Well, I did use some chopped pumpkin seeds for garnish."

"Pumpkin seeds?" Junior looked at his father. Then both started to laugh. When Douglas had recovered, he held his wine glass above his head.

"To pumpkin seeds. A little present from nature that's given me everything I could ever want."

"Hear, hear, to pumpkin seeds." The Andersons touched glasses and drank.

"THE MEETING'S READY to start." Gloria stood in the doorway with what had to be five strings of Christmas lights, three hanging around her neck and one in each hand. A week before Thanksgiving and the hospital was about to get into the holiday spirit.

"What are you going to do with those?" Sandy wanted to make certain that his office would be spared.

"The cafeteria."

"Good."

"I'll probably need some more to do the reception area."

Was that a plea for a donation? Sandy wasn't sure. "Do you need my signature to hit petty cash?"

"That would be nice."

"Okay. Remind me when I get back."

A blast of Christmas music filled the hallway. Now that seemed a little early. Must be testing the new sound system.

The meeting was planned as a debriefing on the Hantavirus but had turned into a going-away party for Ben. He'd be leaving in mid-December. Sandy would miss him. The room was crowded with technicians from the lab, Ben, Julie and hospital staff.

"The quicker we start, the quicker we can tear into that cake. Who wants to go first? Nancy?" Sandy stepped to the side as she walked to the front of the room.

"Thanks to Julie's suspicions about Mr. Chang's lab, we were able to run tests on twelve rodents whose bodies had been left more or less intact by the fire."

"Hey, how can I eat cake if you're going to talk about something gory?" a young doc yelled out to an explosion of laughter.

"Okay. No gore. The fact that there was a bandicoot among the rodents sent to be analyzed pretty much points a finger at Mr. Chang being the originator of the altered virus."

"Where does the CDC go from here?" Sandy asked.

"Well, believe it or not, it's been a major breakthrough for us to have the virus isolated and grown in a lab. It puts us closer to developing simple diagnostic tests to quickly screen for the illness. Ultimately, we're one step closer to preventing something like this happening again," Nancy said.

"What about a vaccine?"

"Another thing that growing the virus in controlled conditions can help with. Right now, a vaccine would be welcomed by our military stationed in Asia. Hantaviruses still kill between ten and forty thousand people annually."

"What about the death of this Anderson guy over the weekend? Wasn't that attributed to the virus?"

"Yes. But we have reason to believe that it was an isolated case and does not indicate a new outbreak of the disease. We'll know more after his son recovers sufficiently to answer questions." Nancy walked back to her chair.

"Anything else, before we hear from Ben?" Sandy had stepped forward. "Ben, I guess the floor's yours." Sandy watched as Ben moved to the front of the room. He'd be an asset to any program. Too bad it would be a few years before he'd be able to come back to Albuquerque.

"As some of you may know, I've been accepted at the University of Illinois. I'll start work on a doctorate in psychology next month." Ben paused for the applause to die down and then continued to thank Sandy and other hospital personnel for helping to make his internship successful.

"Finished? I'd like to make an announcement, too."

Everyone turned to face Julie.

"As of this morning at 10:05 a.m., I'm the rookie member of the *Channel Three News* team in Chicago."

Sandy watched Ben jump over two people seated on the floor to reach Julie. Grabbing her around the waist, he hoisted her in the air before her arms went around his neck and they stood oblivious to the cheers of their audience.

"Hey, one last item of business before this celebration gets out of hand, does anyone remember giving Lorenzo his flu shot before we released him last Friday?" Lost cause, Sandy thought, he didn't have anyone's attention.

THE SUN CAME OUT about noon and quickly melted the light dusting of powdery snow leaving wet streaks across the tops of the adobe houses. Lorenzo watched for his chance to walk to the river. For three days his granddaughter hadn't let him out of her sight. She was in the living room right now retelling the story of *Oku pin*, of his bravery and how the spirits had directed him to save the life of a young woman about to be killed.

He sighed. He hadn't wanted to be a hero. Too much fuss. He knew the spirits wanted him to do one last thing. Then it would be over. The blackness would leave his people, and they could live in harmony.

He sat on the edge of his bed putting first one leg then the other into the new jeans that his granddaughter had left out for him. Their starched stiffness slipped in his grip as he tried to pull them up when he stood. He steadied himself with the help of a chair back before reaching for the warm flannel shirt, then the poncho and a blanket. Ready.

He paused in the doorway. All clear. He darted around the edge of the house to peer in the front window. His granddaughter was occupied. She was talking to four of her neighbors who sat around her at the dining room table, each in rapt attention.

The sun made the wet gravel glisten. The road sparkled and beckoned to him to follow as it unfolded to the West. But Lorenzo knew where he had to go. He pulled the poncho around him and stuck one hand deep into the left pocket. Yes, everything was there. Everything that he would need to make the spirits happy.

There was no wind this early afternoon. Trees in their winter starkness stood unmoving. The grasses along the dry irrigation ditches were a parched brown, bent, beaten down, their roots beneath the ground in limbo, waiting for the warmth of spring. Lorenzo liked the winter time when the plants slept.

This time of year, the Winter Chief spirit might take the form of a crow and accompany him on walks. He scanned the horizon. Surely today, the spirit would be with him to give guidance.

Lorenzo saw the shadow before he saw the great black bird. It landed on a fence post just ahead of him to his right. The crow dipped its head, stretched its wings then settled to preen.

Its feathers gleamed an inky, iridescent jet in the sunlight. Lorenzo spoke to the Winter Chief thanking him for leading him to *Oku pin*. The chief cocked his head, fluffed his feathers and nodded.

Lorenzo laughed, then closed his mouth quickly as cold air rushed down his throat to seek the center of his being. He pulled the zipper of the poncho up to his neck. It was time to get on with their plan. With the crow fly-hopping along the fence posts in front of him, Lorenzo scuttled down the road, finally stopping where the asphalt drive met the dirt and gravel.

The skeleton casino looked forlorn. Sheets of tarpaper had pulled loose at the corners, curled and ineffective against the plywood siding. There was no glass, just empty window frames and a dome open to the sky. Lorenzo started up the long drive, the crow now hopping across the parking lot beside him.

No spirits dwelled in this shell of a building. The emptiness was complete. Stepping inside, Lorenzo looked up at the pale, clear sky and a coldness seemed to settle around him.

He drew the blanket up to his shoulders, then dug deep in the pocket of his poncho. The packet of matches had "Bernies One-Stop Shop" on one side and a telephone number on the other.

But what did he do now? He'd forgotten to bring something to build the fire with, like kindling. He looked around. The Winter Chief had followed him inside and perched on a saw-horse some twenty feet towards the back—on a sawhorse that straddled a pile of refuse—newspapers, insulation, wood.

Lorenzo made a pyramid out of the debris, angling chunks of wood out from the center, rolling newspaper and stuffing it at the base. Then he struck a match and laid it at the bottom of the pile. A wisp of smoke pushed up through the lattice of wood and paper but vanished. Lorenzo got to his knees, struck another match and blew gently. He breathed spirit into the fire and with a pop, it crackled into flame.

He scuttled back, then struggled upright. The smoke was carried upward through the open dome to the sky. He picked out a burning two by four and carried it torch-like to the north wall. The tarpaper and insulation caught fire, flames racing to the bare rafters. In ceremonial silence, Lorenzo repeated his actions holding the torch to each of the other walls. Then he walked through the double front doors and out into the parking lot. He stood in the center and lifted his arms to the heavens and offered a prayer.